TRACKS BENEATH THE CLAY

LEIA KAY

DISCLAIMER

This is a work of fiction. Names, characters, businesses, places, events,
and incidents are either the products of the author's imagination or are
used in a fictitious manner. Any resemblance to actual persons, living or
dead, or actual events, locales, or organizations is entirely coincidental.

ALSO BY LEIA KAY

Before the Tracks Were Laid

Family Bible

Marriages

William Cheney Sr. married Eleanora Fairfax,

William Cheney II married Alice O'Connell, April 21, 1839

Brigid O'Connell (sister to Alice) married Thomas
Whitmore, August 5, 1840

~~Edward~~ Cheney married Margaret Ellis, June 12, 1915

Thomas Cheney married Eleanor Price, April 4, 1946

Ruth Cheney married Edward Dalton, June 14, 1970

Births

William Cheney II, born February 12, 1847 – date unknown

Billy Cheney (William III), born March 2, 1842 – no record

Henry Cheney, born September 14, 1845 –

Abbigail Cheney, born June 22, 1848 –

Natalie Withtmore, born July 14, 1843 –

Benjamin Cheney Whitmore, born October 11, 1861 –

~~Edward~~ Cheney, born 1887 – date unknown

Thomas Cheney, born January 4, 1917 –

Ruth Cheney, born March 3, 1948 – living

Deaths

William Cheney Sr. died October 1859

Eleanora Fairfas Cheney, died February 1860

Margaret Anne O'Connell, died 1828

William Cheney II – date unknown

William Cheney (Billy, William III) – no record

Cheney Family Tree As We Know It

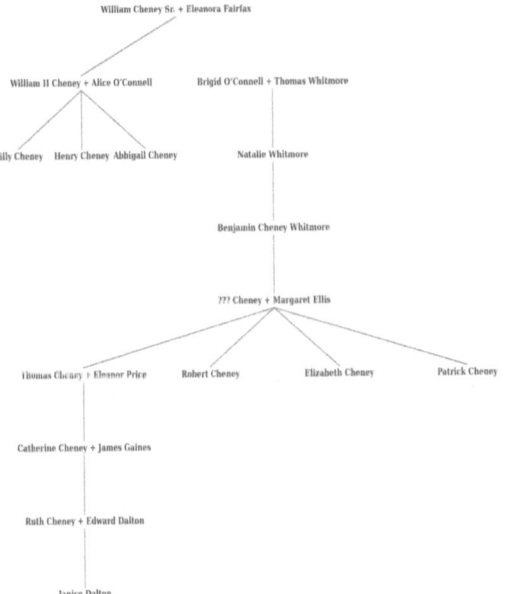

William Cheney Sr. + Eleanora Fairfax

William II Cheney + Alice O'Connell   Brigid O'Connell + Thomas Whitmore

Billy Cheney   Henry Cheney Abbigail Cheney

Natalie Whitmore

Benjamin Cheney Whitmore

??? Cheney + Margaret Ellis

Thomas Cheney + Eleanor Price   Robert Cheney   Elizabeth Cheney   Patrick Cheney

Catherine Cheney + James Gaines

Ruth Cheney + Edward Dalton

Janice Dalton

SYMBOLS

❧❀❧

The following symbols appear at the start of each chapter to guide you between timelines.

They are drawn from history and heritage, chosen for what they represent.

◇◇ Past Timeline

A symbol drawn from quilt codes once used along the Underground Railroad.

Two diamonds could mean a crossroads or safe passage, marking the hidden paths people once walked.

These chapters follow Natalie, Lucy, and the history of Peachtree Plantation.

⚜ Present Timeline

The fleur-de-lis, long a symbol of endurance and legacy.

Here, it represents Janice's journey in the modern day, carrying forward the weight of memory and uncovering truths long buried.

For the family of my blood, and the family of my heart.

PART ONE
ROOTS AND SHADOWS:

"Every family carries beginnings they do not choose and shadows they cannot escape."

"The most common way people give up their power is by thinking they don't have any."
— Alice Walker

CHAPTER ONE
◦◦PROLOGUE

The Orchard
1850s, Georgia

Her sister had dared her.

"Bet you won't walk through the orchard after dark," she had said, her voice half-mocking, half-serious, eyes shining in the lamplight. They had been shelling peas on the porch, their fingers working while the sun slipped low and the rows of pecan trees turned to shadow. By the time the baskets were carried inside, the moon had risen pale and heavy over the fields.

She could have refused. Mama would have scolded them both for the idea alone. But pride had a way of stealing her voice. She would not be the one to turn timid.

So she stepped barefoot onto the dirt path, the night air damp against her skin. The orchard rose ahead, its branches leaning together like old women whispering secrets. She drew a steadying breath and walked on.

There was no reason to be afraid. The neighboring farms were close, and everyone knew everyone. Folks left doors unlatched. Voices carried across fields. Nothing in these trees had ever meant her harm. That was what she told herself.

But her body betrayed her. The hair at the back of her neck prickled. Her arms tightened with chicken flesh. Her mouth went dry. Some deep instinct told her to turn back, though her mind fought it down. She lifted her chin and kept moving, determined not to give in to fear.

The first crunch of boots behind her made her smile. Her sister, of course. She pictured her darting from trunk to trunk, waiting for the right moment to leap out.

But the steps did not quicken. They did not break into laughter. They stayed even. Measured. Following.

Her smile faltered. She turned, expecting to catch a flash of her sister's dress in the moonlight. There was nothing. Only shadows folding deeper between the rows.

Her breath caught. That was when she saw them.

Two red points glimmered between the trees. Watching. Waiting. Not fireflies. Not lantern light. Eyes.

Her throat closed. She told herself it was nothing, only the tricks of the night and moon. But her feet betrayed her, quickening over the dirt.

Then came the laugh.

Low. Male. Amused. A sound without warmth that slid across the orchard and settled heavily in her chest.

She ran.

The last thing she saw was the branches swaying, as if

the orchard itself had shuddered at what it was about to witness.

This was not the first scream the orchard had swallowed, nor would it be the last. Long before Natalie or Ruth, the land had already been keeping its tally of blood.

CHAPTER TWO

⚲BELLEVUE, WASHINGTON

J eff dropped into his chair, sliding Janice's margarita across the table with the kind of flair that always made her suspicious.

"Guess who I just saw walking out of Bellevue Hospital?"

Janice paused mid-sip, the straw still at her lips. "Who?"

Jeff removed his sunglasses like a man revealing state secrets. "Ruth."

She blinked. "My Ruth? *My mother*, Ruth?"

He gave her a look. "Do you know another Ruth who wears Ferragamos to the ER and carries a patent leather bag like it's armor?"

Janice set her drink down and sat back in her plastic chair, her brain trying to catch up. "Why would she be at a hospital?"

"She wasn't limping, no bandages, no visible drama. But she looked off." He made a vague gesture. "Pale.

Rushed. And she saw me. I know she did, but then pretended she didn't."

Janice rested her chin on her hand, her index finger tapping her mouth, her eyes narrowed against the midday Seattle sun. It was one of those rare, brilliant afternoons when everyone emerged like lizards, soaking in the little warmth Seattle offered. But suddenly, the brightness felt harsh.

"I talked to her yesterday. She didn't say anything about being sick," Janice thought aloud.

Jeff tilted his head, studying her. "When your mom keeps quiet, it's usually because she doesn't want anyone stopping her."

That landed. Ruth Cheney didn't do secrets. Or hospitals. She did lunch dates, liberal politics, and long-winded speeches about feminist icons. If something was wrong, Janice should have known. That was the rhythm of their relationship, maybe not warm, but constant.

"You think it's serious?" she asked, trying to sound casual and failing.

"I don't know, Janice. But she looked like a woman carrying more than just a handbag."

A silence settled between them as the waiter delivered their food. Janice picked at a corner of her quesadilla, suddenly uninterested.

"Maybe she was visiting someone," she offered.

"Maybe." Jeff stirred his margarita, not looking convinced. "But if it were me, I'd ask her Directly."

Janice hesitated. Their weekly nail appointments and the lunchtime gossip sessions all suddenly felt like a script

Ruth had been performing. And Janice, the dutiful daughter, had never questioned the lines.

She pulled out her phone.

Jeff smirked. "There you go. There's my Nancy Drew with a side of anxiety."

But Janice didn't respond. She was already scrolling through her recent calls, the memory of yesterday's conversation unraveling under the weight of a new truth:

Ruth *had* been hiding something.

And Janice was about to find out what.

Jeff took a long drink of his margarita and squeezed her hand.

They had known each other since sixth grade, back when Jeff wore braces and carried a Lisa Frank notebook he swore was ironic. Janice was the new girl with too many books in her backpack. They found each other in the corner of the cafeteria, two awkward kids orbiting just outside everyone else's confidence.

Janice had never really had boyfriends in high school. Jeff, ironically, had been her only "date": junior prom, where they slow-danced in borrowed clothes and took pictures in front of his mom's azaleas. She remembered him twirling her like he was auditioning for Broadway. He ended up having more luck with the guys than she ever had with the boys, and the truth was, she had never minded. Jeff made her feel seen when no one else had even been looking.

Since then, he had come out without ever really having to. She had watched him become the man he was now: sharp, self-assured, and adored by his husband and their two rescue dogs. Janice, meanwhile, had chosen a quieter life. A safer one. But Jeff still knew her better than anyone.

He could always tell when something was coming undone.

He reached across the table and placed his hand gently over hers.

"You're like your mother, Janice," he said. "She is the strongest woman I know. If there is a problem, she will either talk it into submission or she'll stare at it until it dies."

Janice laughed softly, the sound catching in her throat.

"Still," he added, his tone shifting, "it wouldn't hurt to check on her."

Janice looked down at their hands. Her thumb grazed his knuckle.

"I will," she said.

And she meant it.

CHAPTER THREE

◦◦THE MENDING BASKET

1858, Spring
Georgia

The bright Georgia morning light filtered through the lace curtains, painting soft shapes across the parlor floor. Lucy sat in the corner armchair with her mending basket, fingers flying over a tear in Abby's Sunday dress. Abby, now ten, was sprawled nearby on the rug, flipping through an old book of bird sketches, legs tucked beneath her like a foal still figuring out how to fold them.

"You stitched this one already," Abby said, pointing at the frayed edge of a hem. "Twice."

Lucy glanced up, smiling. "That doesn't mean it can't come undone again. Things wear out quicker when you run through fields like a wild girl."

Abby grinned. "You say that like it's a bad thing."

Alice's voice floated in from the hallway. "It isn't, as

long as she doesn't outgrow all her dresses before the season's out." She entered the parlor with a small tray: tea for herself, warm milk with cinnamon for Abby, and black coffee for Lucy. Her hair was pinned up in her usual neat twist, but a few strands had come loose around her temples.

"You look like the day's already worked you over," Lucy said gently as she accepted the cup.

Alice laughed softly. Between writing to her sister and straightening out the household ledgers, she needed a few minutes with her girls.

She settled beside Abby, smoothing her skirt. "Natalie's arriving soon," she added. "Your cousin. From Albany."

Abby sat up straighter. "How old is she again?"

"Seventeen," Alice said. "Same age as Lucy, actually. Just finished her schooling."

Abby's eyes lit up. "Then you'll be friends!"

Lucy smiled faintly. "We'll see. We come from different worlds."

Alice placed a warm hand over Lucy's. "That's exactly why it might work. You two are both strong and observant. You'll balance each other."

Abby's curiosity bubbled over. "Does she like books? Will she bring any?"

"I'm sure she will," Alice said. "And likely ones you've never heard of."

Abby turned to Lucy. "Do you think she'll want to play cards?"

Lucy looked thoughtful. "She might. She'll probably want to walk the land first. Get her bearings."

"Do you think she'll like it here?" Abby asked, her voice suddenly more serious. "It's not like a city."

Alice hesitated. "I hope so. She's used to different things. But she's family. And I think... I think she might be looking for something too."

"She'll like the orchard," Abby said, trying to sound certain. "I'll show her where the rabbits nest."

Alice's voice grew firmer. "Just remember, no playing out there after dark. Not even with Natalie."

Abby frowned. "Why not? It's just trees."

Lucy's voice was gentle, but Abby felt the air shift as if the walls were listening to their words. "Because there are things the trees remember. And they don't like to be disturbed at night."

"Stay where the light can find you," Alice added. "That's always been the rule."

Abby nodded slowly. "Alright. We'll stay by the house."

"Good girl."

"What does she look like?" Abby asked after a pause.

Alice smiled. "In the photo, she had dark eyes, a long braid down her back, and a serious expression. But there's laughter just beneath it, if you know where to look."

"She sounds like she has secrets," Abby whispered.

Lucy raised an eyebrow. "Don't we all?"

They all laughed.

Then Alice's tone shifted. "Someone else is coming home too."

Lucy's needle pricked her finger, but she didn't flinch and she didn't stop stitching.

"Billy," Alice said softly.

The room quieted. Even Abby stopped fidgeting.

"He's older now," Alice added, her voice carefully neutral. "Maybe different."

Lucy said nothing at first. Her needle moved in smooth, practiced loops.

Alice looked toward the window. "I just want Natalie to feel safe here. As safe as anyone can."

"I'll look out for her," Lucy said, eyes steady on her thread. "And Miss Abby, too."

Alice reached out and touched Lucy's arm, light but meaningful. "You've always been a gift, Lucy. To both of us." She looked at Lucy, then at Abby, with love in her eyes.

Abby leaned her head against Lucy's shoulder and closed her eyes.

For a moment, the room felt whole, like time decided to stand still just long enough to pause and let in peace. Outside, the wind moved through the pecan trees. Somewhere deeper in the house, a faint creak echoed near the hall, ordinary, but Lucy's spine stiffened for just a moment.

She blinked it away. Not today. Not with the light like this and both of them sitting close.

Natalie was coming. So was Billy.

Whatever darkness he carried through that door with him, Lucy would be ready.

CHAPTER FOUR
⚓ THE KUDZU

Sitting in the chilly exam room, "What can I do now?" Ruth asked, her voice low but steady. "I've done everything you told me. Is this when they do radiation or chemo?"

The doctor sat across from her, hands folded, mouth tight. He did not rush. That was almost worse.

"Ruth," he said gently, "I know this is hard to hear. But it has spread."

She blinked once. The words landed like a stone dropped into a still pond. The surface of her mind fractured, ripples echoing outward as her ears filled with a low, pulsing hum.

Spread. That word again. Spread like a stain, like a vine crawling over everything it touches. Spread like the kudzu that used to swallow the fences behind her grandmother's house in Georgia.

The doctor was still speaking, but his voice had receded, muffled by the rush in her ears. She caught pieces: months, options, and quality of life, but they floated like leaves on water. Out of reach. Unreal.

Her thoughts scattered. Greece. She had never seen Greece. Grandchildren. Janice had never said she wanted children, but still, Ruth had hoped. She had wanted more time. More afternoons sitting by the water. More quiet mornings with a good book. More of the small things that filled a life worth living.

"I feel fine," she said sharply, interrupting whatever the doctor was trying to explain.

He blinked, startled by the edge in her voice. But she meant it. Her body didn't feel like it was dying. She still walked three miles a day. She still handled spreadsheets better than the interns. She still wore heels when she felt like it. She was strong and still could give anyone in the office a run for their money.

This wasn't how it was supposed to happen.

It had started with the mole.

Ed had noticed it first. "Have you always had that?" he asked one morning while she was drying her hair. Just a harmless question, but his tone had been too casual.

She simply replied, "Yes, of course," equally as casual. But later that night, she pulled up her phone gallery and scrolled back through years of photos, searching for proof. There it was: a photo from a weekend trip to Eastern Washington's Apple Festival. She in a swimsuit, turning slightly, laughing at something off-camera. The mole was there, barely visible, but smaller.

Still, she hadn't worried. Who took selfies of their backs? Who panicked over freckles after all those Georgia summers lying on docks with nothing but baby oil and stubbornness? They hadn't used sunscreen back then. She had never burned. Her mother called her skin "Georgia strong."

She'd mentioned it at her next physical, almost offhand.

"I'm sure it's nothing," she said. "But I get regular mammograms, so I figure I should keep an eye on my skin, too." She'd said it like someone reciting a checklist, as if awareness alone could save her.

The doctor had barely looked up from his screen. He asked about weight, about fatigue. She'd answered honestly; yes, she was tired, but wasn't everyone? She had thought it was perimenopause or stress. She had even laughed at the idea that those would be symptoms of something other than a day in the life of a working person. She shared with the doctor that she was ready to retire soon and wanted to do it on her own terms. The doctor didn't smile; no warmth in his eyes. He handed Ruth some pamphlets.

She'd named him Doctor Three Minutes. That was how long it took him to skim her chart, deliver the news, and vanish down the hall. And it felt a little cheap; she waited her turn without complaint, came in, sat in a paper-thin gown exposing her backside even longer. He could have at least pretended to care. Ruth felt like she didn't get her time or money's worth from that appointment. After she was dressed, he told her to head to the window before the exit to speak with the nurse. He couldn't be bothered to walk with her.

The nurse at the discharge window had big black glasses and a messy bun piled high like a bird's nest. She handed Ruth a card with the date and time of her next appointment and told her she would need someone to drive her home. So very sterile and uncaring.

Ruth smiled and nodded, her voice syrupy sweet. "Of course."

Out in the hallway, she pressed the down button on the elevator and eyed the trash can. Without a second thought, she tossed the pamphlets in the trash: *Living with Melanoma, What to Expect When It's Spreading, Talking to Your Family.*

She shook her head.

Why terrify myself before it's necessary?

Outside, the air was crisp and damp. Sunlight filtered through low clouds in narrow shafts, as if trying to remember how to shine. Ruth spotted a green metal bench near the sidewalk and sat down, resting her hands in her lap. Her coat was open. She hadn't noticed the chill until now.

Seattle carried on around her. Pedestrians strode past, coffee cups in hand. A cyclist wove between cars. A mother with a stroller paused to check her phone. Ruth stared past them all, unblinking.

To them, this was just another day.

But to her, it felt like a countdown had begun.

She closed her eyes. And she went to her happy place.

The stream came rushing back.

Not the one in Washington, but the one behind her grandmother's house in Georgia, the place where memories settled into the land like roots. The place where, as a girl, she felt carefree. Where peach cobbler and sweet tea were always available. She remembered that those summers with her grandmother were some of the best in her life.

She saw herself lying in the grass, a girl again. Her knees were wet with dew, and the scent of honeysuckle clung to the air like perfume. Overhead, the willow trees bowed low, their branches trailing in the water like fingers brushing secrets into the current.

Her mother had brought her there many times.

"That's where Lucy used to sit," she'd once said, pointing to the bend in the stream. Ruth had looked, expecting to see a shadow or a figure. But the spot was empty. Still, it felt occupied.

"Lucy?" Ruth had asked.

Her mother nodded. "She was a house girl. Stayed on the land after the war. Her mother said she never married. Said she carried too many ghosts."

Ruth had grown quiet.

"And Natalie," her mother continued, "she came from up North. Alice's niece. She said the orchard still listened if you knew how to speak to it. And Lucy, well, Lucy said the land remembered even when people tried to forget."

Ruth hadn't understood what any of it meant then. But she remembered the hush that fell over the yard when her mother spoke those names. Remembered how the trees sometimes creaked with no wind. How her grandmother would mutter a prayer under her breath when the house grew too still.

Now, in her sixties, Ruth finally understood what the land had been trying to say.

Some women didn't vanish when they died. They became part of the soil. Of the stream. Of the silence.

She opened her eyes with a renewed sense of determination.

A single yellow leaf fluttered down the sidewalk, circling as if it were caught in a current she couldn't see. It skidded past her shoes and disappeared into the street.

She wasn't ready to tell Janice. Not yet.

She wasn't sure what she would say.

But the past had risen like water. Cold and unyielding.

This wasn't just a diagnosis.

Something had been awakened.

And it was calling for her.

CHAPTER FIVE
◦◦THE BLUE RIBBON

1859, Spring
Albany

Natalie rose before the sun. It was her favorite time, when the world paused between darkness and light, when the breeze felt like a breath held in prayer. The birds were just beginning their morning chorus. The silence before them belonged to her.

She stood by the window in her plain cotton nightgown, watching the faint silver mist curling over the ground. This early stillness made her feel, if only for a moment, like anything was possible.

Her dress, a gift for her seventeenth birthday, hung neatly on the wardrobe door. She stepped into it carefully and tied her favorite blue ribbon in her dark hair. Then, kneeling on the wooden floor, she whispered her morning prayers, not out of habit but hope. That something would change. That she would not be trapped forever in this small town, this quiet routine, this role of daughter and helper and girl.

Outside, the yard waited. The chickens were already clucking. She grabbed the pail and moved through her chores quickly, tossing leftovers into the coop, reaching under hens for eggs, and arguing with one particularly bold bird.

"Fine. Keep it," she muttered as she retreated, half-laughing.

The shop door creaked as she passed through it, grabbing an apple from the display pyramid for later. Inside the house, the scent of fried eggs and wood smoke filled the kitchen. She placed the eggs carefully on the counter.

"Merry morn, Mother," she said brightly.

"Go wash your hands, Natalie," her mother replied, not turning from the stove.

"Yes, Mother."

She darted back outside to the basin, splashed her face, dried her hands on her pinafore, and returned, hair slightly damp and cheeks pink from the chill.

They ate together. Her father drank his special coffee, too expensive for anyone but him. Natalie and her mother had hot cocoa. The biscuits were warm and the jam sweet, but Natalie barely tasted them. She had too much energy, too much restlessness, pressing up against her ribs like steam.

Her mother had not always lived in the North. She came from Georgia, from the land of red clay and cane fields, where magnolia trees shaded houses that were large and full of secrets, she would say. Her sister, Alice, had stayed behind, marrying a man from Savannah who owned land and people.

Natalie had only met Alice once, years ago, when she came North for a visit and stayed exactly three days. Alice had been polite but distant, her voice clipped, her posture stiff as starch. She spoke little of her life in the South. What she did say came in careful phrases: the estate, the family, the hands.

Natalie's mother had never hidden her feelings. She said the air in Georgia had grown too heavy, that the house where they had been raised creaked under the weight of silence and obedience, that the land might have been beautiful, but it was soaked in sorrow. She had left as soon as she could, packed her things after her sixteenth birthday, and never looked back.

"She chose comfort," her mother had once said of Alice. "I chose to breathe."

It was the closest Natalie ever got to a full story. Her mother did not like to speak of the past. But when she did, her voice took on a sharpness Natalie never heard otherwise, as if it hurt to remember.

That sharpness lived in Natalie, too, in the way she asked questions and in the way she watched the horizon.

Outside the window, Natalie saw her friend Meredith walking down the hill.

"I'm off," she said, kissing both parents on the cheek and leaving a trail of biscuit crumbs on their shoulders. Her pail bounced in her hand as she ran down the street to meet Meredith.

Their town was neither large nor small, big enough that you did not know everyone, but small enough that everyone knew your business. The dressmaker's shop was two doors down from their own, and the mayor's house loomed above town on the hill. Those who lived up there liked to look down on those below, as if altitude granted wisdom.

The schoolhouse bell rang in the distance, and children began to spill into the streets. Natalie loved the way they greeted each other as though a single night apart was too long.

Meredith, as always, was perfectly put together. Her flaxen hair was tied back with a new ribbon, and her lake-blue eyes sparkled even in the morning haze.

"Is that a new dress?" Natalie asked, already suspicious.

"Do you recognize the fabric?" Meredith beamed.

Natalie narrowed her eyes. "Wait, didn't your father order that fabric specially for your mother?"

"Yes, and Mother had some extra made one up for me. Do you think Grant will like it?" She twirled in the street, showing off the beautiful special-order fabric.

"No," Natalie blurted, louder than she intended. "Well. Probably. But that is not the point."

People passing by gave them space. Natalie barely noticed. Everyone knew who Meredith's father was, and most of them steered clear when she and Natalie were mid-discussion.

"You have to stop thinking something will come of Grant," Natalie said, lowering her voice. "It is foolish."

"He is different," Meredith replied, still swinging her pail.

"You know your father would forbid it."

"Then I will marry him anyway."

Natalie rolled her eyes. "You are dreaming."

"You will understand when you fall in love," Meredith said sweetly.

"Love?" Natalie scoffed. "He barely looks at you."

"Oh, he will today."

Natalie gave her a sideways glance. "What are you planning?"

Meredith just smiled.

As they neared the school, Natalie's pace slowed. Her eyes caught the edge of a folded newspaper resting on a cart beside the dressmaker's shop. She paused just long enough to glimpse the headline:

Southern States Escalate Tensions; Fugitive Slave Law Sparks New Conflict.

Her breath caught.

Just yesterday, she had overheard the dressmaker whispering to a customer about the affair that no one dared speak of publicly. A man helping others escape bondage had passed through town quietly, in the night. No names. Just rumors. But Natalie had listened harder than she was meant to.

She wanted to know more.

More than fabric bolts and school recitations. More than walking straight and smiling politely and waiting for a boy to choose her. She did not want to be picked. She wanted to act.

As Natalie stepped away from the newspaper cart, her fingers itching to take it but knowing better, a voice cut through the air like a broom brushing dirt off a porch.

"You will wear your nose thin sticking it where it does not belong, young lady."

Natalie turned. Mrs. Harper stood at the corner, bundled in her shawl despite the mild air, eyes narrowed beneath her wide-brimmed bonnet. She ran the boarding house two streets over and had a talent for turning her opinions into warnings.

"I was just reading the headline," Natalie said, keeping her tone polite, but her nails began to dig into her palms.

Mrs. Harper sniffed. "Headlines are for the menfolk and the merchants. Not for girls on their way to school."

"But it is important," Natalie tried. "There is a man helping people escape, people who should not have been enslaved to begin with." Her chest started to heave with adrenaline.

Mrs. Harper cut her off with a pointed look. "I do not know where your mother thinks she is raising you, but this is not one of those abolition meetings. This is a respectable town, and respectable girls do not go chasing shadows or whispering about affairs that do not concern them."

Natalie clenched her jaw. "Maybe it *should* concern them."

Mrs. Harper clicked her tongue. "Curiosity like that leads to trouble. And a girl with trouble has no future, no husband, and no name left to carry."

She turned away then, muttering something under her breath about the Southern blood, as if that alone explained everything.

Natalie stood rooted, cheeks burning. Not from shame, but from fury. She wanted to shout back. To tell

Mrs. Harper she was wrong. That silence was what allowed cruelty to thrive. That she would not be one of the girls who grew up quiet and vanished into the dust.

But she did not.

Not yet.

She simply turned and walked toward the school, her fists tight, her heart thudding, and her resolve quietly sharpening.

CHAPTER SIX

⚓ THE WILD BOAR

Ruth remembered her momma saying that a little bit of sugar helped the medicine go down. And today, that lesson felt especially heavy. The truth would have to come out, especially now that Jeff had seen her. Sunday dinner was the setting she chose, a tradition. Safe. Familiar. Ruth called Janice with the invitation.

"Mom, Jeff said he saw you at Bellevue Hospital this last week. Are you okay?" Janice's voice was careful, each word enunciated like stepping on cracked glass.

"Yes, baby, everything is good. Just a regular check-up, you know how those things go." It wasn't a complete lie, just enough to stall.

"Oh? Okay, good. Phew, I got worried there for a second."

Guilt twisted low in Ruth's belly. "Baby doll, can you please bring some of that wine I like so much?" she asked, redirecting, hearing her own voice rise a touch higher than usual. *Breathe, Ruth.*

"Mom, it's the cheapest wine. Can I please bring something better?"

"Why? I like the inexpensive wine." That sounded steadier, she thought.

"Okay, okay, I'll bring it. Anything else you need, give me a call."

"You know I will. See you at five."

"Love you, Mom."

"Love you too, sweetie." It took everything Ruth had not to cry.

When she hung up, the lies pressed down again. It was going to be a difficult dinner.

In the kitchen, Ruth began slicing strawberries for her famous shortcake. The recipe was her mother's, always served after a roast on special occasions. As the sweet scent filled the kitchen, Ruth focused on her breathing. Inhale calm. Exhale dread.

Ed came home from bowling with a bouquet of fresh-cut flowers.

"Oh, Ed, how sweet! What's the occasion?"

"Can't a man buy the love of his life flowers for no reason?"

She laughed and kissed him. He had been her anchor for thirty years. "Go wash up. Janice will be here soon."

He sniffed the air. "That smells amazing. What's for dinner?"

"One of your favorites."

As he went upstairs, she found a vase and placed the flowers in the center of the table. It looked festive, but the reason for the meal made her pause. "It's nothing," she whispered, steadying herself.

The screen door squeaked. Janice walked in holding two bottles of wine.

"Ohhh, two? It's a party, huh?"

"One's for me. Rough week," Janice said with a sarcastic laugh. She looked a little worse for wear, her hair tousled and dark rings under her eyes.

"Come kiss your momma first."

Janice kissed her cheek. "Love you, Mom. Now, where's the corkscrew?"

"In the drawer by the fridge," Ruth said.

As Janice dug through the drawer, Ruth thought about how food had always been the language of love in her family. Conversations, plans, and confessions all happened over full plates and shared desserts.

"Janice, can you set the table? Your daddy is washing up."

"Oh?" Janice glanced over. "What's Dad been up to?"

"Just bowling, dear. Nothing crazy."

"Remember when he fell off the roof and didn't tell anyone until the doctor visit for his—what did he call it?"

"His bum leg." Ruth smiled.

"That's right. And it turned out to be broken!"

"It was just a hairline fracture."

"Mom, that's still a break. I didn't hear about it until he had a cast on!"

"Well, we just don't like to make a big fuss." Ruth continued with the dinner prep.

"HA! "Falling from the top of a two-story building, not worth a fuss?"

"Sweetie, it's all good now. Can you please tell your daddy that dinner is ready?"

These were the moments Ruth wanted to bottle like preserves. Just the three of them at the table. She had wanted more children, but Janice had been their miracle baby. Now retirement and travel were finally within reach. She only needed to get through this little bump in the road.

At dinner, she started to bring it up slowly.

"You know," Ruth said after swallowing a bite and straightening her napkin, "I think I may want to do that family tree thing we talked about."

"What's that, dear?" Ed asked.

"She wants to learn about her family tree, Dad," Janice explained.

"Oh."

"That's kind of cool, Mom," Janice added. "I'd love to know where the relatives are. I only know Dad's cousins."

"Huh?" Ed said again.

"Nothing, Daddy. Just talking about family."

"They're a good lot. Just don't loan them money," he joked.

Ruth chuckled. "You know, my mother's side was interesting. They were from Georgia. But not all of them stayed. A branch moved north to New York. Then, one of them, a girl named Nancy—no, Natalie, went back down during the Civil War. Caused quite a scandal."

Janice perked up. "Really? What happened?"

"She was a spy. For the North."

Janice's eyes widened. "That's wild."

"I have a necklace made from a coin that's been passed down," Ruth said, touching her collarbone as if to feel the memory of it. "I'll show you later."

Ruth smiled, enjoying the moment. Maybe this wasn't the right time for bad news. But the weight pressing on her chest wouldn't let her wait."

"Mom, how did your appointment at Bellevue go?" Janice asked, too casually.

Ed looked up. "What appointment?"

The air shifted. Warmth drained from the room. Ruth's throat tightened, but there was no soft way to say it now.

"Skin cancer," she said at last. It landed on the table like you would expect a wild boar to, sudden, violent, impossible to ignore.

The silence that followed was thick and unkind.

Janice's tears came fast. Ed said nothing, just reached out, one hand on Janice's back, the other finding Ruth's.

"So that's why you were at Bellevue?" Janice said.

Ruth nodded, a lead ball sinking in her stomach.

"So you lied to me." Janice's hand curled into a fist.

"I didn't mean to."

"We're not super close, but God, Mom, I'm your only daughter. You can talk to me."

The weight snapped Ruth's temper. "This isn't all about you. This is about me. What I'm facing. Either help, or don't say anything at all." She stood, threw her napkin down, and left the room.

Behind the locked door, her strength gave out. She slid to the floor, knees to her chest, tears falling freely. For a few minutes, she let herself break. Then, as always, she pulled herself together.

When she returned, her face was washed, shoulders

squared, apron freshly tied. The silence was awkward and thick.

Ruth leaned against the counter, drying her hands. "You know who I thought about the other day?" she asked softly.

Janice looked up. "Who?"

"That boy you brought home. You were crazy about him. What was his name? Sean. Sean from Nashville."

"The math tutor?"

Ruth nodded. "Lord, you were over the moon. Always blushing, writing his name in your notebooks."

"You never liked him."

"I didn't trust him. Too smooth. Southern boys like that, always polished, always knowing what to say. But underneath…" She shook her head.

Janice smirked. "You and Jeff said he was 'all charm and no spine.' You were right. He thought women should stay home and raise kids. Said that's what 'real family values' looked like."

Ruth raised her brows. "He said that out loud?"

"Not at first. But it came out."

Ruth folded the towel. "Then he found what he wanted. But it was never going to be you."

"No," Janice admitted. "Back then, I just wanted someone to choose me."

"You did choose someone," Ruth said. "You chose yourself."

The kitchen fell quiet.

"Mom," Janice asked softly, "who did Natalie end up marrying?"

Ruth's brow furrowed. "I never really knew. Last I

heard, she stayed down South. Barely eighteen. Maybe younger."

Janice traced her glass. "Strange how someone like her, someone who spied to change things, ended up staying."

"Maybe she did change things. Just not in the ways we'd expect."

The screen door creaked. Ed sat alone outside in the porch light, shoulders heavy.

Janice touched his shoulder. "She's going to need you." Janice tipped her head to the inside of the house.

"I know." His head bobbed; he rubbed his hands on his legs and blew out a long breath.

When Ruth joined them, he said quietly, "You should've told us sooner."

"I didn't know how."

"You always know how. You just didn't want us to know."

"That's not fair."

"No, it's not. But I can't help wondering what I missed."

"You didn't miss anything. I was hiding it."

He brushed her cheek with his thumb. "Strong doesn't mean alone. You know that, right?"

"I'm learning."

And for the first time that night, Ruth let herself be held.

CHAPTER SEVEN
⚴ THE FIRST BRANCH

I t was not the night anyone thought it would be.

The word still hung in the air long after dinner ended. Skin cancer. Janice could still feel the echo of it in her chest as she helped clear the dishes, every scrape of a plate too loud, every silence too sharp.

Her emotions were a storm she could not name: Anger. Sadness. Fear. Guilt. All crashing into one another until she felt raw.

She was not sure what she could do, but she knew she could not sit in it alone. Pulling her phone from her back pocket, she sent a text to Jeff.

Janice: Hey, can you come get me from Mom's?
Jeff: Are you OK?
Janice: No. Please come.
Jeff: OMW. Thirty minutes.

Glancing at her watch to mark the time, Janice paced. Through the window, she saw her father still sitting on the porch, one hand buried in his hair, staring blankly into the night. She opened the second bottle of wine, filled her glass to the rim, and stepped outside to sit beside him.

"Dad, are you okay?" she asked.

"No, Janice, I'm not." He stood and left her sitting alone on the porch. "But, for the first time," he said, "we will take care of Mom."

He was right. Ruth had always been the glue, but Janice had never thought of her as a whole person. That realization settled heavily on her.

Janice stared into the night sky, struck by how little they truly knew of each other's lives. The basics, yes, but not the undercurrents that shaped decisions. That distance was its own wound.

Her phone buzzed.

Jeff: Ten minutes.

When Jeff arrived, she left quickly, sliding into his car without looking back.

They drove to a rundown corner bar, dark and tired. Janice sank into a booth, trying to disappear.

"Two of whatever is on tap," Jeff ordered.

He leaned back. "Okay. What happened?"

A few beers and soggy nachos later, Janice finally whispered, "What if she does not make it?" Tears burned in her eyes.

"They do not know anything yet," Jeff said gently.

"Thank you for telling me you saw her. I am not sure she would have ever told us."

"Cancer," he said, shaking his head. "Are you going to move back in?"

"I don't know. Maybe. I can work from home, take her to appointments…"

"How is Ed taking it?"

"He seems…stunned. Lost."

Jeff sighed. "Do you want me to take you back or home?"

"What about your place?"

"No room at our place, the in-laws are camped out. Trust me, you don't want that circus tonight"

Despite everything, she smiled faintly. "I'm sorry."

"Don't be. You gave me an excuse to breathe. My mother-in-law could win gold in passive aggressive."

Janice pressed her hand to her heart. "Thank you for being here."

He dropped her off at her condo. She felt both physically and emotionally numb but lighter after talking. Jeff had always been her chosen brother, closer than anyone else.

Inside, she opened her laptop. Build a family tree, she typed. Dozens of sites appeared. She drummed her nails against the keys. This was going to be a long night. But maybe, finally, a way to make sense of it all.

Janice settled on an ancestry website and purchased the year's subscription. What she thought would be a quick peek turned into hours. She lost herself in names and birth dates, piecing together branches that reached further than she expected.

She sent a text to her boss, letting him know she'd be working from home that day. He didn't respond until after lunch, not that she was surprised. No one ever really noticed when she was gone.

There was always this feeling, like she didn't quite fit

in. She wasn't sure why; it had always been that way. The odd one. The quiet one. The one overlooked. It didn't always hurt, but sometimes it did. Not being invited to weddings or parties. Not being thought of first. Then again, she wasn't sure she would have gone anyway.

Still, it stung.

She typed in her parents' names, then her grandparents'. The website offered hints, birth years, places, and even a few family matches that looked promising. She cross-checked them against what little she knew and found they seemed accurate, but she wanted confirmation.

Janice scrolled through census records, the names stacking one after another until her eyes blurred. She leaned back, dragging both hands through her hair, tugging lightly at the roots as though she could pull clarity straight from her scalp. The gesture steadied her, a release of nerves she hadn't even realized she carried. Then she bent forward again, jaw tight, determined to chase every name until the truth surfaced.

She looked up at the clock. Time to call Mom.

As she made the move toward her phone, it rang, and she saw "Mom" flash on the caller ID.

"Hello." She was surprised they were on the same wavelength.

And then they both spoke at once.

They stopped. Ruth started, but Janice rushed ahead. "I just wanted to apologize for what I said and for running out." She exhaled, relieved to have gotten it out, and leaned back in her chair.

"Oh, Janice," Ruth replied softly.

There was another pause. Then both of them started again at the same time, stopped, and laughed.

It was exactly what they needed to break the ice.

"Mom?"

"Janice?"

"Before we talk about anything else," Janice rushed out, "I need all the names you can remember in the family."

"Why, honey?"

"I started building our family tree. This site is really cool; it gives hints, record matches, and all sorts of stuff."

"Really?" Ruth sounded genuinely intrigued. "Oh, I want to see!"

"You can log in under my name. I'll text you the username and password."

"Okay. But why don't you come over? We can talk about it in person." Then, after a pause: "Wait, aren't you supposed to be at work today? You usually don't call until after."

"Nah. I'm working from home. I just wanted to check in and see how I can help you. And show you what I've found so far." Janice was proud of herself, proud to have *done* something instead of just worrying.

There was a long breath on the other end of the line. Janice recognized it instantly, the careful inhale, the heavy exhale. Her mother was measuring her words.

"The doctor said I'll be alright," Ruth said finally. "Please don't worry. But... I do have a favor to ask."

Janice sat straighter. Her mother never asked for favors.

"Of course. What is it?" She grabbed a pen and a scrap of paper.

Another pause.

"I think it'd be better if we talked in person," Ruth said carefully, calculating each word.

"Well, of course," Janice said, glancing at her calendar. No meetings. Good. "Let me wrap up a few things here, and I'll be over."

"I can be there in about an hour. Still need to shower."

"Great. And bring your laptop," Ruth added.

Just as Janice ended the call, her phone buzzed.

Jeff: We're going to start flipping homes! Found our first one!

Janice smiled, genuinely happy for him—but also a little envious. Jeff always did what he wanted. Took risks. And somehow, it always worked out. She, on the other hand, stayed on the sidelines, calculating every what-if.

She texted back:

Janice: WOW. Master Realtor, now Master Flipper, what's next?

Jeff replied with a heart emoji.

"Good for you, Jeffery," she muttered, then hurried to the bathroom.

True to her word, she was at her Mother's within the hour. She'd answered a few emails from her phone, but nothing urgent. Dressed in worn jeans and a faded "Peace, Love & Coffee" T-shirt from her favorite local café, Janice felt... herself again.

Ruth opened the door before Janice could reach for the knob and pulled her into a hug. At first, Janice stiffened; they weren't usually huggers. But then she softened, leaning into it. The strap of her laptop bag dug into her shoulder, but for once, she didn't care.

Inside, Ruth led her straight to the kitchen. Of course. All family things happened in the kitchen.

On the table sat an old, well-worn Bible and a velvet ring box with frayed corners. Janice furrowed her brow.

"This," Ruth explained, "is the record of births and marriages." It's been passed down."

She reached for the ring box.

"And this…" She opened it gently, revealing a delicate silver necklace with a tarnished coin dangling from it. "This is the coin I mentioned."

Janice leaned in.

One side read: *Confederate States of America Half Dollar.*

The surface was scratched, dulled by time, but undeniably real.

"Wow. Look at the date, 1861. Right before the war." A shiver ran down her spine. "I bet that's worth something."

"This was handed down," Ruth said, "but no one's ever been sure from whom. Maybe you'll find out. I don't think it's worth much money, but it's priceless to our family."

Janice set her laptop down, opened it, and pulled up the ancestry site.

"This is what I've got so far," she said, turning the screen. "See the little leaves? Those are hints. I just need help confirming."

Ruth slid on her reading glasses and studied the screen, then the Bible. She flipped carefully through brittle pages until she reached a handwritten list of names. The ink had faded to a ghostly brown, but one stood out, barely legible in elegant looping script: *Benjamin Cheney Freeman.*

Janice stared.

"That's odd," she whispered. "Why would he have two last names? And who were his parents?"

Ruth squinted. "Does the computer say anything?"

Janice typed his name in. Nothing useful surfaced.

"I'm going to take some photos," she said, pulling out her phone.

"I'm going to try Natalie's name."

Janice typed in "Natalie" with other fragments, and soon the site suggested she'd had a child whose name matched her grandfather's.

It was something.

She realized this wasn't going to be a one-weekend project.

"Mom, do you remember grandma telling you any stories of people?"

"Well, she often told stories of Natalie and Lucy on the farm."

"Lucy? Was she a Cheney?"

"No, I think she helped out around the house, but she always comes across as close to the family in the stories," Ruth responded thoughtfully.

"Mom, you said earlier you had something to ask me?"

Ruth moved toward the stove, peeling potatoes.

"Remember how I told you Grandma's great-great-grandmother was from outside Atlanta?"

Janice nodded.

"Well, they still have a house down there. I inherited it from your grandmother."

Janice blinked. "I didn't know that."

Ruth busied herself at the counter, not meeting her eyes.

"I never told you because I wasn't sure what to do with it," Ruth admitted. "And truthfully, I wasn't ready for the memories that came with it."

Janice felt the air shift. "Yes…" she said slowly,

"You told me you wanted to help," Ruth said, the scrape of the peeler marking time.

"I was thinking doctor's appointments. Maybe making dinner." Janice's voice was sharper than she intended.

"This wouldn't be terrible," Ruth said gently. She set the peeler down, turned, and placed her hands on Janice's elbows. "It might even be fun."

"Fun?" Janice blinked, caught between dread and curiosity.

"Your father and I have decided it's time to retire early."

Janice lit up. "That's wonderful, Mom!"

Ruth smiled faintly. "We'll still need income, though."

Janice's stomach tightened. "You want to do what with the house in Atlanta?"

"Well," Ruth said carefully, "we thought maybe you

could go down there. Check it out. Fix it up. Maybe rent it out."

Janice swallowed. The floor seemed to tilt beneath her. She wanted to protest. She wanted to say she wasn't ready, that she barely kept her own life together. But beneath the fear, a flicker of something else stirred.

Possibility.

CHAPTER EIGHT
⋄⋄THE RULER

1859, Albany
Late Spring

The injustice of it all was staggering. Natalie had been defending Meredith, yet she was the one in trouble. Meredith had been sent home crying, her plan to get Grant's attention backfiring on them both. She had made him a heart cut out of red parchment paper and offered it to him during morning break. Grant had thanked her, barely, and immediately run to his friends by the tree line to show them what she had given him.

Meredith had stood frozen, caught between the school steps where Natalie sat and the boys under the trees. They had all laughed, Grant most of all. Laughed. The audacity. Natalie's jaw had dropped. Meredith had spun around and bolted back into the classroom, and Natalie had followed without hesitation.

It had taken Natalie the entire break to calm her

down. Poor Meredith, dressed in her best, her hair braided into delicate coils at her temples, had given Grant her heart, and it had become a cruel joke. She had just wanted to go home, but Ms. Aims had refused.

They had eaten lunch on the steps, keeping to themselves. But Grant could not let it go. He kept circling, hurling vulgar remarks and ugly words. Natalie had looked at him, wondering, what could she do? Meredith was her best friend, like the sister she never had. This was not how people should treat one another.

So she had done what any good friend or wannabe sister would do. She stood up and shoved him away. A little harder than she meant to. He stumbled down the stairs. Then he escalated it, pointing, laughing, and calling her a shopkeeper's daughter.

While technically correct, it was the tone that did it, the mockery, the laughter. The way his friends snickered behind him made heat begin to rise in Natalie's chest like a tea kettle just before the whistle.

Then he sneered, "So what are YOU going to do about it?" in a sing-song voice.

That was when everything went red.

Grant turned back to his friends for approval, but when he spun around, his cheek met Natalie's hand with startling speed. A sharp slap echoed against the trees and the school walls.

The world stopped.

She remembered thinking absurdly: *Who needs a school bell when a slap will do?* And then: *Who did that?*

For a second, she was not even sure it had been her.

Her palm tingled. Grant clutched his face, eyes wide with confusion. Blood trickled from his lip.

"Wow," she whispered. "Did I do that?" She was stunned, equal parts proud and terrified.

Before the first drop of blood hit the dirt, Grant cried out for the teacher. His friends gasped and sprinted toward her, desperate to be the first to tattle. Natalie stood motionless in the middle of it all, her heart hammering.

Heartsick, she looked for someone, anyone who might stand beside her. Her eyes found Meredith. Her friend's face was wet with tears and twisted with something else—disdain, shame, even a flicker of fear. Meredith's gaze locked with hers for a breath, then broke away. She shook her head slowly, turned her back, and walked away.

Natalie's stomach dropped. How could Meredith not see? She had done this for her. She could withstand almost anything, but Meredith's disappointment was unbearable.

"I—I… he was saying such awful things," Natalie called after her, but Meredith kept going, her shoulders stiff.

Natalie's chest hollowed. She had never felt so alone.

Ms. Aims seized her arm and dragged her into the back room without a word. From the desk she snatched the ruler, that thin strip of polished wood that served as judge, jury, and executioner in the classroom. It whistled once through the air before cracking down hard, the sharp edge of order striking against Natalie's skin.

Natalie bit her lip. She knew how to take her licks.

But this was unjust. The ruler was meant to straighten crooked lines, yet here it struck her for trying to do what was right. Protecting someone who could not protect herself should never have been considered a crime.

Tears welled, not from the sting of the ruler, but from the thought that Meredith might never understand.

"Natalie," Ms. Aims said, exasperated, "you talk back. You ask too many questions. And now you've struck a boy." Each charge landed in rhythm with the ruler's arc, as if the wood itself were keeping time with her condemnation.

When Ms. Aims finished, her hair had come loose from its bun. Her cheeks flushed, perspiration dotted her forehead, and she was breathing hard.

Natalie rubbed her backside, defiant even in pain. "But you are not listening to me," she said. She wanted to speak as her parents did when they disagreed, reasonable, firm, logical. But Ms. Aims was not interested in reason.

Natalie's mind raced. *What does she want? What can I offer her? Think, Natalie.*

"Ms. Aims, I will stay after school all week. I will clean the classroom for you." She watched the teacher hesitate, then added quickly, "It is always such a mess. It could use a good scrubbing."

The wrong words. Ms. Aims folded her arms, huffing, frowning, and offended.

Why do I keep offending people without trying? Am I not speaking the same language?

Then came the unmistakable sound of her mother's heels approaching. Natalie's stomach sank.

. . .

LATER, in the kitchen, her mother tried to explain to her father.

"She got in a tussle at school and punched a boy."

Natalie sat silently, facing her father, biting her lower lip.

"What is this you say?" he asked, his brow rising.

"What will people say?" her mother continued with a weary sigh.

Her father turned toward Natalie, eyes wide. "Did you really hit a boy, Natalie?"

"Yes, Father," she said softly, eyes downcast, fingers fidgeting on the table.

With her back still turned, her mother did not see him reach over and tap Natalie's hand. She looked up. His face was angled so only she could see, and on it was a broad smile.

"So, my girl knows how to stand up for herself, hmm?" he whispered.

Relief washed through her like a warm tide. She smiled back, loving her father more in that moment than ever before.

Her mother, sensing something, turned around sharply. "Go to bed without dinner, young lady. And think about what you did."

Natalie stood. *Think about it? I already have. And I am fine with it. Maybe she is the one who needs to think.*

She climbed the stairs, her feet landing heavily, the old wood creaking beneath each step. Every movement reminded her of the sting. It was hard to get comfortable, her backside still resonating with the correction, each throb an echo of Ms. Aims's ruler.

By the time she reached her room, her emotions were beginning to boil over: anger, confusion, shame, and a strange pride all churning beneath the surface. She tossed her satchel onto the bed and crossed to her desk, where her most treasured book rested: *The Genius of Universal Emancipation*. She picked it up and opened to the page she had marked days earlier. The familiar scent of old paper and ink grounded her.

Benjamin Lundy's words stared back at her with quiet force. His conviction, his tireless voice against injustice—this was the reason she had stood up to Grant. It had not been impulsive. It had been righteous. The courage she had summoned had come from these pages, from the clarity they gave her when the world seemed unjust.

She traced the underlined lines with her fingertip, her breath slowing as her thoughts caught up to her pounding heart. Her eyes lingered on a passage about silent complicity, and she felt again the snap of her hand across Grant's cheek. It had been her choice. And it had been the right one.

Her mother entered with a sandwich on a plate. "May I come in?" she asked, lingering in the doorway.

"Of course, Mother." Natalie was sitting on her bed, holding the book tightly to her chest, as if just having it in her hands gave her strength.

"Natalie," her mother began, "you are in your final years of school, and I realize now I have done you a disservice."

Natalie tilted her head, puzzled.

"By moving us to this small town, I have kept you from the life you were meant for. In the South, you would be attending balls, wearing gowns, preparing for a husband, not asking questions and stirring up chaos in school. Wouldn't that be so much nicer, my dear?"

Fear bloomed in Natalie's chest.

"No, Mother," she said quietly. "I enjoy being here with you and Father. I would not trade it."

Her mother set the sandwich beside her. "You must understand something."

Natalie leaned in.

"Defending someone who cannot defend themselves is admirable."

Hope flickered in Natalie's chest until her mother spoke the next words.

"But you have to know your place."

She stressed "your" and "place" with pointed clarity.

"You are a young woman. That kind of behavior is not acceptable for a lady."

Natalie's heart thudded in her chest, a strange sick feeling settling in her stomach.

"But what should I do next time if something like that happens again?" she asked.

Her mother leaned closer.

"Use your wit," she said. "Remember: the meek shall inherit the earth, but so shall the intelligent." She tapped her temple.

"Now, finish your sandwich and turn down the lantern." She smoothed her skirt. "You will stay home from school tomorrow. We will continue this conversation then. Good night, daughter."

"Good night, Mother," Natalie whispered, the bread

sitting like a stone in her uneasy stomach after the first bite.

Outside the window, the light faded against the horizon. A storm gathered in the sunset sky.

CHAPTER NINE

◦◦THE EXILE

1859, Albany
Summer Begins

Natalie awoke to the sound of her mother's and father's voices drifting up from below.

"I just don't know about this," Father said. "Do you really believe that this is the best thing for her?"

"Yes. Look how she turned out," Mother replied.

Natalie sat up, the words striking sharper than any schoolmaster's ruler. She was not going to school today, and deep down, she knew she would not be going back at all, not after the disgrace of yesterday.

The memory stung. The shame of it clung to her skin, and the certainty of it filled her bones: she would not walk back through those school doors again.

She hurried down the stairs, heart drumming, and glanced out the window, half-hoping, half-dreading to see Meredith.

"Mother, did anyone call on me today?" she asked, her voice too eager.

Mother turned, looking past her to Father, and waved her hands as if in despair.

"See? Such bad manners." She cannot even manage a simple good morning."

Father gave Natalie a pleading look.

"My apologies," she said quickly, backtracking. "Good morning, Mother, Father. I do hope you slept well."

Mother turned back to the fire with a sharp flick of her wrist. "Yes, yes, yes. And no, no one called on you. Meredith must be very upset with you, and you have no one to blame but yourself."

Natalie sank into her chair, the weight of it pressing down.

"Daughter," Father began, clearing his throat, coffee in hand, "how would you feel about taking your summer break elsewhere this year?"

Her brows knitted. "I beg your pardon?"

"What your father is trying to say," Mother said briskly, "is that it would be best for you to spend some time away from Meredith and that boy."

"You mean Grant?" Natalie blurted. "There isn't a place on earth I'd rather avoid more."

Mother folded her arms. "I sent a telegram to my sister yesterday. We are arranging for you to spend the summer at her plantation house. She has three children, plenty of land, and you will learn to ride a horse and conduct yourself as a proper young lady should."

Natalie's mouth fell open. "You want to be rid of me?"

She turned to her father, the sting of betrayal burning her throat.

"No, darling. Your place is always with us. But your mother has raised some valid points."

Her anger flared hot. "But Mother, why? That scoundrel deserved it. He mocked Meredith's new dress and pulled her hair when she only meant to give him her heart. He had it coming!"

"Do not speak in that tone," Mother snapped. "Instead of helping us, you caused your father embarrassment. If we were not the only store in town, I am sure we would have lost customers over your behavior. Until this blows over, you will go to Georgia. It will do you well to spend time with your cousins."

"My cousins? I do not even know them! And you want to send me to a plantation?" The word stung on her tongue. "Aunt Alice and Uncle Will probably live like it is the Stone Ages. They could learn a thing or two about decency from us here in the North."

She crossed her arms and bolted up the stairs, trying to slam her door. The warped wood only thudded weakly before creaking back open.

"Ugghhh!" she screamed, throwing herself onto the bed. The world was not fair, not at all.

FOR THE NEXT WEEK, Natalie tried everything to redeem herself. She helped in the house, restocked shelves in the mercantile, and even smiled at customers she normally wished would vanish. Each effort was a pebble tossed into a well with no bottom.

Her mother remained unmoved, and her father was distracted.

At night, Natalie lay awake, staring at the ceiling, replaying the moment over and over—the sting in her hand, the shock on Grant's face, Meredith's tears. Was it truly so wrong to stand up for her? Or was she everything her mother claimed: wild, unruly, shameful?

The more she thought of it, the more uncertain she became. She wanted to believe it had been justice. But in the silence of her room, doubt seeped in. And with school no longer hers to return to, the walls of her world seemed smaller than ever.

Then, one afternoon, while scouring the newspaper between ads for patent medicine and shipping notices, her eyes caught a line that made her breath hitch. Benjamin Lundy would be speaking in the square on the abolition of slavery.

Her heart thudded. She had read his words by candlelight, traced them with her finger until they felt like her own. And now he would be here, in her town.

She pressed the clipping flat on the counter, excitement coursing through her. "Father," she asked in her sweetest tone, "may I go to the square tomorrow?"

"Why?" His voice was gruff, his patience thin since the quarrel with Grant.

"Well… a few of my classmates are going," she said, fumbling. Her finger tapped her lip as she reached for something plausible. "I only meant to say goodbye."

He studied her, flour dusting his sleeves, hands on his hips. "It is only for the summer, daughter. You will see them again."

"Please, Father." Her voice softened to almost a whisper.

He exhaled, glanced toward the stairs, and then lowered his voice. "Keep it between us. Your mother does not want you out of her sight. Not after everything you did last week."

Natalie rushed forward and hugged him. He stiffened at the sudden display but patted her back once.

"Thank you, Father," she whispered.

That night, as she set her bonnet and gloves neatly on the chair by her window, Natalie stared into the dark. Tomorrow, she would see him. Tomorrow, she would hear his voice. And tomorrow, she promised herself, nothing would keep her away.

CHAPTER TEN

◦◦THE AWAKENING

1859, Albany
Mid Summer

The next morning, Natalie slipped out through the mercantile instead of the front door, bonnet pulled low and gloves clutched in her hand. Besides, if she got caught, they could not exile her twice to Georgia now, could they?

She paused on the step, chest trembling, and looked both ways up and down the street. No one seemed to notice her, but still she checked the windows, half expecting her mother's sharp face to appear behind the curtains. A pang of guilt pressed hard in her ribs. She had lied to her father, and the weight of it burned.

Still, she pressed forward, tucking her strawberry blonde hair beneath her bonnet and fixing steps toward the square. Each footfall felt louder than it should, her heart thudding to match. The murmur of a gathering crowd reached her before the words did, a low hum of voices carried on the morning air.

Then, rising above them, a voice rang out: "There cannot be a United States if there are slaveholders."

Natalie froze mid step. On the corner, standing tall on a wooden box, was Benjamin Lundy.

"This great nation of theirs is founded on a contradiction," he cried.

Natalie's breath caught in her chest. Her entire body felt charged, as if every hair on her arms stood on end. The words struck like a thunderclap. They hold these truths to be self evident, that all men are created equal.

Her eyes burned. Her pulse thundered in her ears. She pressed a gloved hand to her chest, as if to still the trembling within. She did not just hear those words. She felt them echo in her bones, shaking something long sleeping awake. It was as if a bell had rung inside her, a summons she had not known she was waiting for.

"All men are created equal," Lundy repeated, stamping his foot.

And then a tomato flew. It burst against his sleeve, spattering pulp across his coat.

Natalie gasped, her hand flying to her mouth. She craned forward and spotted a group of boys laughing. When one turned, her fury burned hotter. Grant. Of course it was him.

Benjamin brushed the tomato aside and pressed on, unfaltering. "A United States cannot be united with slaveholders."

But Natalie barely heard. She had already gathered her

skirts, ready to march straight to Grant and deliver another slap across his smug face.

Before she could, her arm was yanked back hard. The sudden force stopped her like a tethered horse pulled short. She spun around.

Her father stood there, holding her arm, his expression tight with disappointment.

"Natalie." His voice was low, heavy with warning.

"Father, let me explain."

"No need. I see you are about to make more trouble for yourself again." He tipped his head toward the cluster of boys.

Natalie's breath quickened. "But Father."

"No, daughter. Not today." His grip softened, though his gaze held firm. "Fight with your head, not your hands."

His words stilled her, even as shouts rose around them. The crowd had erupted into chaos, voices clashing in a roar of infighting. People surged back and forth like a single angry thing.

"Go, Natalie." Her father guided her with one hand while pushing through the mob with the other. "Before your mother catches you somewhere you should not be."

Once free of the crowd, Natalie turned back. Benjamin still stood on his box, voice rising above the noise. What struck her most was not his words. It was the faces of the people she had known all her life. Neighbors. Customers. Fellow churchgoers. They were shouting him down. Good Christians, siding with the bully, not the brave.

Her stomach churned. Every kind smile and Sunday sermon now felt like a mask, thin and brittle, crumbling in the heat of hate. She wrapped her arms around herself, as if to hold together her ideals, her innocence, maybe even her sense of belonging.

Silence was no longer safety. Silence was agreement. And she would not agree.

Father and daughter walked slowly, their pace like a Sunday stroll, though the air around them still crackled with unrest. Natalie finally spoke.

"Father, why is it legal to own another person?"

His lips pursed. He let out a long breath and shook his head. "I do not know, daughter. Your mother moved from the South because of the cruelty. Did you know that?"

Natalie stopped short. "What? Truly? I thought it was because you married and started the store."

"That too," he said with a small chuckle, "but we could have started it anywhere. Your mother wanted to be as far north as she could get."

Natalie frowned. "But she hates the cold."

"Yes, but she hated the ways of the South more."

Natalie walked on in silence, chewing on his words. If Mother had once resisted, why did she now speak only of obedience? And why send Natalie to the place she had fled?

As if hearing her thoughts, Father patted her hand. "Your mother sees more of herself in you than you realize."

Natalie's reply came out sharper than she meant. "So, I am a handful who must learn her place."

His eyes crinkled beneath his mustache, and a smile tugged at his lips. "That may be true too."

By then they had reached the mercantile. He leaned close and whispered, "How about we keep today between us."

"Yes, Father," she said softly, her anger cooled but her mind ablaze.

Inside, he pulled a package tied with twine from a drawer and handed it to her. "For you, my inquisitive daughter."

She raised a brow but tore it open without ceremony. Inside lay a book: *Running a Thousand Miles for Freedom* by William and Ellen Craft.

Natalie's heart skipped. She traced the cover with reverence. "May I read it tonight."

"I would prefer you did," Father said warmly. "We can speak of it tomorrow."

She stood on her toes, kissed his cheek, and slipped away to her room.

Upstairs, she settled into her chair by the window, the book heavy in her lap, her thoughts heavier still. She opened it and read of Ellen Craft, light-skinned and disguised as a white man, and her husband traveling as her servant. Courage breathed from every page.

At last, the tangle inside her began to loosen. She was not wild. She was not unruly. She was not a disappointment. She was a girl who could not abide cruelty. The slap, the shouting, the restless questions were not flaws. They were her.

Georgia no longer seemed only exile. It was a test, a proving ground. She intended to meet it. And this time, she would not remain silent. She had seen today that silence was its own form of acceptance. She also knew that with her voice, her face, her place in this world, people would have no choice but to listen. She would use that power not to hide, but to fight.

CHAPTER ELEVEN

◦◦ THE DEPARTURE

1859, Albany
Autumn

Standing on the podium of the first train, the morning dew still on the grass. Natalie had decided to wear her best traveling attire. She held her carpet bag at her side, a parasol, and a matching reticule, which held her ticket and some money from Father for incidentals and to give to Uncle for her stay.

Natalie's mother and father were standing behind her, and it looked as if her mother might change her mind, her handkerchief in hand, dabbing the inside corners of her eyes. But after Natalie's conversation with her father about the book, she *wanted* to go to the South now more than ever.

It wasn't to hurt her mother, but now Natalie wanted to see what she'd heard about and read her entire life for herself.

She wanted to see what a plantation was like and if

there was any way she could affect change in her uncle's way of doing things. It was a cotton farm, according to what Mother said; that farm was her father's, and his father's before him. Over fifty acres, with a river she said she used to cool off in, behind a lush pecan orchard in the summer, and a tree in the back that used to produce the most delicious peaches. Natalie's mother made sure she would eat a peach for her and write when she did.

"There's nothing better than picking your own fruit when it's ripe and eating it right off the branch." She was wistfully entranced in a past memory.

Now Natalie had eaten apples off the tree before, but a peach would be nice. So, she promised her mother she would, and there was something called iced tea, odd considering they had tea all the time, but it was usually hot. So she was a little confused by how this could taste good, but so far, the food sounded odd but intriguing.

Natalie's mother advised her to stay to herself, that she couldn't behave like she did here.

"The South is different; you have to behave like a lady," she continued. "Let the men talk but direct your questions to your cousins or your aunt in private. You don't want to make yourself appear silly in front of others. "

Well, that did sound like good advice. As they were talking about the delights of peach cobbler, her mother glanced above her right shoulder and smiled a tight smile. Then, she felt a small but pronounced tap on her shoulder.

She turned to see Meredith; without thought, Natalie engulfed her in a hug. She pulled back and smiled.

"I had to make sure I saw you off," she said sheepishly.

"Where on earth have you been, Mer? I have been trying to get in touch," she said quickly, knowing her time was running short.

She cut her off. "My parents thought it best I keep my distance... from anything that might stir trouble," she said apologetically.

"So I'm controversial?" Natalie asked, her eyebrows making a poignant question mark on her face.

Meredith glanced at her hands, down in front of her, that held a package and shoved it to Natalie.

"Here, Natalie, I wanted to give you this." She handed it over.

Natalie still wasn't over the shock that Meredith's parents kept her away, but she glanced down at Meredith's hands. There was a square, similar to what Father had given her, but this one was wrapped in beautiful cloth and a ribbon of emerald green.

"Oh, Mer, this ribbon is beautiful," she said.

Meredith smiled. "I thought it matched your eyes."

Natalie pulled as gently as possible with one hand while the other held the package in front of them. Four pairs of eyes were on the smooth, emerald-glimmering bow on beautifully patterned fabric. Natalie pulled one of the loose ends from the bow, shrinking it to just a ribbon, and at that moment, the fabric opened to reveal a book.

"Oh?" Natalie said. Meredith picked it up from its resting place in Natalie's hand and showed it to her. It was a bound book with the letter M in gold inlay on the front.

"So you don't forget me while you're gone."

It had a deep red color unlike any she'd ever seen before. It carried a sort of prestige with it. Natalie opened up the first page, where there was a paragraph in beautiful, looped script written in her hand.

Dearest Natalie, I give this book to you so you may capture every moment you and I are separated. Instead of letters that I may or may not receive, this will be a record of events that, once you're back, you can share with me. Keep this safe, as I look forward to our time to revel in all that occurs during your absence.

She'd signed her full name.

"Brilliant, Meredith, I love this so much. Thank you." She hugged the book. She was beginning to cry when the train started loading up with passengers. Their time was coming to an end. Natalie held the book in her left arm and hugged Meredith with her right.

"I will write in it every day, thank you, Mer." Her throat seized, tears sprouted, not because she didn't want to go, but because she was actually going to miss everyone so much.

It could be felt by everyone on the platform: there was a lot of change on the horizon. Natalie could feel it in the air around her, crackling with anticipation; she was excited but also hesitant, and being her first time away from her parents, she wasn't sure what to expect.

"Now behave for your uncle and aunt. They will be waiting for you at the station, and please send word once you arrive." Her mother sniffed, hugging her one last time.

Father hugged her next and tucked a renegade hair behind her ear.

"You're leaving a young lady and will come back to her a fearless woman. Make me proud, daughter." "

She bent at the knees to pick up her bag and placed her new prize inside, a book to which this summer would be scribed. She stood straight, parasol and reticule on her left and her bag on her right. She squared her shoulders and walked forward onto the train, not looking back until seated. Drawing her handkerchief from her sleeve, she dabbed her nose. She couldn't help herself; an emotional tug of war was taking place.

Meanwhile, no one had moved from their positions on the platform. Natalie's father, mother, and Meredith stood stoic, dabbing at their eyes every so often.

The train blew its whistle, startling her, and slowly began to pull away. She waved her handkerchief at them and watched for as long as she could before the train sped up and around the bend for its first stop.

It was hard to believe that she was leaving, she thought, both with trepidation and excitement about the new adventure that was about to unfold.

She left just past noon on a Monday; it was a chilly start to the day, so thankfully, she was prepared. She had her favorite book to accompany her, but it would be a full day, night, and another day before she arrived at her final destination. This was her first time alone on her own and with many stops in between. Her father warned her not to talk to strangers, to only get off the train to relieve herself, and to eat sparingly what she had with her, or to visit the food car if absolutely necessary.

She sat across from a nice young couple who stayed to themselves, offering the occasional smile in her direction and niceties, but she daydreamed them into being a couple on their way to their first home together. Just married and ready to start their lives; she assumed she was becoming a romantic at heart, as something about the train lulled one to such thoughts. She scribbled her first entry. She counted and found that the book had close to 300 pages, and if she wrote only one page a day, there would be plenty left, so, unhindered, she started her first entry.

JOURNAL ENTRY:

Today, Meredith and I said our goodbyes. We promised we'd always be best friends. I told her I was sorry for everything. For how it all unfolded. I do know better now; I truly do. She hugged me so tight I almost cried. Almost.

Still, I can't help but feel something stirring inside. A strange kind of anticipation. I'm actually looking forward to the summer; imagine that. To learn more about where Mother came from, to walk the same land she once walked. Maybe I'll understand her better. Maybe I'll understand myself better.

I met a nice couple on the train. I'm glad to have someone respectable nearby for such a long journey.

The train ride lulled her into a trance. The landscape blurred past like a runaway buggy, cows, trees, and long empty stretches of nothing. The sun gave one last fiery glow before sinking beneath the hills, and then all was gray and still. She had to close her eyes. The motion, the hum, the thoughts, they were all too much.

Tomorrow begins something new. She felt it.

CHAPTER TWELVE

☿ THE ROAD SOUTH

Janice left before the sun had fully climbed, coffee steaming in a travel mug and a grocery sack of snacks on the passenger seat. The apartment looked strangely bare in the rearview mirror when she pulled away. She had watered the plants, wiped the counters, and placed her mother's photo facedown because she could not stand the way the eyes followed her. She told herself she would be gone only long enough to see what shape the Georgia house was in and what it might be worth. She told herself the drive would give her space to think and to plan. She told herself a lot of things.

She had packed the car and small trailer with everything she could manage. The rest went into her parents' garage, boxed and stacked like a life on hold. She had ended her month-to-month lease two days ago, handing back the keys without ceremony. It was frightening, the way the tether snapped, but also liberating. For the first time in years, she had no address that felt fixed. No lease. No safety net. Only the road.

The highway opened, and the car settled into its hum. She queued a podcast called Care for the Caregiver and another called Walk Beside Me. The host's voice was gentle and practical. Keep a notebook for appointments. Ask the doctor for the words you do not understand. Speak to the nurse navigator. Offer help that is specific. Sit and be quiet when there is nothing to fix.

Janice said the words out loud, as if studying for an exam. Notebook. Questions. Nurse navigator. Specific help. Quiet. She repeated them until the car knew them too.

She thought of the night at the dinner table. The way Ruth had said the word "cancer" like it was a chore to be handled and not a storm. The way Ed had stared at the rim of his water glass. The way she had felt shrinking and growing at the same time, like someone pulled in two directions. She wondered if her mother would listen to anything she brought back from these voices in her speakers. She wondered if there would be a day soon when Ruth wanted to hear them, and another day when the voices would only make her tired. She pressed pause and let the tires carry the silence.

The road curved through low hills and stands of pine. At a rest area, she stretched, rolled her shoulders, and watched a line of birds lift from a wire all at once, a ribbon of black that folded and reformed as if one mind moved them. The morning smelled like cut grass and gasoline. A man in a neon vest waved a litter grabber like a flag and nodded to her, and she nodded back, strangers sharing a small piece of the day.

Back in the car, she started a new episode. A survivor

described how her daughter learned to sit through chemo days. Bring a soft scarf. Bring something cold to suck on. Ask about mouth sores. The woman's voice was matter-of-fact and kind. Janice wrote on a sticky note without looking down. She tucked the note into the visor. She imagined walking into a clinic with Ruth, imagined the cool light and the hush, imagined her mother's jaw set against the hurt, and felt both steadier and more afraid.

The miles unspooled. She switched from podcasts to music when her brain felt thick. A song from years ago filled the cabin, and she sang with it even when her throat ached. She let the chorus pull her forward. She let herself think about the house. Not a museum. Not a burden. A place she might scrub and paint and air out. Floors she could make shine. Windows that would open after years of being stuck. She pictured white curtains that actually moved. She pictured her mother sitting at a small kitchen table there, late afternoon light on her face, the kind of light that forgives. The image arrived so clearly that she had to blink it away to keep her eyes on the road.

At a gas station outside a town she did not know, a cat lounged beneath the ice freezer and blinked at her, slow and sovereign. A woman at the next pump had a church fan in her back pocket. Two teenagers laughed loudly and easily near the windshield squeegees. Janice felt like she had stepped into a film that had already begun.

She bought a pack of mints and a bottle of water and texted Jeff a photo of a billboard that read, **Jesus is coming. Are you ready?**

He answered with three laughing emojis, then: **You good?**

She typed: **Driving. Podcasts. Scared and okay.**

He replied: **That is the right order. Call if you need to hear a dumb story.**

She smiled and tucked the phone away.

The state line came with a welcome center and a flag that cracked in the wind. The air was warmer here. Heavier. Pines gave way to a different green, lush and a little wild, and vines climbed wherever they found a hold. Kudzu, she realized. She had seen pictures of it, but never this much. It clung and smothered, swallowing fence posts, trees, whole stretches of road. She pressed her palm against her stomach as if she could calm the feeling there.

The feeling was not only fear. It was a lift in her ribs, a small rise, like the first crest of a roller coaster before the drop. She had not felt it in a long time. Maybe since school. Maybe since the last time she let herself believe that a door could open instead of close. The feeling scared her almost as much as it thrilled her.

She started another episode. This one was for friends and adult children. Do not say, "Let me know if you need anything." Say, "I will come by Wednesday with soup if that is all right."" Say, 'Would you like me to handle the insurance call?" Say, 'I can sit with you during the scan." The host said, 'Your job is not to be heroic. Your job is to be faithful."

Janice closed her eyes for one breath at the red light and said, 'Yes." She pictured writing those sentences on a notecard and taping it to her mother's refrigerator. She pictured Ruth reading it and lifting an eyebrow and saying, 'We will see.' "

She drove through a long stretch of trees where the

light broke into coins across the hood. She thought about names she had read in her mother's family bible: .Natalie. Abby. William. Names that belonged to people who had lived, worked, endured, and left their mark on the same land. she was heading toward. She could not explain why it felt like those names were not just history but a set of keys, and that somewhere along this road she had begun to carry them in her pocket. She had told herself she was going to Georgia for practical reasons: to assess, to clean, to see. But now the car felt like a line drawn between her and something older than any of her plans. She did not have a word for it and did not need one.

At midday, she pulled into a diner that leaned against a wide parking lot. The sign said "Open" in faded red letters. Inside, the air smelled like coffee and fry oil. A waitress with a silver braid set a menu down and called her "baby" without apology. Janice ordered eggs, toast, and fruit she did not finish. She listened to a couple at the counter discuss high school football. She caught a headline on the small television in the corner about storms rolling up from the Gulf.

Back on the highway, she spoke into a voice memo and made a list. For Ruth: bring a soft blanket, bring favorite tea, ask for copies of reports, ask about fatigue, ask about winter plans if treatment runs long, ask who to call after hours. She added a second list and titled it "House": mop and bleach, check the well, Windows. Roof. Photographs. Legal papers. She said the last item twice: legal papers. The words steadied her. There were things to do. She could do them.

Afternoon leaned toward evening, and the sky grew

sweeter. She clicked the air conditioner lower and cracked the window for the smell of heat and dust. Now and then, the trees broke, and she saw fields of something golden, and then a flash of red earth in a cut bank where the road had bitten through. The color startled her, bright and alive. She had seen it in pictures, but the real clay glowed. *There it is.* She did not know what she meant. She only knew she meant it.

Traffic slowed near a road crew, and she crept along beside cones, blinkers, and men in hard hats. One of them lifted a hand in a weary wave, and she lifted hers back. A small boy stood barefoot in a front yard beyond the cones and watched everything as if it were a parade. No one in that yard looked toward the forest just behind them, toward the dark that began early under the trees. Janice looked there instead. For a breath, she felt watched. The feeling was not dangerous. It felt like standing in a doorway and knowing someone was in the next room, quiet and waiting for you to speak first.

She did not speak. She drove.

By the time the sun began to fall, the signs for the county she needed had started to appear. She turned the music off and rolled the window down again. The air was soft and thick, and the sound of insects rose up like static. She left the interstate for a two-lane road that ran between pastures and low houses with wide porches. Porch lights blinked on one by one as if someone were testing a circuit. She slowed when a dog trotted across in front of her, tail held high, then trotted on as if she belonged to this place and always had.

She passed a small church with a white steeple and a

marquee that read: **Potluck Saturday.** She passed a produce stand closed for the day, a hand-lettered sign promising peaches that were already gone. She passed a water tower with the town name painted in a faded blue and felt the name settle on her tongue like a word you know you will say often. She tried it out quietly and liked how it sounded when the car held the syllables.

The last podcast of the day was a short one. A chaplain spoke about how to stand beside pain without rushing to cover it. "Ask what matters to you today. Ask what you are afraid of. Ask what would help and mean it." The voice was calm and plain, and Janice thought that calm and plain might be a kind of miracle. She turned the volume down and let the words sit with her like a passenger.

She did not drive all the way to the house. The light was almost gone, and her eyes had begun to ache, so she pulled into a roadside inn that promised clean rooms and cable. The clerk slid a key card across the counter and told her which way to turn for the best biscuits in the morning. In the room, she sat on the edge of the bed, rubbed her calves, and listened to the air unit start and stop. She texted Ruth a photo of the sunset from the parking lot. Peach and violet, a color the sky only makes when it has been warm all day. Ruth answered with a heart, then, *Call me in the morning.*

Janice: I will. Sleep well. She stared at the bubbles that did not fill with a reply. She set the phone on the nightstand and plugged it in.

She brushed her teeth and stood at the window with the curtains open. The parking lot light made a pale circle on the asphalt. A moth battered itself against the glass and then disappeared into the glow. Somewhere out there were the trees and the red earth and the house that waited. Somewhere out there were the names she had begun to carry. She pressed her palm to the cool pane and felt the smallest current of air at the edge where the seal had worn away.

Excitement rolled through her again, that rise in the ribs, and right behind it a rush of worry. She let both live in her. She did not try to choose. She whispered three words to the dark, not sure who she was addressing. "I am coming."

Then she turned off the lamp, lay back, and listened to the hum of the room and the long breath of the road still in her body. She did not dream, or if she did, she could not remember. Morning would bring the rest.

CHAPTER THIRTEEN

◦◦ THE RIVER

1859, Somewhere in the Midwest
Autumn

The gentleman in front of her had asked for two blankets and handed one to his wife and one to Natalie, a soft smile on his face. "Don't worry, I'll stand guard," he said.

His wife looked at him, then at Natalie, and giggled. "He never sleeps. I would think he hides in his office during the day and naps if I didn't know better." "

She had her mother's cadence, that Southern, sing-song way of carrying you along as though every sentence were a gentle swing. Natalie couldn't help but smile in return and thanked them. She rested her head against the train window, the cool glass easing her temple as the steady clatter of the wheels lulled her into sleep.

That was when the dream came.

She stood barefoot in a field, the grass damp against her soles. The orchard stretched before her, not tidy rows but a wild, tangled expanse of moss-draped pecan trees. Their thick limbs curled like bent, accusing fingers. The air was humid and close, heavy with the scent of wet bark and decaying leaves. Spanish moss swayed in the breeze, whispering secrets she could not quite understand. A low wind stirred the branches, and in it, she thought she heard her name. Or maybe it was a cry.

Then she saw him. A man stood at the edge of the orchard, tall and lean, his face too calm to be kind. The soil clung damp to her bare feet, as though the ground itself meant to hold her there. He smiled; the moss above him swayed like a noose.

He looked to be in his twenties, tall and lean, his dark hair slicked back from a face too calm to be kind. He was handsome in a disarming way, the kind of face that might have drawn admiration in another setting, but something in it unsettled her. He stood perfectly still beneath one of the older trees, its bark split and hollow like a wound. He was watching her. Not with curiosity, but with recognition. As though he had been waiting for her to arrive.

Fear rose sharp and sudden inside her, though she could not have said why. Natalie tried to move, to step back, but her feet were rooted in the soil. Her throat locked. She could not call out.

The man was Billy, her cousin, the same cousin her mother had once spoken of. He stared at her with empty, soulless eyes. He tilted his head slightly. The moss above him stirred like a curtain drawn by an unseen hand. Then he smiled, and the orchard darkened.

When the shadows deepened, he appeared again, his

shirt streaked and dripping with blood. But somehow Natalie knew, with bone-deep certainty, that the blood was not his.

Somewhere behind her, a woman sobbed. The sound was muffled and thick, as if the earth itself were grieving.

Natalie turned toward the crying, but when she looked back, Billy was gone. In his place lay a single ribbon, red as blood, half-buried in the moss, fluttering faintly as if stirred by breath.

Her chest ached as she woke, the train whistle echoing in her ears. She pressed her damp palms to her lap, her heart still racing. Why Billy? Why now? She had only ever heard his name in passing, a whispered cousin from her mother's stories. Why was he finding her in her dreams?

The whistle blew again, longer this time, and she shivered. Maybe it was only nerves, the fear of leaving everything familiar behind. Or maybe it was something more. A warning. She remembered her father's words about fighting with her head, not her hands, but the dream lingered, twisting around her thoughts like vines. If even in her sleep she was being pulled toward Billy, what did it mean for her summer in Georgia?

Outside, dawn was breaking pale and uncertain over the horizon. She told herself it was only a dream, but deep down she knew better.

Her neck ached with a crick, and her palms were damp. Dawn was breaking pale and blue along the horizon.

"Perfect timing," said the woman across from her.

Natalie gave a small smile. "Good morning."

"And good morning to you," the woman replied, her

voice lilting with an edge of familiarity, as though she had seen Natalie somewhere before.

Natalie stood to gather her things, nearly forgetting the blanket. She folded it carefully, her fingers trembling. Something about the dream clung to her skin, heavy as dew. She did not know why the trees felt alive, but a chill had settled deep in her spine. She could not shake the feeling that what she had seen was not just a dream. It was a warning.

Outside on the platform, she followed the couple to stretch her legs. The air smelled of coal smoke and damp wood.

The woman in blue was striking, her gown the shade of a summer sky. Her hair was a polished chestnut, touched with warm auburn highlights that caught the light when she moved. It wasn't like Natalie's strawberry-blonde or Meredith's flaxen, but its own rich hue, deepened by her piercing steel-gray eyes. Her constant, saccharine smile never seemed to leave her face, even when no one was looking.

"Do you mind if I ask where you're from?" Natalie asked.

"Why, of course not, darlin'. I'm from Georgia," she said, making Georgia a three-syllable word.

Natalie brightened. "That's where I'm headed." "

The woman laughed. "Well, of course you are. This train is full of us going back home."

Natalie flushed, realizing her foolishness. "I didn't think about that."

"And you don't sound like you're from Georgia. Where are you from?"

"Buffalo. New York," Natalie replied.

"New York!" The woman clapped her hands together in delight.

"Well, yes, but the countryside. My father owns a store, and we moved there to get away from the city."

"Isn't that a hoot? My husband's family is from New York. That's where we were visiting. But it's time we headed back home. The estate won't tend to itself." She looked at Natalie as though the girl might have the answer.

Natalie only managed, "I couldn't say."

The woman laughed again and patted her arm. "I'm Kathleen. And that," she pointed with her gloved hand, "is my husband, Walt."

Natalie smiled and extended her hand. "So nice to meet you. I'm Natalie. Spending the summer with my aunt and uncle."

Kathleen leaned closer. "Oh, a summer, you say? Most who go South for the summer never leave," she giggled. "It's beautiful. You'll never want to go home." Then, lowering her voice behind her gloved hand, she whispered, "Now let's get back on before we're stranded in this Godforsaken place." Her saccharine smile stayed fixed even as her eyes flicked restlessly around the platform.

Natalie blinked. Ohio hardly seemed Godforsaken to her. The rolling pastures and tidy towns were lovely. Yet Kathleen's unease lingered.

As the train pulled forward again, Natalie caught her first glimpse of the Ohio River stretching wide and silver. She whispered to herself, "Get her over that river on the right side of everything."

That river wasn't just water. It was the dividing line between bondage and freedom. South of it, human beings were sold, hunted, owned. North of it, they might find liberty. It was called the Jordan, the Promise, the Threshold. Many had died trying to cross. Even more had dreamed of it.

Natalie sat with the weight of that thought when she remembered her errand. From her carpetbag, she drew three carefully addressed letters: one to Mr. and Mrs. Craft, one to Mr. William Still, and one to Mr. Benjamin Lundy. She needed them posted before reaching her aunt's house. She did not want her family to see those names, not yet.

As she smoothed the envelopes, Walt glanced down and pressed her hand closed around them before anyone else could see. His voice dropped. "Madam, allow me to post those for you. We're limited on time."

Startled, Natalie shook her head. "No, sir, you can't."

He held her gaze. His eyes were firm, knowing, protective. "I am the best person here to do this."

Walt slid the envelopes into his coat, his voice low enough that Kathleen didn't stir.

"Letters won't reach you safely once you're south," he murmured. "Too many eyes, too many hands eager to open what isn't theirs. If you write more, don't risk sending them. Tell me what you need carried, and I'll see that word makes its way north by mouth. Safer that way."

Natalie's throat tightened. "Why help me?"

His gaze was steady. "Because some words must live. And because no one fights alone." He tipped his hat and was gone before she could answer.

For reasons she could not explain, she believed him. She handed over the coins from her reticule. He tipped his hat and strode off down the street.

By the time he returned, Kathleen was still humming and fixing her hair, oblivious. Walt slid into his seat without a word but gave Natalie a single nod. That nod said more than words could.

Natalie opened her journal.

JOURNAL ENTRY:

Something peculiar happened today. I wrote three letters I meant to send before reaching the plantation, addressed to people whose names are known in certain circles— abolitionists, yes, but people I trust. I am not ashamed of the names, but I am cautious. I do not want my family to see them. Not until I understand more.

I was about to post them myself when Walt, Kathleen's husband,—the nice couple from the train— quietly offered to do it for me. He did not explain, only gave me that steady nod, as if to say he understood. I do not know what made me trust him. But I did.

There is something happening beneath the surface of this journey. I feel it. And somehow, so does he.

CHAPTER FOURTEEN
⚓ THE THRESHOLD

J anice eased the car to a stop at the edge of the drive, gravel crunching beneath her tires. For a long moment, she just stared, taking it all in. Her fingers tightened on the steering wheel, slick with sweat, though the air-conditioning still hummed. A shiver rose across her arms, gooseflesh against the thick Georgia heat, the kind of contradiction she couldn't name. Part of her longed to put the car in reverse and escape back to Seattle, but another part just as strong, told her she had to go inside. Her mother needed this, her family needed this, and she was the only one who to do it.

The house stood with the weary dignity of something that had outlived its builders, its late 1800s bones still upright but undeniably tired. The two-story farmhouse was framed in weathered clapboard, the white paint now barely more than a memory, peeling in strips like old parchment. It wasn't ruined, not exactly. But it was a place that remembered too much.

A wide, covered landing spanned the front, its steps

sagging and crooked with age. The porch railings were laced with delicate spindle work, their curves and flourishes still visible beneath vines and dust. One post leaned at a doubtful angle, propped against a cement block someone had wedged beneath it long ago. The rocking chair by the door moved slightly in the breeze, empty but stirring, as though someone had just left or was about to arrive.

Her eyes followed the trim up to the second story. A covered deck jutted from the upper floor, the kind that might once have caught a breeze on sweltering Georgia nights. Its roof dipped at the center like a spine too long burdened, and a single iron chair sat facing the orchard in the distance. The railing was mismatched, some pieces ornate, others clearly replaced with scrap wood in a pinch.

The house looked aware, as if the years of silence had turned it into a patient witness, studying her approach with an unblinking eye. Like it remembered everything and wasn't sure yet whether to let her in or keep its secrets buried.

Janice stepped out of the car, the summer air pressing in on her as cicadas buzzed in the trees beyond. The orchard behind the house was wild now, moss-covered pecan trees stretching their arthritic limbs like old men reaching for the past. She could almost picture someone, Natalie maybe, or the girl, Lucy, she had only heard of in fragments, standing barefoot at the edge of it all, gazing back at this very house with secrets still tucked behind the shutters.

She shaded her eyes against the sun and took a slow

breath. "Well," she murmured, "guess this is home for a while."

She pulled out her phone and hit call. Her mother picked up after the second ring.

"You there yet?" Ruth asked, her voice edged with fatigue but steady.

"Just pulled up," Janice said, eyes still fixed on the weathered clapboards and the sagging porch. "It looks... older than I expected. You didn't tell me it looked like something out of a Faulkner novel."

Ruth gave a dry laugh. "Don't you go scaring yourself with old stories. That house has stood longer than most people in this family. Good bones. Just needs a little love."

"Mom, it needs more than love," Janice replied. She let her gaze wander to the upstairs balcony where a single chair faced the orchard. "It needs paint, a roof, maybe a miracle."

"Don't fuss. You've got the card. Just do what you can. Nothing fancy, just enough to make it livable again. You'll see, it'll feel different once you're inside."

Janice hesitated, pressing her lips together. "It feels... like it's lonely."

Her mother grew quiet for a moment. Then came the clink of ice in a glass. "That house has always waited for someone to tend to it. Maybe it's your turn."

Janice swallowed, unsure if that was meant to reassure her or not. "Alright. I'll call you later with pictures."

"Good girl. Now go on and get inside before you melt in that Georgia sun."

"Love you, Mom."

"Love you too, Janice."

She hung up, slipped the phone into her pocket, and finally mounted the leaning stairs. The foyer smelled of dust and old cedar, the kind of scent that clings to wood after generations.

Her grandmother's trinkets and photos were still placed on almost every flat surface. She picked one up and rubbed the glass clean, revealing a group of people in black and white on the porch in rockers, laughing at a joke she would never know. It warmed her to see laughter and history right where she stood. She thought of her mother running across these very floors in diapers.

She placed her keys on the kitchen counter and wandered through the rooms, taking stock the way her mother had told her to. The kitchen held little beyond a dented metal table, its surface pocked with rust, and a pair of mismatched chairs pushed against the wall. The old refrigerator, an off-olive green color, surprised her by humming to life when she tugged its stainless steel handle. Cold air drifted out, and she smiled then quickly wrinkled her nose. "Better than I thought, but it needs a serious cleaning before anything can go in there." She waived her hand in front of her face

The front parlor offered a sagging sofa with sun-bleached floral fabric. Dust puffed from the cushions when she pressed a hand to it, and she sneezed into her arm. The flooring looked original, though water damage near the sink had warped a few boards. The back door opened onto a covered porch that seemed to connect the house and orchard seamlessly. She noticed the lock was flimsy, adding it to her growing mental list.

Toward the rear of the first floor, she found a large

bedroom with a view of the orchard and a fashionable walk-in closet. A small bed with a delicate spiral frame sat under rose-patterned wallpaper. She imagined her grandmother's last days here. Instead of frightening her, the thought filled her with comfort.

Upstairs, the rooms were bare except for a toppled chair in one corner and a cracked dresser missing its mirror. She ran her fingers along the chipped wood, then opened a window with a groan, letting in a thin slice of sunlight. Another bathroom greeted her in the hall, unexpectedly updated, tiled, and functional. She decided this would be her bedroom and set to work, sweeping and wiping until the air smelled less of cedar and more of effort. Carrying up her suitcase, bedding—and dragging her mattress, took the better part of the afternoon. By the time she returned downstairs, her shirt clung with sweat, and her throat was raw from dust.

As she reached the curve of the staircase, her eyes caught a small cupboard tucked beneath it. The knob was tarnished with age. She knelt and tugged, coughing as dust bloomed into her face. Inside, the cedar-lined space was shallow. Too shallow.

She tapped along the back wall. Hollow. Her fingers brushed a groove at one edge. She hesitated. "Here goes nothing." She pulled, and the panel slid forward reluctantly, revealing darkness beyond.

She switched on her phone's flashlight and leaned in. A shiver crossed her shoulders, but she reached inside anyway. Her hand closed on a small wooden box, no bigger than a loaf of bread, tied with a frayed leather cord.

At the kitchen table, she untied the cord and lifted the

lid. Inside lay an embroidered cloth, faded but soft, stitched with roses around a single ivory button. She traced the threads, her chest tightening as though the cloth itself carried memory. Beneath it was a folded envelope. The script was looping and deliberate: *To Meredith. In case I do not return.*

Her breath caught. She set it aside, unable to open it yet.

Below the envelope were yellowed newspaper clippings.

Local Girl Missing After Church Picnic.

Third Disappearance Rocks County. No Leads.

Sheriff Urges Caution: Curfew in Place After Fourth Incident.

Her stomach turned. Different names, different years, but the same dark undertone. At the bottom of the box was a hand-drawn map, the orchard circled, an arrow pointing to the root *cellar* with the note: *where the land splits.*

Janice held the page up to the window, turning to match the angles to the orchard outside. For just a moment, it seemed the trees leaned closer, shadows stretching toward the house.

"Get a grip, Janice," she muttered.

But the feeling of being watched stayed with her.

She slid the box back into its hiding place and brushed dust from her hands. "Enough for tonight."

Upstairs, she washed and crawled into bed, but her mind would not rest. Every creak of the farmhouse set her on edge. She pulled the blanket beneath her chin, eyes fixed on the dark doorway, until at last, she drifted into uneasy sleep.

And when she dreamed, the orchard was searching. Branches stretched down, heavy with moss and shadow, brushing against the windows as if searching for a way inside. Faces seemed to form in the bark, eyes hollow and unblinking, mouths open in soundless cries. Whispers tangled in the leaves, low and urgent, like prayers spoken too fast to follow. A woman's voice wept beyond the trees, mournful and low, then broke into laughter sharp as breaking glass. She strained to see her, but the sound scattered like leaves in the wind.

Janice woke with a start, her heart pounding. For a moment, she swore the orchard pressed against the very walls of the house, crowding closer, leaning in to learn more.

"It's just a dream," she whispered into the dark.

But the unease lingered, thick as the night air.

CHAPTER FIFTEEN
◦◦THE THREAD

1859, Georgia
Autumn

The train wheels screeched against the rails as the cars began to slow, and the scent of red clay and honeysuckle drifted through the cracked window. Natalie pressed her forehead to the glass. Georgia was nothing like New York. The air hung heavy with heat, thick as wool and just as irritating to the skin. Not even the strongest breeze seemed to push it away.

Her stomach fluttered with nerves. For weeks, she had told herself she was ready—ready to see the land her mother had spoken of with both longing and disdain, ready to prove she was more than a headstrong girl who could not hold her tongue. But as the platform came into view, lined with strangers and expectant faces, a hollow ache rose in her chest. What if she did not belong here? What if all her ideals, all her books, all her talk meant nothing in this place?

Excitement and dread twisted together, pulling her tight from within. She wanted to rush forward, to set her feet on this strange new soil, and yet she wished the train would keep rolling, carrying her back to everything familiar.

The cars lurched to a halt. She drew in a breath and sat up straighter. No turning back now.

Walt helped Kathleen down the steps first, then offered Natalie a hand next. As he steadied her, he leaned close.

"Remember what you carry," he whispered.

Natalie blinked, startled by the weight in his tone. "The letters?"

He gave the faintest nod. "They've gone to the right people. But this," he tapped the side of her bag gently, "this is about more than paper. You'll understand soon."

Her heart skipped. She snatched her hand back, cheeks flushing. "Thank you," she said stiffly.

Kathleen turned just in time to miss the exchange. She brushed a curl behind her ear and smiled warmly. "Welcome home, Natalie. Social life down here is a whirlwind; you'll see. I expect to see you again soon." She gave a little giggle, the kind that drew people in without effort.

Natalie forced a smile. "I'll look forward to it."

As they parted ways, Walt appeared beside her one last time. "Be mindful of whom you trust here. Not everyone wears their loyalties on their sleeves."

She straightened, meeting his eyes. "I understand."

"Atlanta's a web, Miss Natalie," he said, the hint of a

smile tugging at his mouth. "Best to move through it like a thread. Quiet. Careful. Strong."

Then, with a tip of his hat, he was gone into the crowd.

A voice called her name from the edge of the platform. First a man's, then a boy's. "Natalie?"

She turned to find two figures approaching. One older, dressed sharply in a navy suit with round spectacles perched on his nose. The other, a lanky boy with a mop of light brown hair and an eager smile.

"I'm your Uncle William," the man said, extending his hand. "And this here is your cousin Henry."

Natalie smiled politely as she shook their hands. "It's very nice to meet you both."

William snapped his fingers. "Isaac! Get her bags, come on now."

From around the carriage stepped a young man about Natalie's age, barefoot, dressed in patched work clothes. His head was shaved close, his eyes steady and curious. He paused when their gazes met. For a moment, she felt an unspoken connection, as if something passed between them. Then it was gone.

"No, thank you, Uncle," she said quickly. "I've got it."

William waved her off with a firm hand. "Isaac is here for just that."

Reluctantly, Natalie passed her bag over. "Thank you, Isaac," she said softly.

He gave her the briefest smile, but it disappeared the moment he turned toward William. His face went blank, his posture folding inward. The change unsettled her.

"You must be tired," William said, steering her away from the awkwardness.

"I am," she admitted. "It was a long ride."

"Your aunt has a room prepared. You can rest until dinner."

Natalie nodded. Henry skipped at her side as they walked toward the carriage. He was full of questions.

"Do you really get snow so deep it covers fences?" he asked, eyes wide.

Natalie smiled faintly. "Sometimes. And sometimes it's so heavy the roofs nearly cave in."

Henry whistled. "I'd rather pick cotton in the sun than shovel that."

Natalie's smile faded. "You don't choose it. You just live in it. Same as here."

Henry tilted his head, confused, but William cleared his throat, cutting the conversation short. "Tell me about your mother and father, Natalie. How are they holding up with the business expanding?"

She answered politely, but her mind stayed with Isaac and the weight of Walt's warning.

The carriage rattled along the dusty road. Henry pointed out the homesteads as they passed.

"That's the Walshes'. They grow tobacco and sugar."

"And over there, the Lancasters'. Cotton. They tried indigo last year; total disaster." He laughed at his own joke, and William chuckled. Natalie forced a small smile, but the words left a sour taste. Her eyes strayed instead to the endless rows of bent laborers working the fields.

"Are those all enslaved folks?" she asked quietly. "Or are some of them employed?"

Henry frowned, uncertain. William's jaw tightened. "In the South, Natalie, things are different."

Natalie opened her mouth to protest, but William cut in smoothly. "Tell me, what was it like on the journey? Did you make any friends?"

The question shut down her protest. She leaned back, giving polite answers while her thoughts churned elsewhere.

The road narrowed, shadowed by trees draped in gray moss. The air cooled, but the silence was heavier than the heat. No birds sang. No insects hummed. Only the creak of carriage wheels and the clip of hooves against stone.

Natalie sat straighter, her reticule tight in her grip. She kept her expression carefully composed, answering William's questions and smiling faintly at Henry's chatter. Outwardly, she must have looked calm, even curious. But inside, her thoughts twisted restlessly. She would not let them see her nerves, not here, not yet.

Something in the stillness felt alive, as if the land itself were alive.

JOURNAL ENTRY-

Mer, you would not believe the ground here. The clay is red, the kind of red that clings and stains like dried blood. Even the honeysuckle, sweet at first, leaves something bitter in the air.

I will admit this to you and no one else: when the train slowed and I saw the families waiting, I felt my chest seize. For weeks, I have been so bold in my letters, telling you I was ready, telling myself I was brave. But the truth? I was afraid.

Afraid I would not belong. Afraid I was stepping into a world that would swallow me whole before I even understood its rules.

It is a strange thing, Mer, to want something so fiercely and dread it in the same breath. I wanted to see this land, to test myself against it. But I also wanted to turn the train around and go home, back to our school steps, back to everything I knew. My heart twisted both ways at once.

Walt told me to move like a thread. Quiet. Careful. Strong. I do not know why, but it keeps replaying in my head. Kathleen, his wife, tried to make things light. She hugged me like family, but Walt, he looked at me as if he knew more than he was willing to say.

Uncle William is every bit the gentleman, maybe too much so. He asked about Mother and Father, about the store, but when I asked about the fields, he said only, "In the South, things are different." Different. That was his only answer.

Henry pointed out the farms with such pride. "That is the Walshes; that is the Lancasters." When I asked if the workers were free, Henry just stared at me, not knowing what to say.

And then there was Isaac. He carried my bag without a word, but when our eyes met, it startled me. He looked at me directly, steady, alive. Then William barked his name, and it was like watching a door slam shut inside him. I do not know why, but I cannot stop thinking about that look.

The ride grew quiet beneath the trees. Moss hung down like curtains, gray and heavy, and not a bird sang. It was silence thick enough to choke. Mer, it felt like the land was waiting for something. Or maybe waiting for me.

Walt was right. This is more than letters, more than family ties. Something here is older than all of us, and I intend to understand it. He said to move like a thread. Quiet. Careful. Strong.

I will. I will be the thread.

PART TWO
HAUNTINGS AND BURDENS:

"Secrets fester beneath the clay, and what is buried does not stay silent forever."

"What the dead remember binds the living. What the living forget binds them even more."
— Traditional Southern saying

CHAPTER SIXTEEN

⚓ ROOTS AND RUINS

T he light filtered in through the warped slats of the blinds, catching dust motes that swirled in lazy spirals above her head. Janice lay still, watching them drift like tiny planets suspended in a universe of their own. The old house seemed to breathe with her, every timber expanding and groaning in its own rhythm. She had slept more soundly than she expected, though not without interruption. At least three times, she swore she heard footsteps outside her door, the faint scuff of movement. At other times, she felt as if unseen eyes were on her. It creeped her out enough that she had wedged kitchen chairs beneath both the front and back door handles. Just in case.

Now the morning air was cool, but she could already feel the press of humidity promising a sweltering day ahead. She swung her legs over the side of the mattress, her bare feet landing against the worn wood floor with a thump. Her coin necklace, which had slipped off during the night, lay tucked into the sheet. She slipped it back over her head and adjusted it against her collarbone.

Her stomach rumbled, a low reminder that she had not eaten anything proper since yesterday.

And there it sat.

The box.

The one she had found behind the cedar panel, tucked deep beneath the stairs where the risers dropped much lower than expected. Even now, hours later, it seemed to hum with its own presence. She had stayed up late into the night, combing through its contents: the embroidered cloth, the yellowed clippings, the map, and the letter.

Especially the letter.

On the outside, it read in looping script: *To Meredith, In Case I Do Not Return.*

Inside, Natalie's handwriting stretched dense and emotional, her words pulsing with urgency. Though the letter was not dated, Janice felt the weight of finality in every line. Words like "truth," "forgiveness," and "witness" clung to her mind. She did not yet understand all of it, but she knew she held something far heavier than paper.

She leaned against the back of the chair, her gaze drifting toward the rear window. Out there, past the waist-high grass and twisted piles of brick, was the orchard. Was that where the map pointed? Was that what Natalie and Lucy, too, if the embroidered cloth was any sign, had wanted someone to find?

Not just patching a house, Janice thought, pressing her palm against the letter as though she could still feel the heat of Natalie's hand through time. She was stitching together a history she had only known in fragments.

She set the letter aside and decided to walk through the house in full daylight.

The house had already revealed its fragments: the dust-heavy sofa, the crooked dresser with its cracked mirror, the penciled grocery list fading in the kitchen drawer. Now, when Janice thought of them, they no longer seemed like relics of neglect but pieces of a story. She imagined the hands that had touched them, her grandmother's hands, her mother's as a child, threads of history both loved and forgotten. Somehow, having them here felt like part of her own legacy, though she could not quite explain why.

The daylight showed what she hadn't noticed before. Upstairs, the air thickened beneath the pitched roof. In the back bedroom, a crooked dresser stood, with a mirror cracked in a jagged line that split her reflection. Inside its drawer, she found a single child's sock balled in the corner, stiff with age.

In the hall, she paused. The wallpaper was yellowed and peeling in places, and something faint caught her eye. She leaned closer.

There, just above the baseboard, were pencil lines.

Her breath caught.

She crouched down, fingers brushing the wall as if afraid the marks might vanish at her touch. Names and numbers were written in a careful hand. *Benjamin – age 6. Benjamin – age 7.* Another just above: *Benjamin – age 8.*

Her breath caught. Oh, was this the same Benjamin she had found on the ancestry website? The graphite was faint but steady, etched into the house itself. She ran her fingertip over the grooves, feeling a strange intimacy, as though she were trespassing on a family's private ritual. A lump rose in her throat. Whoever Benjamin had been, he had lived here, had grown here, and had left proof of himself in a place no one had thought to erase.

Janice whispered the name aloud, tasting it. "Benjamin."

The sound of it lingered in the stillness of the hall. She gave a small nod, as if acknowledging him.

She stood there longer than she meant to, her palm pressed against the faded wall before finally stepping back. The marks remained, quiet witnesses, wanting someone to remember.

When she circled back downstairs, her phone buzzed. Her mother.

"Janice? Are you there yet?" Ruth's voice was thin, carrying a distracted edge.

Janice's heart sank. "Yes, Mom. I called last night when I pulled up."

There was a pause, then a soft chuckle. "Yes, yes, I remember now. Silly me, it's these meds. They make me feel like I'm always two steps behind."

Janice swallowed against the knot in her throat. "That's all right. How are you feeling today?"

"I wish everyone would stop asking me that." Ruth coughed lightly, then softened, her tone gentler. "I'm fine, darling. Send me pictures of the house."

Janice leaned against the porch post, choosing her words with care. She remembered the podcast: Offer something specific, not vague. "Mom, what if I called your doctor about the prescriptions, so you don't have to juggle it all yourself?"

A silence followed, long enough that Janice worried she had overstepped. Then Ruth exhaled, her voice weary but grateful. "That might be useful. I hate being placed on hold. And Janice, don't forget to send me those pictures."

Janice's fingers tightened around the porch post, the weathered wood digging into her palm. The second request landed heavier than the first, threaded with the fear her mother might not remember much else.

Ruth cleared her throat. "And how's the family tree coming along? Have you added anything new?"

The question caught Janice off guard, though she forced a smile into her voice. "A little. I found something yesterday that I think belongs there. I'll tell you more once I've sorted through it."

Ruth hummed softly, content with the answer. "Good. Keep at it, darling. Someone has to remember for all of us."

Janice let out the breath she had been holding. "Then I'll handle the calls. I'll keep a notebook of everything they tell me, so you don't have to remember."

"You always were the practical one," Ruth murmured. A beat passed, then she added, "Your grandmother used to keep roses on the kitchen sill. Maybe you'll see if any bushes are left."

Janice's throat tightened. "I will check."

"That's good," Ruth said softly, her voice drifting toward weariness. "I should make some coffee for Ed before he heads out, or maybe I'll lie back down. Either way, I love you, darling."

"I love you too, Mom," Janice whispered.

She sat there a moment longer, the phone cooling in

her hand. Ruth's words lingered, simple, ordinary things like roses and coffee, but beneath them, Janice heard the strain. It made her ache with worry, yet at the same time, it drew her closer, as if each conversation was stitching something between them that had frayed too long.

At last, she slipped the phone into her pocket and headed toward the yard.

The shed stood crooked at the far end of the property, boards grayed and warped. Its door resisted before finally giving way with a shriek, releasing a bloom of musty air and a cascade of cobwebs. She coughed, waving her hand as her throat stung. Tiny feet scurried into shadow.

"Please do not let there be spiders. Please do not let there be spiders," she muttered.

The shed was barely five feet square, its roof sagging but intact. Tools leaned against one another in tired poses: a shovel, a pickaxe, a wood axe, and trimming shears. In the corner rested a wheelbarrow with one sagging tire. She dragged it into the sun with a grin. The tire was spongy, and rust gnawed at the frame, but it would do.

Along the axe handle, someone had carved faint letters: WL. She traced them absently, the grooves shallow and uneven, worn down by time. Whoever had pressed them there was long gone, their story forgotten. The house had a way of keeping pieces of people, even when the family tree did not. Janice let her hand fall away, struck by the weight of it all. So many hands, so many names, and now hers among them. The history of this place was tangled and dark, but it was hers, and she felt a strange, fierce pride in claiming it.

Above the doorway, a bent horseshoe had been nailed

for luck. She touched it lightly. Whatever luck it had promised had long since run out.

As she stood there, cicadas began their droning chorus. The sound pressed against her eardrums, an unbroken buzz that seemed to vibrate in the marrow of her bones. She shaded her eyes and looked toward the orchard again. Moss hung like curtains from the pecans, and the pile of bricks near the center looked almost purposeful. The map came to mind, and with it, a prickling awareness that something out there waited. She shivered and turned back toward the house.

By the time she reached the porch, a truck pulled into the drive. A young man in a company shirt and ball cap climbed out, grinning crookedly.

"Guy, Lawn Guy Maintenance," he introduced himself.

"Is that really your company name?" she asked, raising an eyebrow.

He flushed under the brim of his hat. "Yes, ma'am."

She laughed. "Clever. But why not just The Lawn Guy?"

"Because we do more than lawns," he said, puffing up a little. Behind him, two workers unloaded equipment.

"Well, I may need more than lawns done around here. Can I get a card?"

He handed her one, simple and white, with a list of services scrawled on the back. "And we do even more," he added. Then his tone softened. "My grandma says not to walk in that orchard at night. She says the land remembers."

Janice stilled, caught by the seriousness in his eyes.

"Thank you," she said, pocketing the card.

By noon, the AC repairman had come and gone, leaving the unit humming steadily. She sat at the green-topped kitchen table, the box of relics spread before her again. Her fingers hovered over the map. She lifted it, held it against the window light, and turned it this way and that. The landmarks were sketched faintly: the orchard, the line marked *"root cellar,"* the cryptic words "where the land splits."

She whispered, "Where the land splits... what does that mean?"

Her eyes drifted to the backyard. The orchard loomed, its tangled branches a barrier and a beckon. An eerie feeling crept over her as if someone stood just beyond the tree line, watching. She shook her head, telling herself not to be ridiculous, but the unease clung like humidity.

Janice folded the map carefully, slid it back into the box, and tied the bootlace around it. She sat for a long moment, the hum of the AC filling the silence, the taste of the energy drink still sharp on her tongue.

For the first time in years, she felt a calm settle deep inside her chest, something steady and grounding. But there was still something else too. Something unspoken. The calm was only half the truth. The other half was the gnawing sense that the house had chosen her for a reason.

CHAPTER SEVENTEEN
◦◦ PEACHTREE PLANTATION

1859, Georgia
Autumn

B y the time Natalie finished answering questions about her family's store and their place in the community, the carriage turned off the main road onto a smaller tree-lined path. Oaks arched overhead, their limbs draped with heavy moss that swayed like gray ghosts clinging to the branches. The air cooled in their shade, but the humidity clung to her skin like wet linen. Resin scented the breeze: pine and earth and something sweet that she could not name. Sweat gathered at her temple and slipped past her ear despite the drift of air that moved through the open window.

The cicadas screamed so loudly that they drowned the clatter of wheels and the steady clip-clop of hooves. The sound was a blanket that settled over everything until even her thoughts seemed to hum. Natalie leaned out of the carriage window, eyes wide, trying once again to take in the landscape. The trees whispered in a language she did not understand. The wild, tangled green stretched in every direction, thick with vines and the rich, damp smell of soil that had been turned and turned again. Ferns crowded the trunks. Sunlight dropped through in coins that blinked and vanished. There was beauty in its strangeness, but also unease. The deeper they drove, the more the air seemed to shift, as if they had passed through an unseen veil into another world where the rules would be different, and the house might breathe when it slept.

Then she saw it. A gleam of white through the trees, and then the full splendor of the house revealed itself, grand and unapologetic, set at the end of a circular carriage path. Flowers bloomed in the roundabout's center: roses and something pale that lifted its face to the heat. The vast porch, wrapped around the house like open arms, held tables and empty chairs that waited for guests who were not there. The shutters were a clean dark green, and the roof shone faintly in the sun. The place did not look built so much as posed.

"She is a beauty, is she not?" Uncle William asked, breaking the silence.

Natalie startled, realizing her mouth had fallen open.

"It is stunning," she whispered.

The house stood in whitewashed grandeur, fronted by towering Greek columns and a staircase that spilled down like a gown. It looked less like a home than a statement. Something plucked from a dream, or a dream that might sour if you stared at it too long.

She glanced back and saw that the tree-lined entrance had hidden broad fields of cotton. Beyond the house, rows stretched toward the horizon, endless white bolls glowing in the afternoon sun. The plants looked like snow had fallen and refused to melt. It was the first working plantation she had ever seen. Distant figures moved in a slow line under the light. Heads bent. Shoulders lifted. The rhythm of labor was older than the house itself. Her hand twitched on the window frame, part of her wanting to wave, part of her unsure if a wave would comfort or wound.

"You only grow cotton?" she asked, her voice thinner than she intended.

"Well, Momma and Miss Patty tend the vegetable garden out back," Henry offered quickly, eyes darting between her and his father. "The workers have one too."

"Oh, how lovely," Natalie said, hands clasped near her chin. She was not sure what else to say. The word lovely felt wrong in her mouth. The field shone prettily, and the edges of it felt sharp if you looked straight on.

Isaac pulled the reins gently. "Whoa." The horses slowed, answering more to his quiet presence than the word itself. He touched one on the neck, and it shivered as if relieved.

As they drew near, the porch filled the front of her vision. At the top of the grand staircase stood a woman in a butter-yellow dress, posture regal, a little girl clinging to her side. Aunt Alice. Ribbons fluttered in the child's braids as the warm air stirred. Somewhere on the side of the house, a wind chime lifted and fell and then stilled again.

Natalie stepped forward, hand outstretched, but Alice drew her into a firm embrace instead.

"Welcome home, niece," Alice said, her voice a soft Southern lilt that settled around Natalie like a shawl. "This is Abbigail, your youngest cousin."

Natalie blinked, startled by the warmth in the woman's touch. Alice's face was strikingly similar to her mother's, the same high cheekbones and deliberate poise. But where her mother often seemed restrained, Alice's eyes crinkled with genuine affection. Her smile carried ease. Lavender water clung to the fabric at her throat. For a moment, Natalie felt as if she had stepped into a gentler version of her mother, one touched with light rather than steel.

Abbigail peeked from behind her mother's skirts, then launched herself forward, arms wrapping Natalie's neck with the fierce joy only a child could muster. The girl smelled like sun and starch and a trace of sugar.

"Oh my," Natalie said, laughing as she steadied her footing.

Only then did Natalie notice the figure standing just behind Abby. Not a child at all, but a girl nearer her own age, slender and tall enough that her presence seemed diminished only because she carried herself with deliberate quiet. Her apron bore a faint dusting of flour, and her cap shadowed dark eyes that flicked up once before lowering again. In that quick glance, Natalie sensed a steadiness beyond her years, a watchfulness that unsettled her.

Abby tugged Natalie's sleeve. "And this is Lucy. She helps me with everything."

Lucy inclined her head, the smallest of acknowledgments, her gaze sliding away as though such introductions were not hers to make. But Alice's hand reached gently for her shoulder, a gesture of reassurance that lingered longer than it needed to.

"This house is livelier already," Alice said warmly, drawing Natalie into an embrace again. Yet her fingers pressed lightly against Lucy's shoulder a moment more before she let go, as though she needed to feel the girl anchored near her.

Natalie's smile softened. "Hello, Lucy."

Lucy's lips parted as if to answer, but no words came. Abby quickly filled the silence with another burst of chatter, tugging Natalie further into the hall, Lucy following at an even pace, her quiet presence trailing like a shadow that knew its place.

The moment shifted quickly. Abbigail's bright expression faltered, her gaze flicking past Natalie. She pulled away and slipped back to her mother's side, fingers tucked into the folds of the yellow dress.

Natalie turned. A man had stepped forward, and the air drew taut. He was tall, broad shouldered, handsome in a bronzed way, and glaring. His sharp gray eyes locked on hers with disdain. Something in the space stilled. Even the cicadas seemed to thin for a breath.

Natalie lifted her chin and offered her hand. The gesture hung in the heat. Shame and anger rushed through her chest in equal measure. He did not greet her. Did not acknowledge her as family. Just looked her over as if measuring and finding her wanting, as if she were a parcel that had arrived with the wrong seal.

She lowered her hand slowly. Alice's embrace

evaporated in her memory, replaced with the weight of this silent refusal.

"Allow me to introduce our eldest," Uncle William said quickly. "William the third. We call him Billy."

Natalie drew herself up and arranged her voice. "How do you do."

Billy scanned her from head to toe. The corner of his mouth pulled.

"This is the one from the North." The words slid off his tongue like something spoiled.

"Yes, son. This is your cousin Natalie. She will be staying with us for a while," William answered evenly.

Billy spat into the dirt, eyes still on her. The sound was small, but it landed like a stone.

William stepped between them. "Now, now, son. Natalie is family." Whether warning or plea, Natalie could not tell.

Isaac had already dismounted. Head bowed, he moved with quiet efficiency. He lifted her traveling case as if it weighed nothing and passed it to a woman in an apron streaked with flour. Her gray-streaked hair framed a face softened by years of kindness and work.

"Miss Patty," William said, with a nod that held respect and habit in equal parts. "See that Natalie gets settled. She has had a long journey."

"Of course, sir," Miss Patty replied. Her voice carried its own strength, the kind that did not need to raise itself to be heard.

Natalie exhaled and let Billy's stare fall away like a weight. She followed Miss Patty across the threshold. The coolness of the interior raised the small hairs on her arms.

Beeswax and lemon oil clung to the banister. The marble tiles beneath her shoes gleamed where the sun touched them and turned dull where the corridor curved. A tall clock ticked with a steady patience.

Leaning close, Natalie whispered, "Miss Patty, please, you do not need to serve me. Just tell me where to go."

Miss Patty's smile deepened, lines of humor and wisdom crinkling her face. "Now, I will do no such thing. Mister William asked me to look after you, and that is that." Her eyes shone with a glint that said she had seen many nieces arrive with fine talk and fine shoes and that she loved them anyway.

Natalie laughed softly, charmed despite herself. "Well, thank you. But if you ever need anything, I am not helpless. I promise." She pressed a finger to her lips in mock secrecy.

Miss Patty chuckled, a full, round sound that filled the hallway. As it faded, her expression shifted. Not cold. Not fearful. Just careful, as if setting a cup down without a rattle. Her voice dipped low.

"Mind yourself around that eldest boy. He was born with the land's mark on him. Some say the trees went quiet the day he came into this world." She lifted her chin slightly toward the windows that faced the orchard. "Some say the owls do not take the pecan branches near his window. Some say the dogs refuse the steps when he sits on the porch. The land remembers, child. It blesses and it warns."

Natalie blinked. "The land's mark?"

Miss Patty only turned, the light catching the silver in her hair. "Come along. Let us get you washed and rested.

This house does not always welcome new blood easily. But I reckon you are meant to be here." She paused beside a tall arrangement of roses on a side table and plucked a brown petal free. "Roses will show you if the air is right. Keep an eye on them."

They moved through a parlor dressed in velvet that had seen too many summers. A pair of portraits regarded them from the wall, their painted faces watchful. In the dining room, sunlight made a bright river across the long table. Through the back windows, Natalie caught a glimpse of another world behind the grandeur: A yard full of heat waves, A kitchen garden with rows of beans and okra reaching for trellises, and a wash line that snapped once and fell still. Beyond that, the orchards lifted a dark green edge.

Upstairs, Miss Patty opened a guest room that smelled faintly of lavender and starch. A pitcher of water waited on the washstand. A small Bible lay near the pillow. The cover was worn where fingers had worried it smooth. The window looked toward the side lawn, where a pair of women carried baskets and spoke in low voices that drifted up without words.

"If you need anything, you call for me," Miss Patty said.

"Thank you," Natalie answered. The words felt thin beside the weight of all she did not know how to say.

Miss Patty smiled again and left the door ajar as she went.

Natalie stood a moment in the quiet room and listened to the house settle. Wood sighed. The great clock downstairs spoke the hour, then held its breath again. She washed her face in the basin and watched the water ripple, her own face wavering there, new and not new. When she lifted the pitcher, she saw that a petal had fallen beside it and was already curling at the edge.

She set the petal on the sill and closed her eyes. A memory rose unbidden: her father's hand on a ledger, his voice even as he spoke of accounts and costs. How value is always a question of who is doing the counting. She opened her eyes and looked down toward the white rows beyond the porch. Beauty is never free, she thought. Not here.

When the bell rang for the evening meal, the sound carried through the house like a gentle order. She smoothed her dress and went down. The dining room glowed. Aunt Alice stood at the head of the table with an easy grace that made the crystal catch light. Uncle William smiled in a way that was both welcoming and warning. Henry pulled out a chair for her with a small, proud flourish. Abbigail slid onto the seat beside her and tucked her hand into Natalie's for one quick squeeze that felt like allegiance.

Billy was already there. He lifted his glass and watched the window instead of the people. When Uncle William offered grace, Billy's mouth pressed thin, and his eyes stayed open. When the amen rose, he held his fork like a small weapon. No one remarked on it, which told Natalie more than words.

Miss Patty and two women moved through the room with practiced ease. Plates were set down. Bowls were passed. Slices of ham that shone with glaze. Cornbread that broke with a soft sound. Greens that smelled of smoke. Natalie thanked each server by name when she could, and each time Miss Patty's mouth flickered at the corner as if she took measure and filed the moment away.

"Tell us about your journey," Aunt Alice said, warm and curious.

"It was long," Natalie said with a smile. "But I saw stars from the last stop that looked close enough to touch." She glanced at Henry. "Do you always hear the cicadas like this in the evening?"

"Every summer," Henry said. "They sing until you do not notice."

"I still notice," Abbigail said primly, then giggled and hid her face against her arm.

Uncle William spoke of weather and planting, and a neighbor's new mill. Aunt Alice asked after Natalie's parents with sympathy that felt clean rather than performative. Henry chattered about a bird's nest he had found under the eaves. Billy cut his ham into precise squares and ate them like a man timing himself. When Natalie lifted her water glass, her hand steadied itself with effort.

Later, as the air cooled by degrees and the lamps were trimmed, Natalie slipped out to the back veranda alone. The boards were warm under her shoes. Fireflies lifted at the edge of the yard and went dark again, a slow signaling that felt like language. Farther off, the field held its pale quilt and its silence. The orchard a dark line that watched.

She heard the kitchen door open and close. Miss Patty joined her with a small plate and set it on the railing.

"Peach slice," she said. "You did not finish yours."

"Thank you." Natalie took a bite. The fruit was soft and warm from the day and tasted like the color of the sky over the cotton. Sweet. Slightly sad. "Everything is so beautiful."

"And?" Miss Patty said.

"And costly," Natalie finished.

Miss Patty nodded. "You will learn the rest in time." She looked toward the orchard, and her voice went soft again. "Keep the lamps burning if you hear the wind pick up. The mothers do not like the dark here."

"The mothers," Natalie repeated.

Miss Patty did not answer. She touched the rail where the plate had been, as if smoothing a wrinkle there, and left the way she had come.

Natalie stayed until the fireflies faded and the first bats cut through the air. She folded the last bite of peach into her mouth, swallowed, and told herself she would find the kitchen garden in the morning. She would find out where the water was drawn. She would learn the names of the women who carried the baskets, the names of the men who guided the mules, and the names of the children who slept in the cabins beyond the orchard. If she was meant to be here, she would act as if meaning had work to do.

When she returned to her room, the petal on the sill had curled tighter. She set the Bible aside and took up her journal.

JOURNAL ENTRY-
I arrived safely in Georgia, and it is both more beautiful and more sorrowful than I imagined. The house is tall and

white as bone, its porch ringed with columns that make a person feel small. The cotton fields roll on and on, soft in the sun, but knowing what they cost changes everything I see. Beauty is never free.

On the train, I met a man whose name I will not write, and he spoke as if he saw not only who I am but who I might yet become. He hinted at people who help and people who act. I think he believes I could be one of them. I do not know if I am brave, but I know that silence feels like a lie in a place like this.

Abbigail is a sunbeam in lace. She nearly knocked me over with her hug. Henry is curious and kind and still half-lit with wonder. I feel protective of him already. Aunt Alice is my mother softened, a familiar face washed in gentleness. I did not know I needed that until she held me.

And then there is Billy. Cousin Billy looked at me as if I were an enemy before I said a word. He called me the one from the North as if the word itself were filth. I think he hates what I represent: that I see not only the beauty here but the pain that underwrites it.

There was also Lucy. She is about my age, though she carries herself with a stillness that makes her seem older. She stood just behind Abby, silent but steady, her eyes sharp even when she lowered them. I cannot stop thinking of the way Alice's hand lingered on her shoulder, as if she needed Lucy near to steady herself. Something in me stirred when our eyes met, though it was only for a moment. I feel as though she will matter, though I do not yet know how.

Miss Patty warned me in a voice that felt older than the house. She said Billy was born with the land's mark and that the trees went quiet when he came into the world. I do not know exactly what that means, but I believe her. There is something wild in him. Not free. Cruel. Something that waits in the dark and thinks about its teeth.

I am frightened, Meredith, not of what he has done, but of what he may yet do. Still, fear is not the same as surrender. If I am to stay here, I will learn the ways of this place. I will keep the lamps burning. I will find the paths that run beneath the clay. I will listen for the mothers in the wind. I will not look away.

CHAPTER EIGHTEEN

◦◦ SHADOWS IN THE
ORCHARD

1860, Georgia
Summer

The day had been long and heavy, the kind of late summer afternoon where the air itself seemed to sag. Alice and Natalie had gone into Marietta for flour and lamp oil, leaving Abbigail and Lucy with the rare gift of an afternoon to themselves. Abby clung to it eagerly, savoring the chance to keep Lucy close without interruption. For once, the house seemed to belong to just the two of them. Cicadas screamed from the trees, their endless chorus drilling into every corner of the plantation. Most of the hands were still in the fields, but the yard lay quiet, almost too quiet, as if it were watching with anticipation.

Abbigail tugged on Lucy's hand the way she always did when she wanted something and would not be denied. "Come on," she pleaded, her dark eyes wide and bright, a ribbon slipping loose from her braid. "Just to the orchard. I'll show you where the rabbits hide."

Lucy hesitated, her gaze flicking toward the line of pecan trees beyond the yard. The orchard loomed like a growing shadow, the branches thick with leaves that never seemed to stir even when the wind bent the pines nearby. She wanted to say no, but Abby's small fingers clutched hers with such trust that the word caught in her throat.

"Only for a little while," Lucy said softly.

Abby grinned, triumphant, and skipped ahead, tugging Lucy into the path that curved toward the orchard. Their bare feet pressed into the dry grass, and the smell of dust and resin thickened with each step. The shade swallowed them slowly, a coolness that should have been a relief but settled instead like damp cloth on the skin.

The orchard stretched wide, its rows unnervingly even. Gray moss hung from the branches, swaying in long drifts like tattered curtains. A few pecans had fallen early, scattering across the ground. Abby darted to one and cracked it against a rock. She grinned, holding up the broken shell.

"See? Fresh," she said, slipping a piece into her mouth. "Want one?"

Lucy shook her head. "Not from here."

Abby frowned but popped the rest into her mouth anyway. "Mama says the orchard's been here since before we were. Before even Grandpapa bought the land. Is that true?"

Lucy nodded, her voice low. "Older than the house, older than me." She glanced at the trunks, the bark ridged and split like old scars. "Some say older than anything that was meant to grow here."

Abby crouched, brushing her fingers along the grass where wildflowers tangled with weeds. "Bitsy told me the orchard takes things. Firstborns. Is that true?"

Lucy's chest tightened. She wanted to hush her, to tell her children they ought not to speak of such things, but Abby's gaze was searching, serious in a way too heavy for her age.

"Bitsy hears stories," Lucy said carefully. "Old stories. Sometimes stories keep you safe."

"What kind of stories?" Abby pressed.

Lucy drew in a slow breath, her eyes scanning the darkening rows. "That the orchard remembers the ones who came before us. That it doesn't let the firstborn stay. The Huxleys lost their boys here, one by one. Their mama too, in fright. The land took them all."

Abby shivered but leaned closer. "But Billy's the firstborn. And he's here."

Lucy pressed her lips tight. She did not want to answer. She did not want to give shape to the fear that everyone in the cabins whispered when they thought no one could hear.

Abby's hand slipped into hers again, small and warm. "Then why's he still here?"

Lucy forced a smile she did not feel. "Because sometimes the land don't take. Sometimes it gives back something else."

Abby tilted her head, unsatisfied. "Something else like what?"

Lucy opened her mouth but stopped. A crow shrieked

overhead, the sound jagged, splitting the silence. Abby startled and pressed close against Lucy's side. The air seemed to thicken around them, the shadows deepening though the sun still burned in the sky beyond the orchard.

Lucy crouched, brushing Abby's ribbon back into place, her hands steady though her stomach knotted. "We should go back now. Your mama will be worried."

But Abby lingered, her eyes fixed on the far row where the trees grew thickest. "It feels like someone's watching," she whispered.

Lucy followed her gaze. Nothing stirred. No hand, no shadow, only the droop of moss and the slow sway of branches. And yet Lucy felt it too. That prickle at the back of her neck, the way the orchard seemed to lean closer the longer you looked at it.

She took Abby's hand firmly this time. "Come," she said, her tone leaving no room for argument.

Abby obeyed, but as they stepped back into the light, she glanced over her shoulder one last time. The orchard stood quietly, but the silence felt less like peace than like hostility.

Lucy did not look back.

By the time Lucy and Abbigail stepped back into the yard, the sun had lowered a hand along the horizon, and the heat pressed heavy on every surface. Natalie had just come out from the hallway carrying folded linens when Alice called from the porch.

"Come sit," Alice said, her voice soft but firm. "There is sweet tea enough for all."

They climbed the steps. The porch boards burned

with the last of the day's warmth, but the shade made it bearable. Alice poured the tea into sweating glasses, the ice chiming like bells. Natalie took a long sip, the sweetness cutting through the dust that had gathered at the back of her throat.

"You went to the orchard," Alice observed, eyes settling on Abbigail and Lucy.

Lucy's hands folded tight in her lap. "Only a little ways."

"It feels like church," Abbigail said brightly, then lowered her voice. "But not always in a good way."

"Church is a fine word for it," Alice said gently, though something tightened in her jaw. "Some places ask for respect."

Abbigail twisted toward Natalie, eyes wide. "Bitsy says the orchard takes the firstborn."

Alice stiffened, the gentleness gone from her expression in an instant. "Bitsy hears too many stories," she said, though her hand pressed against her daughter's back with a protective weight.

Natalie set her glass aside. "People tell stories to make sense of fear," she offered carefully. "In Savannah, they say the river keeps tally. Boats that take too much often pay it back in storms."

Alice looked at her, something like gratitude flickering in her eyes.

That day, Alice had taken Natalie into Marietta for flour and lamp oil. The depot was alive with men's voices, and Lincoln's name went around like a lit match.

"He'll split this country in two if he wins," one said, grinding his boot into the dust.

"Blood will be what binds it back, not ballots," another answered.

Alice tightened her grip on Natalie's arm and steered her past. "Do not linger," she said, as if to herself as much as to her. Once they had turned the corner, Natalie let out the breath she had been holding.

"In Albany," she whispered, "they said his name like it was a promise. Here it sounds like a threat."

Alice glanced at her sharply, her eyes flicking back toward the depot. "Careful. This is not Albany."

Natalie bit her lip but did not look away.

"Still, it is the same man. The same country." Alice's grip softened but did not release her arm. "And that is why you must be wiser than them."

In Albany, his name had been a hopeful whisper. Here, it felt like tinder.

But the porch fell quiet. The cicadas swelled, filling the space with a shrill hum. Then the ground itself began to shake. A horse thundered into the yard, foam dark against its bay coat. Billy leaned low over the animal's neck, eyes sharp, posture more suited to war than home.

"Not near the porch!" Alice called, her voice rising to command.

At that moment, a toddler darted from the yard's edge after a ball, more legs than balance. The horse's hoof clipped the child with a sickening thud. The boy crumpled, his mother's scream splitting the air.

Natalie was on her feet, breath locked in her chest.

Billy wrenched the reins, the horse fighting him in the churned-up yard. He swung down hard, crop dangling in his hand. It was a rough braid, something darker woven through, uneven strands that caught the light. He flicked it against his leg once, twice, a sharp crack that made Natalie flinch.

Lucy flew from the porch, crouched over the child with quick, steady hands. The mother dropped to her knees beside them, sobbing as Lucy wiped grit and pressed cloth against scrapes. The boy whimpered but began to calm, no bones broken, only skin raw and pride bruised.

Alice held Abbigail close, her arm like a shield.

Billy looked at the child only briefly. His eyes climbed slowly to Natalie instead, fixing on her as though no one else existed. His head tilted to the left. He held it there, still as a hunting cat. Then tilted to the right. The faintest curl tugged at his mouth, not joy, not apology, something colder.

Natalie's body refused to move. She felt pinned beneath the weight of that look. The crop cracked against his thigh again, setting a rhythm only he understood.

Abbigail pressed her face into her mother's dress. "Mama," she whispered.

"Enough," Alice said, her voice low but edged with steel.

Billy flicked the crop once more, then turned without a word. He mounted the porch steps with an easy gait, opened the front door, and disappeared inside. A moment later the clink of plates carried faintly from the dining room.

The yard exhaled as if life had been held still. The boy's mother gathered him in her arms, Lucy steadying her with one hand.

"Bring them to the kitchen," Alice ordered.

Natalie and Abbigail followed Lucy and the boy's mother into the house. The cool dimness of the hallway swallowed them whole. In the kitchen, pails of water waited near the wall. Alice wrung a cloth, her hands calm though her mouth pressed tight. She dabbed at the boy's cuts, her touch as tender as her voice had been fierce. Lucy steadied the child, speaking low until his sobs quieted.

"Thank you," the mother whispered again and again, as if gratitude were the only thing keeping her upright.

Natalie sat with Abbigail at the table, trying to still the tremor in her own hands. She could hear plates set down in the dining room, deliberate and casual, as if the same man who had nearly crushed a child now dined without a second thought.

The kitchen door to the study closed hard. Alice's voice rose sharp and urgent. William's answered, firm and unyielding. Their argument swelled and broke against the walls, words muffled but fierce.

Lucy's head bent lower over the child, but Natalie could see her listening with every line of her body. Abbigail pressed her fingers to her ears, though her wide eyes stayed fixed toward her mother's voice.

Natalie sat straighter, her own pulse hammering. She could not make out every word, but she knew. They were speaking of Billy. And the house itself seemed to listen.

The kitchen had fallen into a brittle kind of silence once the boy and his mother were sent home, the pails emptied and the cloths rinsed. Lucy moved quietly at the table, smoothing Abbigail's hair, though her ears tilted toward the closed study door across the hall. Natalie sat opposite, her spine straight, her own hands folded so tightly her knuckles paled. The house seemed to press in, listening with them.

Alice's voice rose first, muffled but sharp. "You will not pretend again. You saw it, William. You saw the way he looked at that child. What if it had been Abbigail in his path?"

William's reply came quick, low, and cutting. "Do not let fear make you hysterical. He has a temper, yes, but he is my son."

"He is your son, and you blind yourself to what that means," Alice shot back. "How many more, William? How many children must we watch stumble half-dead from his shadow before you admit what he is?"

Natalie's stomach tightened. She glanced at Lucy, whose lips pressed into a thin line, eyes refusing to meet hers. Abbigail shifted uneasily, her small hands cupped over her ears, though her gaze darted to the door again and again.

William's voice dropped, iron hard. "You will not repeat tavern tales in this house. We do not know what happened in Macon. We do not know what happened with the neighbor's girl. Gossip grows wings."

Alice's voice cracked, fierce through the break. "Gossip does not leave bodies. It does not carve girls until their mothers cannot recognize them. Do not speak to me of wings when we are standing over graves."

Natalie's hand clamped over her mouth. The air in the kitchen thickened, hard to breathe. Lucy shifted closer to Abbigail, her arm slipping around the girl's shoulders.

William thundered again, sharp enough to rattle the door. "We don't know it was him!"

Silence fell, heavy and choking. Then Alice's voice, low and trembling. "It is him. It has always been him. Even as a child, he left scars. You sent him away, and he did worse there. And now you bring him back under this roof with our daughter."

Her words dissolved into quiet sobs she did not bother to hide.

William's tone softened, though it was steeped in denial. "He is the firstborn. He lives when others did not. Perhaps the land spared him for a reason we do not understand."

Alice's reply was a whisper sharp enough to cut. "Or perhaps the land marked him for what it lost."

Natalie's pulse hammered. She stared at the grain of the kitchen table, willing herself not to look at Lucy, not to reveal the terror pressing inside her chest. Abbigail burrowed against Lucy's arm, trembling.

The voices in the study dropped lower, more like a hiss and mutter than speech. Natalie caught fragments, "name in town," "our standing," "appearances", and she thought she might be sick.

Then a sound shattered the fragile stillness. From the dining room came the hard clank of a plate against wood. Another, louder, deliberate. The scrape of a chair.

Billy.

Natalie stiffened. Every muscle in Lucy's body tensed, her hand flattening protectively over Abbigail's back. They did not move, did not breathe.

Footsteps passed slowly through the dining room,

unhurried. Another dish clattered, this one rolling a little before settling. The doorframe creaked as though a shoulder brushed it. For a moment, Natalie thought he might come into the kitchen.

Instead, the front door opened with a long, groaning hinge. The slam shook the walls, and then there was only the cicadas outside, shrilling as though nothing had happened at all.

The kitchen exhaled in unison. Lucy leaned her forehead against Abbigail's hair. Natalie forced her hands to unclench, though her palms bore half-moons where her nails had dug deep.

From the study came Alice's broken voice again, softer now. "And what if the next body we bury is hers."

Natalie's chest ached. She closed her eyes, knowing she would not sleep that night, not while the memory of hooves clattering across the yard and a child's scream rang like a warning in her mind.

The house had quieted, but the silence was uneasy, as though the walls still hummed with the argument behind the study door. In the kitchen, the lantern flame wavered low, throwing long, trembling shadows up the plaster.

Lucy sat at the table with Abbigail curled into her side, the child still shaken, thumb tucked against her mouth in the way of a much younger child. Natalie lingered across from them, her hands folded tight in her lap, her thoughts darting like startled birds.

"Is he all right?" Natalie asked softly, meaning the boy who had been carried home.

Lucy nodded once. "Scratches. Bruises. He'll mend.

His mama…" She trailed off, eyes far away. "She'll not forget."

Natalie pressed her palm flat against the table, grounding herself. "Why does he—" She stopped, her throat tightening. "Why does Billy look at people that way? As if…" She could not bring herself to say the word prey.

Lucy's hand smoothed over Abbigail's hair. She did not answer immediately. The air between them grew taut. Finally, she said, "Abby, sweet pea, it's time for bed. Your mama will be looking for you."

"I don't want to," Abbigail whispered. "He'll be in the house."

Lucy bent, kissing the crown of her head. "Miss Natalie and I will be right here. Nothing will come for you."

Reluctantly, Abby slid from the bench. Natalie rose, offering her hand, and walked the girl to the stairs. Halfway up, Abby paused and looked back, her eyes wide in the flickering light.

"You'll stay?" she asked.

"I'll stay," Natalie promised. "Now go on."

Abby hurried up, her small feet pattering until they were swallowed by the second floor. Natalie returned to the kitchen.

Lucy had not moved, save for folding her arms on the table. Her eyes, when she lifted them, were weary and hard.

"You asked what's wrong with him," she said at last.

Natalie sat slowly, her breath shallow. "Yes."

Lucy's gaze dropped, fixed on a knot in the wood

grain as though she feared to look Natalie in the eye. "He was born this way. The others before him didn't last—the Huxley boys, their mama, even his own kin here. No firstborn should've survived on this land. But Billy did. And it marked him."

Natalie felt her stomach turn. "Marked him how?"

Lucy hesitated, her lips parting and closing again. She glanced toward the door, then leaned forward, lowering her voice. "Have you seen his crop? The one he carries?"

Natalie nodded. She had noticed it earlier, dangling from his hand when he dismounted, the leather rough and dark. "Yes."

"It ain't just leather," Lucy said, voice nearly a whisper. "He braids hair into it. Different colors, different lengths. Braids he's taken."

Natalie's blood ran cold. "Horsehair?" she murmured, though the words sounded hollow, a lie even to her own ears.

Lucy shook her head. "Not horsehair." Her voice cracked. "Trophies. He don't let it out of his sight. He keeps count with it, like the land keeps count of him."

Natalie pressed her hand to her mouth, bile rising. She had thought the strands odd, uneven, but never once imagined... She closed her eyes, seeing the braid in her mind, the way it caught the light. Not horsehair. Not rope. Lives.

"What can we do?" Natalie whispered. "If it's true—what can stop him?"

Lucy leaned back, her face shadowed, her voice weighted with defeat. "Nothing I know. Miss Alice tries to guard Abby, but he's blood. The master shuts his eyes.

The hands pray and tie ribbons in the trees, same as Sibella once taught. Rootwork, charms, little things to keep the dark from crossing our doors." She lifted her eyes at last, and they were full of something heavy, a knowledge too old for her years. "But he is the dark. And you can't charm away what's born into the house itself."

Natalie shivered. Her fingers found the edge of her glass, circling it, though she did not drink.

Lucy's eyes softened, though her words did not. "You keep close to Miss Alice. You keep close to me. And if you hear him coming, you don't linger. You run."

Natalie's throat burned, but she nodded. She felt the weight of the house above them, of footsteps she could not hear but knew were there. Billy's presence pressed in even when he was nowhere to be seen.

The lantern sputtered. The shadows shifted.

Lucy rose, her movements brisk now, as though the conversation had already gone too far. "Best get to bed, Miss Natalie. Morning comes early here."

Natalie wanted to ask more, to demand answers, but the look on Lucy's face told her the door was closed. For tonight. Perhaps forever.

She stood, her knees weak, and followed Lucy's lead, dousing the lantern. The kitchen plunged into darkness, broken only by the faint glow from the hallway candle.

Natalie could not sleep. She lay in the narrow bed, the candle still burning on the table beside her, its flame bent by each sigh of air that moved through the cracks of the old house. The sheets clung to her skin. Every creak in the timbers made her body tense.

At last, she sat up, pulling the satchel from beneath

her bed instead of her journal. Her hands trembled as she drew out a folded sheet of paper and dipped the nib into the ink. She meant to steady herself with her diary, but the words pressing at her heart belonged to another page entirely.

Dearest Mother and Father,

I know you hoped my stay here would be brief, but I cannot come home. This house is not what you think it is. It is not only a home but a threshold, and something walks within it that will not stop at the door. Miss Alice tries to hold the light for her daughter. Lucy stands between the shadows and the child. And now I find I am standing here too.

You asked me once what I meant when I said I felt called. I think I understand now. This is where I am meant to be, not because it is safe but because it is not. If I leave, I will carry the weight of what happens here. If I stay, perhaps I can change it.

Do not write to demand my return. Pray for me instead. Pray that what is hidden here comes to light before it takes another life.

Your loving daughter,

Natalie

She folded the page once, twice, and slipped it into the lining of her satchel with the other letters she meant someday to send. The act left her both lighter and heavier. Lighter for having spoken her resolve, heavier because the words could not yet leave this house.

Only then did she draw her journal back into her lap. These pages were for truths no post rider would ever carry, truths meant only for her hand to remember. She dipped the nib again, steadier this time, and began to write what Lucy had told her about Billy's crop and the braid of hair.

Journal Entry-

September 1860

Today Lincoln's name was spoken like a curse in town; back here, the house holds a different kind of danger.

I thought the land heavy, but it is nothing compared to the weight of what walks inside these walls. Lucy said he was born marked. She said the braid is not leather alone, but hair. I cannot unsee it. What kind of soul collects such things?

The candle sputtered. She lifted her head, listening. A sound had risen from the hall— measured, deliberate.

Footsteps.

They stopped just beyond her door. The silence that followed was worse than the tread itself, a silence thick enough to press against her chest.

Natalie's quill hovered over the page. Her throat tightened. Slowly, the doorknob shifted, turning just enough to rattle the latch. It held there, unmoving, as if whoever stood outside was savoring the pause.

Her breath came shallow, her pulse loud in her ears. She gripped the edge of her blanket, paralyzed.

Then came the scrape.

A fingernail, slow and steady, dragged down the wood. The sound was faint, but it sliced through her like a blade. Again it came, higher this time, tracing a line across the paneling. The message was clear. He knew she was awake. He knew she had heard him.

The doorknob stilled. The footsteps began again,

retreating down the hall with casual ease. One. Two. Then nothing.

Natalie's body trembled with the effort not to cry out. She pressed her hands over her mouth until the silence seemed safe again. The candle flame shivered beside her, throwing the room into uneven light.

She bent over her journal once more, forcing herself to write though her vision blurred.

I do not know for certain it was him. But in my bones, I know. It was him. He wanted me to hear. To fear. To wait. He will choose his moment, and until then, the house itself will conspire to keep me from rest.

Lucy said the land marked him, that no firstborn had lived here before him. Perhaps that is why Miss Alice trembles when she speaks of her son. She does not trust him. She does not even want him here. I see it in her eyes — the way they follow Abbigail's every step, the way her hand shakes when his voice cuts across a room. She fears him, though she tries to hide it.

Uncle William will not see it. He speaks as though blindness is protection, as though refusing the truth might make it less so. He says Billy is only a boy with a temper. He calls the stories gossip. But silence will not hold him back. It never has.

And so, Alice lives with dread under her own roof. Lucy shoulders it beside her. And I — I have stepped into their prison.

That crop he carries… The braid knotted into the leather is not horsehair. It is human. Lucy all but told me so. Trophies cut from the heads of girls whose names are already lost. He keeps them close, counting the lives no one will speak of.

What sort of mother must it be to look at your child and know you birthed the terror that keeps your daughter awake at night? What sort of father is it to defend him still, knowing silence only feeds the dark?

The candle is low. The scrape of his nail across my door rings still in my ears. He knows I am here. He knows I hear him.

If I am to remain, I must learn every creak of these floors, every whisper of the orchard. I must learn when to keep watch and when to hide. Because Miss Alice is right. Billy is not just cruel. He is waiting. And one day soon, he will choose.

She closed the journal, slipped it beneath her pillow, and blew out the candle. Darkness swallowed the room. She lay still, eyes open, listening for the scrape of fingernails that might return before dawn.

CHAPTER NINETEEN
⚓ THE CALL

The hardware store smelled of old wood, oil, and dust baked into the walls. Janice pushed open the door and stepped onto scuffed floorboards that had been worn thin by decades of boots. Behind the counter, an older man in overalls looked up from a ledger. His hair was silver, his face a map of sun and years, his eyes a sharp gray that seemed to take her in all at once.

"Afternoon," he said. "What can I do for you?"

Janice placed a list on the counter—deadbolts, screws, and weather stripping. "The farmhouse out on the old Cheney property. I'm trying to make it feel more like home."

His pencil stopped mid-tap. "Not the big house. The smaller one."

She nodded. "Yes. My family's place. I'm here to fix it up."

Something flickered across his face, recognition, maybe, or discomfort. He slid the paper closer, his fingers rough and deliberate. "We can get you fixed up. Old places like that, you'll want sturdy locks. Fancy breaks. This won't."

He turned, moving more slowly than necessary, pulling boxes from the shelves. Janice glanced at the rows of nails and tools, everything lined up neat as soldiers. When he returned, he set the stack down with a thud.

"You staying out there by yourself?" he asked.

"For now. My parents might visit later, but it's just me."

His gaze lingered. "You keep a light on. Always. Windows are invitations after dark."

Janice blinked. "That's... specific advice."

"Take it or leave it," he said, his voice flat. Then, as though remembering manners, he added, "If you need help with more than locks, I've got names. Folks around here are handy with boards, roofs, even plumbing. But locks, locks you can do yourself."

She thanked him, gathered her bag of hardware, and left with the feeling that she hadn't been given everything he knew.

The farmhouse sat patiently when she pulled into the gravel drive, its white paint tired, its windows wide and bare. The orchard swayed behind it, pecan branches shifting in the late afternoon breeze. She cut the engine and sat for a moment, staring at the dark panes. After Mr. Collier's words, they didn't just look empty anymore. They looked open.

She carried the bags inside, nudging the front door shut with her hip. The hinges squealed, offended by the effort. She set the hardware on the kitchen table and leaned both palms on the wood, listening. The silence was never quite silent in this house. The boards sighed. A cupboard clicked faintly as though settling back into place. Outside, the cicadas droned their endless hymn.

Janice shook out the deadbolts. Their solid weight comforted her. She gathered the screws and screwdriver and carried them to the front door. It took longer than she expected. The old brass knob clung to the frame as though it had grown roots there. She braced one foot on the floorboards and pulled hard, nearly toppling backward when the rusted plate gave way with a groan.

"Guess you didn't want to leave either," she muttered.

At last, the bolt slid home with a firm click. She leaned her forehead against the door, sweat damp at her temple. "That'll do," she whispered.

But the windows mocked her. She crossed the room, staring out at the orchard where shadows had begun to lengthen. Pecan trunks stood like black pillars, their crowns whispering together overhead. She could almost believe the branches leaned closer, listening.

The light outside thinned to amber. She wished she could close the curtains, draw a line between herself and the world pressing against the glass. But there was nothing to reach for, no fabric to soften the view. Just bare panes reflecting her face and the dark yard beyond. She dropped her hands to her thighs, palms pressing hard, as if to ground herself in something solid.

Her phone lay on the counter, its screen dark. For a long moment, she resisted, staring at the orchard. Then she snatched it up and thumbed the screen alive, dialing the one number that steadied her.

It rang twice.

"Jan?" Her father's voice came through, warm but rough at the edges.

Relief caught her in the throat. "Hey, Dad."

"Well, there you are. How's the farmhouse holding up? Got that old plumbing figured out yet?"

She glanced toward the sink where the faucet dripped, slow and steady. "Sort of," she said with a half-laugh. "One thing at a time."

"That's the spirit." He coughed lightly. "Your mom's dozing. I'll tell her you called when she wakes up."

Silence stretched. Janice pressed her free hand to the counter, fingers tight against the edge. "Dad... it's different out here. At night."

"Different how?"

She let out a breath she hadn't realized she was holding. "Spooky, I guess. The house creaks all the time. And the orchard..." She broke off, searching for words. "It feels like something's moving in it. Watching."

Ed chuckled softly, though not unkindly. "City girl ears. Out there, it's deer, possums, raccoons. Maybe a fox if you're lucky. They'll come right up to a porch if the grass is tall. And every board in an old house has something to say. You'll get used to it."

She wanted to believe him. Wanted the shadows to be nothing more than deer nosing at pecans. But the memory of Collier's words pressed down on her: *Windows are invitations after dark. Keep a light on.*

"I don't know," she said quietly. "It doesn't feel like animals. It feels... menacing. Like it's aware of me."

Her father's voice softened. "Jan, you've got a lot on

your shoulders. The house, your mother's health. Fear makes its own ghosts."

Tears burned behind her eyes. "I just… sometimes I think I see things. Like figures where there shouldn't be. Maybe I'm losing it."

"No," Ed said firmly. "You're tired, that's all. You've been running on adrenaline since you drove down there. It'll settle. And listen, you're not alone in this. You call me, any hour, if it gets too much. Promise me."

"I promise."

"Good girl." His voice cracked a little. "Your mother's stronger than she looks, but I know you see how it's wearing on her. She's resting in her chair. You being there, taking on that house, it gives her hope. Don't underestimate that."

Janice turned toward the window again. Her reflection hovered in the glass, pale against the deepening night. "I'll do my best. For her."

"For all of us," he said softly. "That place carries family in its bones. Just remember, it doesn't carry you, you carry it. That's the difference."

She hesitated, then took a breath. "Dad, there's something else I need to tell you. When I first got here, I found a box. It was tucked behind a false wall under the stairs, as if someone wanted it hidden. Inside was a map, old and hand-drawn. There were names on it, and strange markings. Places around the house, the orchard, maybe even something underground. Do you know if any of that means anything?"

Silence hummed across the line. She thought for a moment that the call had dropped. Then Ed exhaled slowly, a long, weary breath. "A map hidden in the wall?" His voice had changed, no longer casual, but careful. "I can't say I know every marking you're talking about. But your grandmother used to tell stories, half history, half warning. There were always whispers about tunnels, about the orchard having places no one should walk at night. I never saw a map, but... Jan, if someone drew one, they had a reason."

"What kind of reason?"

"The kind that doesn't get written down in the family Bible," he said. "The kind people keep quiet about. Maybe things that happened on that land, maybe people who needed hiding. All I know is, if the words or symbols don't make sense now, keep them safe until they do. Don't go showing it around town. Not everyone wants old truths dug up."

Her pulse quickened. "So, I should hold on to it?"

"Yes. Hold on tight. And keep your eyes open. That house has ways of revealing things when it's ready." He cleared his throat, gentler again. "In the meantime, leave some lights on. And for tonight, put on some music or one of those podcasts you like. Something steady in the background. It'll keep your mind from turning every creak into a ghost."

Janice smiled faintly, even through the lump in her throat. "That's a good idea."

"Promise me."

"I promise."

She climbed the narrow stairs with the phone still in her hand, her thumb grazing the worn edges of its case. Upstairs, her bedroom smelled faintly of cedar and dust, the air stale from years without a window being opened. She switched on the lamp by the bed, the yellow glow spreading across the warped plaster.

The quiet was too loud. She set her phone on the nightstand, queued one of her favorite podcasts, and let the familiar voices fill the room. It didn't chase away the dread entirely, but it dulled the edges.

She stretched out across the bed, fully dressed, the coin necklace cool against her collarbone, the lamplight steady. Outside, the orchard whispered with the night wind, branches brushing together like voices just out of reach.

On the nightstand, her notepad lay open. Before letting her eyes close, she scrawled a quick line in uneven handwriting:

Deadbolt — done

Curtains — circled twice

Then she set the pen down, switched off the lamp, and let the voices of the podcast blur into the hush of the orchard.

Sleep came slowly. And when it did, it was shallow, haunted by the sense that someone or something stood just beyond the yard, waiting.

CHAPTER TWENTY

◇◇ THE WRONG PLACE
TO PLAY

1860, Georgia
Autumn

The afternoon light dappled through the pecan trees, throwing long, shifting shadows across the clearing near the old Huxley graves. It wasn't a place children were supposed to linger, but the headstones stood like crooked teeth, the grass clipped short enough to make a fine hiding place.

"Count to twenty, Bitsy!" Abbigail cried, darting behind a leaning slab of stone with Lucy close at her side.

Bitsy squeezed her eyes shut, pressed her palms over them, and began counting in a singsong voice. "One, two, three…"

Lucy tugged Abbigail's hand. "Come on, this way." Her bare feet padded silently through the grass. She knew the lay of the land better than the other girls, knew which trees held low branches and which patches dipped toward the creek.

They crouched behind a mound where weeds had overtaken a broken headstone. Abbigail stifled her giggle with both hands. Lucy hushed her. The game was part fun, part fear—always aware they weren't supposed to play so close to the graves.

Bitsy's voice drifted nearer. "Seventeen, eighteen... nineteen..."

Then, silence.

Lucy leaned forward, peering past the weeds. She froze.

At the edge of the creek, where the water caught the last burn of sunlight, a figure stood. Tall, rigid. Billy.

Her first thought was to duck, to pull Abbigail back into hiding. But her eyes locked on what lay at his feet.

A girl.

Her dress, pale and fine like something out of Sunday best, was stained dark across the bodice. Her hair spilled in tangles across the mud. Her head lolled at a sickening angle, neck bent wrong, and bone jutted pale where it should not.

Lucy's breath caught in her throat.

Abbigail shifted, following her gaze, and gasped so loudly that Lucy clapped a hand over her mouth. Bitsy, drawn by the sound, stumbled out of her hiding place, and stopped dead. Her eyes widened, her lips trembling.

Billy crouched, his shoulders stiff. His hand reached down, not to touch the girl's skin but to gather a strand of her hair, slicing it roughly with a small knife. He slipped the lock into his pocket, movements quick, furtive.

Lucy's stomach turned. She knew, without knowing how, that they weren't supposed to see this.

Billy straightened, eyes sweeping the tree line. The girls ducked low, hearts hammering. Lucy prayed the grass would swallow them whole. For a long, breathless moment, the only sound was the buzzing of flies around the body.

"Run," Lucy whispered. She didn't wait. She dragged Abbigail's hand and motioned frantically for Bitsy. The three darted through the headstones, skirts catching on brambles, breath sharp in their chests.

They didn't stop until the house came into view. Alice was on the porch, needlework in her lap. She rose when she saw them barreling toward her, panic etched in their faces.

"What on earth?"

Lucy couldn't get the words out at first. Her chest heaved, her mouth dry. Finally, she stammered, "By the creek... a girl... she's dead, Miss Alice."

Alice went pale, her embroidery slipping from her hands. "What girl?"

"She ain't one of us," Bitsy blurted. "White. In a dress. But her head, her head–" She broke off, covering her mouth.

Abbigail clutched Alice's skirt, her eyes wet. "She's just lying there. Billy was–"

Alice's face tightened. She gathered them close, lowering her voice. "Hush now. Don't say more till we tell your father."

Together they hurried inside, skirts swishing, hearts still thudding. William was at the desk with his ledger, spectacles perched low. He looked up at the commotion, frowning.

"What is this?"

Alice steadied her voice. "They found a body. By the creek. A girl."

William's pen slipped from his fingers. His expression flickered, shock, then something darker. He rose too quickly, the chair scraping.

"You three, out," he barked. "Out of this room. And you," he jabbed a finger at Alice, voice sharp, "say nothing. To no one. Do you hear me?"

"But, William–"

He cut her off with a glare. "Go."

The girls scurried, fear tightening their throats.

LATER, in the dim safety of the cabin yard, Lucy caught Isaac alone. He leaned close as she whispered what they'd seen. His face went grave.

"I know," he murmured. "Your uncle went to the creek afterwards. Billy was there."

Lucy's pulse raced. "And the girl?"

Isaac's eyes hardened. "She'd been there longer than a night. Days, maybe. Her hair cut. Her body spoiled." He shook his head. "His father was sickened, but Billy swore he found her that way. Said it wasn't him."

Lucy looked toward the orchard where the shadows grew thick. She didn't believe him. Not for a second.

JOURNAL ENTRY-

I scarcely know where to begin. The air itself feels heavy tonight, as though it too carries the weight of what we saw by the creek. Abby will not sleep, Lucy keeps her silence, and Bitsy trembles at every sound in the dark. I keep replaying it all in my mind: the crooked graves, the game of hide and seek, the laughter cut short. And then him, Billy, standing like a shadow at the water's edge.

I saw it with my own eyes, though I wish I had not. A girl, lifeless, her dress stained, her body twisted. He touched her hair with a blade, as if she were some object to collect, a trophy. What sort of creature does such a thing?

Uncle William's command rings still in my ears: say nothing. His voice was iron, cold, and final. Miss Alice tried to protest, but he silenced her with a look. They wish to bury this as they bury all else here, beneath silence, beneath clay.

But how can I keep silent? How can any of us? If a life can be taken so easily, so cruelly, and all we are told is to hush, then what worth is our own? Lucy's eyes told me everything. She already knows the truth of Billy's nature. Perhaps she has always known.

I write this by candlelight with my hands still trembling, wondering what courage demands of me. Am I to turn my head, as the rest do, or will I find the strength to speak? I fear the answer may cost me dearly. Yet I cannot unsee what I have seen.

—Natalie

CHAPTER TWENTY-ONE
◦◦ THE FIRST THREAD PULLED

1861, Georgia
Spring

Natalie woke to shouting that split the quiet of the morning like a thunderclap. For a breath, she did not know where she was. Pale light pressed through the curtains, and the room swam in that soft gray that comes before full day. The house below her seemed to shake with a voice that was all heat and iron. Her pulse climbed to meet it.

She snatched her dressing gown, pulled it tight, slid her feet into slippers, and hurried for the door. The hallway air was cool and still. The runner on the floor swallowed her steps at first, then the boards after it began to complain under her weight. As she descended, the smell of coffee and soap and the faint bite of ash rose to meet her. The shouting grew louder. It had a shape now. A name inside it.

At the foot of the stairs stood Billy. He towered over

Lucy. Sweat had darkened the white cap on her head. Her shoulders drew tight, but her chin stayed lifted, as if her bones had learned to hold the line when nothing else could.

"What did you say?" Billy snarled. Spit clung to his lip. "You think you are above being spoken to."

Lucy did not look at him. Her eyes fixed on a place beyond his shoulder, a blank wall that held her attention with the stubborn focus of a prayer. The quiet of that resistance seemed to pour oil on his temper. He leaned closer. The veins in his neck jumped.

His arm lashed out. The back of his hand struck Lucy's cheek with a sound like a green branch breaking. She folded and hit the boards. The crack of it hollowed Natalie's stomach.

Billy drew back his boot.

Natalie moved before she thought. Her body knew faster than her mind. She dropped to her knees and threw herself across Lucy, arms wide, ribs pressed to ribs, breath shaking like paper in the wind. She felt the floor through the thin cotton of her gown and the fast drum of Lucy's heart under her own. If he meant to strike, it would be her he struck.

The kick did not come.

She opened her eyes. Billy stood above them. His fists clenched and unclenched as if he were working a rope that burned. His jaw twitched. His eyes were wrong. There was nothing in them but a dark gleam, as if something older and colder were looking out through him.

"You had no right," he said, voice low and dangerous. "She belongs to this house. She follows my rules."

Natalie's voice shook, but she pulled breath into it and made it steady. "You were going to kill her."

His nostrils flared. "Do not preach to me, Yankee girl. You know nothing of this place."

Natalie rose, placing herself between him and Lucy. Her knees wobbled. She set her feet until she felt the boards answer her weight.

"She is a human being," she said.

The air between them tightened until it sang.

A second voice cut through it.

"Billy." William's tone came low and even, the sound a man uses to steady a restless colt. He stepped forward from the shadows of the hall with one palm open and lowered. His eyes did not leave his son. "Look at me, son."

For a long moment, Billy did not move. His chest heaved. The tendon in his neck jumped again and again. Then something in him clicked over. He took one hard step backward. His gaze slid to Natalie and sharpened.

"Never stand between me and this house again," he said. "That is your only warning, cousin."

He turned, shoved through the front door, and spat into the dust just beyond the threshold. The slamming of the door rang through the foyer like a lid dropping on a pot.

Henry came running and slammed into Natalie's side with a force that almost knocked her down again. He wrapped his arms around her waist and held on. She put a hand on his head without looking away from Lucy. Blood welled slow at the corner of her lip and tracked down to her chin.

"Natalie, are you hurt?" William asked, voice thin with shock.

She shook her head. "No. But Lucy is."

Alice swept in, her face white with fury that pulled all expression into a single narrow line. She sank beside Lucy and put both hands out as if to gather her back into the world.

"Lord help us," she breathed. "Not again."

Miss Patty followed with calm that came from the far end of long corridors. She knelt, cupped Lucy's jaw, looked into her eyes, and spoke low. "Come now, child. You are safe. Up we go."

She and Alice lifted together. Lucy stifled a flinch and leaned into their hands.

As they passed, Miss Patty gave Natalie a look that held more words than the house had rooms. Approval was in it. Warning was in it too. Then she and Alice were gone down the corridor and through the swing door toward the back of the house.

Henry still held on. Natalie placed her hand over his and felt how small his fingers were. "I am all right," she said, though the words shook. "You did right to come."

Later, the parlor held them all like a jar holds heat. The drapes were open, and the light came in thick and golden. It made the dust look like snow that would never fall. A glass of iced tea sweated beside Natalie's hand, and she could not make herself drink it. The chair held her like a soft trap. Alice moved in a straight line from window to mantel to doorway and back, a measured pacing that kept the room from breaking. Fury rippled under her composure like a river under ice. Henry sat close enough that his knee touched Natalie's skirt. He had stopped shaking, but he watched the doorway the way a boy watches a storm line.

Lucy came back in on quiet feet. She was clean now, and her hair had been smoothed. The mark on her cheek had risen like a slow bruise. Her eyes stayed low as she crossed the threshold, but when Natalie stood, Lucy lifted her gaze and held it.

"You do not need to speak," Natalie said, taking her hands. "I only want you to know that what he did was wrong. I saw you."

Lucy's lip trembled once. She nodded, the smallest bow a person can make to another person without bending at all.

Across the room, Miss Patty set a basin on a side table for later. One eyebrow lifted. Her chin dipped once. A message received and returned.

Lucy turned to go, then glanced over her shoulder. It was not trust. Not yet. But it had the shape of something that might become trust if fed and guarded.

Alice stopped moving. The silence after her steps was so sudden that Natalie looked down to see what had changed. At Alice's feet lay a folded paper that had fallen from the pocket of the apron still clutched in her hand. She bent and picked it up. The creases knew where to go. The headline broke open across her palm.

Young Girl Found Dead in Riverbank Woods.

Neck Brutally Broken.

The ink had faded to a weak brown. The dread inside it was as fresh as blood.

Alice folded the paper again and pressed it to her chest as if she could keep the words from escaping the room. Her face did not crumple. It sharpened, and all the color left it.

"She reminds me of the other one," she said. more to herself than anyone in the room

"The other one?" Natalie asked.

Alice's breath hitched. She sank into the chair across from Natalie as if her bones had been removed. "There was a girl. Not so long ago. Sixteen, maybe seventeen. They found her by the creek with her neck broken clean. As if by brute force."

Natalie lowered her voice. "Do you mean Billy?"

Alice closed her eyes, and a single tear cut through the powder on her cheek. "I do not know what I mean. He has never been right. The orchard fell silent the day he was born. Even the owls kept away from the pecans by his window. His first cry did not come. He only stared, as if he had been marked."

She pressed her fingers to her brow and breathed through them. "And yet he is my son. The first time he wrapped his hand around my finger, I thought my heart would break from the size of it. How do I stop loving what I carried? How do I not fear what he has become?"

Words crowded the back of Natalie's throat and refused to come. She did not know whether to take Alice's hand or to fold her own in her lap and look away. She had never been taught how to hold two truths that cut in opposite directions.

Alice reached across the small table and took hold of Natalie's fingers. The grip was steady but warm. "You must be careful," she said. "He feeds on fear. Do not give him yours. Do not bend either. He despises weakness. He hates defiance more. It is a dangerous line you must walk."

Natalie answered before she had time to count the cost. "Then I will walk it. Quiet and careful." She drew a breath and set her jaw. "I will not look away."

Alice studied her for a long heartbeat, and something in her gaze changed. Recognition flickered there, and something like relief. "Yes," she said softly. "That may be the only way."

Miss Patty appeared in the doorway with a folded cloth and a dish of crushed ice. She placed them on the side table and touched the back of Natalie's chair with her fingertips. "The girl is resting," she said. "I sat with her until the tremor left her hands. She is made of stronger stuff than the boy knows."

The day lengthened. Voices in the yard rose and fell and rose again. Somewhere in the kitchen, a pot lid chattered and then settled. A robin scolded from the oak near the porch and then thought better of it. The house returned to its ordinary rhythm, and yet none of it felt ordinary any longer. A thread had been tugged from the weave, and the whole fabric creaked.

That evening, Lucy found Natalie in the parlor, lowering her voice so no one else could hear. "Miss Natalie, come with me. There's someone out back for you."

Natalie followed her through the darkened hall, heart

beating faster with every step. Lucy led her to the rear door that opened onto the kitchen porch. The night pressed close, the orchard whispering beyond.

Isaac stood there, just outside the lamplight spilling from the kitchen window. His cap was in his hands, his face half-shadowed. He glanced toward Lucy, then fixed his eyes on Natalie.

"Word carried," he said quietly. "Walt sends his regards."

Natalie froze, the breath rushing out of her chest. She had never spoken Walt's name aloud since the train, not here, not anywhere on this land. Yet Isaac spoke it plainly, as though he had been entrusted with it all along.

The message was clear: her letters had reached their mark. She wasn't cut off after all.

Her pulse raced as she met Isaac's gaze. Something passed between them, fear, yes, but also a spark of hope. Lucy shifted closer, protective, as though to guard what had just been spoken.

Natalie returned to the house with her secret burning bright. She had a lifeline now, carried not only by Walt but by those who risked everything to pass his words along.

Henry stood. He toyed with the laces at his wrist and would not meet Natalie's eyes. "You were brave," he said at last, the words quick and small. "I didn't know what to do."

"You did the bravest thing," Natalie told him. "You showed up."

He nodded, jaw set in a boy's imitation of a man's promise. "I will again."

When the lamps were lit and the first cool air edged in from the yard, Natalie returned to her room. Her hands still shook in small, invisible ways. She washed her face and watched the water ripple. She could not wash away the sound of knuckles on cheek or the way Lucy's breath had hitched in her ear.

She drew the journal toward her and smoothed the page.

JOURNAL ENTRY-

This morning, the house showed its ugliest face. Billy struck Lucy so hard she fell, and then he raised his boot. I did not think. My body moved. I threw myself across her and waited for the hurt. My hands shook like leaves in the wind, but I stayed.

He did not strike again. I do not know if it was because I put my body there, or because Father William called his name, or because Miss Patty arrived, but the look in his eyes said he wanted to. That look is a thing I do not know how to name. It has no heat. It is a cold that moves.

Lucy did not cry. She did not plead. She simply endured as if she expected this and expected to survive it. That knowledge broke something inside me. Alice was furious. Not loud. Fierce. Her hands trembled as if the fury had to live somewhere and chose her bones. She cares for Lucy more than she will say out loud.

Billy hates me. He decided it the first time he looked at me. Perhaps it is because I am from the North. Perhaps it is because I did not bend. I know cruelty when I see it. I know also that pretending not to see it is another kind of cruelty.

Henry held on to me and would not let go until the world felt solid again. Miss Patty gave me a look that said two things at once. Good and careful.

I have heard now about the girl by the creek. I will not write the name of who they suspect. The county carries that story like a bruise under a sleeve.

The man who will help told me once to move like a thread. Quiet. Careful. Strong. Today I felt the first pull. Perhaps Lucy is the reason I am here. Perhaps this is where the work begins.

CHAPTER TWENTY-TWO

⚓ IT WAITS FOR THE DARK

J anice had started to frequent the corner café so often that the place was beginning to feel like an extension of her new life. The bell above the door gave its usual chirp as she stepped inside. The morning crowd was thinning out, and she spotted the same hostess with the long blonde ponytail, perfect posture, and a smile more suited to a runway than a roadside diner.

The smell inside was a mixture of strong coffee and sweet pancakes, exactly what a person needed to start the day.

"Morning again," the woman said brightly, grabbing a menu and leading Janice toward her usual booth. "You're getting to be a regular."

"Habit-forming," Janice replied with a smile. "This cornbread has me hooked."

"I get it," the woman said, sliding the menu across the table. "I'm Matty, by the way. Figured it's time I introduce myself since you've been keeping that booth warm for a week straight."

"Janice. Nice to finally meet you."

Matty lingered, tilting her head. "Mind if I sit for a minute? Place is slow, and I've been wondering what keeps bringing you around."

"Sure," Janice said, surprised but glad for the company.

Matty slid into the booth across from her. A couple wandered in through the door, and without looking, she called, "Take a menu. I'll be right with you."

Janice raised a brow. "You won't get in trouble?"

Matty smirked. "Maybe. But I know the owner. Me."

Janice blinked. "You're kidding."

"Nope." Matty took a sip from her own mug. "I graduated from Georgia Tech in computer engineering, but sitting behind a screen all day wasn't my thing. I wanted to work with people. When this place came up for sale, I jumped. My grandma worked here back in the fifties, so it kind of feels like carrying something forward."

"That's amazing."

Matty shrugged, but her smile was warm. "Figure I'll probably die in this diner, slinging pancakes and pouring coffee, but if it's a good life, who cares?"

Janice's eyes drifted to the framed photos on the wall. "Did your family grow up around here?"

"Yep. Born and raised. My people go way back. I know just about every brick and rumor in this town."

That caught Janice's attention. "You don't happen to know anything about the Cheney place, do you?"

Matty's brow lifted. "The big white house that's a museum now?"

"That one is my cousin's place."

Matty gave a low whistle. "Girl, that place has stories. You're not telling me you're staying there?"

"Next door, in the smaller Cheney two-story house. It belonged to my mom's family. I'm fixing it up and... doing some digging."

Matty leaned closer, curiosity flashing in her eyes. "Finding anything good?"

"Depends on what you mean by good."

Matty laughed softly. "Around here, good usually comes with ghosts."

The couple at the counter raised their hands for service, and Matty slid from the booth. "Don't run off. I'll be right back."

Janice watched her move effortlessly between tables, ponytail swaying, her coffee left half-full on the table. It wasn't an accident. She intended to return.

A few minutes later, Matty came back and slid into the booth. "So," she asked, wrapping her hands around the warm ceramic mug, "what's your plan with that old place?"

Janice traced a finger around her own cup. "I wish I knew. At first, I thought I'd flip it or rent it. But the longer I stay, the harder it is to think about leaving."

Matty tilted her head, thoughtful. "It's like it won't let you go?"

Janice looked at her sharply. "Exactly. Like there's something under the surface I'm supposed to understand first."

Matty leaned back, eyes unreadable. "That house has roots. If you're going to dig, be ready for what you find."

Janice hesitated. "What do you mean?"

Matty's smile was there, but it didn't touch her eyes. "Some folks stop asking questions. Some can't help themselves. Which kind are you?"

Janice took a breath. "Would you want to come by later? I could show you around. Maybe you could tell me what you know. History, rumors… anything."

Matty looked surprised, then grinned. "You sure? I've got an unhealthy love of ghost stories."

"Perfect," Janice said.

THAT EVENING, Janice waited outside the house. The sun had dipped low, throwing long shadows across the gravel path and the orchard beyond. Matty's little hatchback crunched up the drive, and she stepped out, eyeing the property with raised brows.

"You're out here alone?" she asked, hands on her hips.

Janice nodded. "Was supposed to be a quick flip, but now I want to know more about the family. About the place."

"You never get scared?"

Janice shifted her weight. "Sometimes. It's a new house, new sounds. But some nights…" She hesitated. "Some nights it feels like more than that."

Matty chewed her lip, then held out her hand. "Phone."

Janice fished it from her pocket and handed it over. Matty typed quickly, then slid it back. "If you ever feel like something's off, text or call. I live above the café. I can be here before you put the phone down."

Relief warmed Janice's chest. "Hopefully I won't need to but thank you."

They walked the property, Matty's eyes drawn again and again to the orchard. "That's where it feels heaviest," she murmured. "Like something's there watching."

"You need lights out here," Matty said.

Janice didn't answer. Her eyes stayed locked on the windows, uncurtained, open to the night. For the first time, she realized how exposed she was.

When Matty left, Janice shut herself inside. The house was too dark, so she left one light burning in the kitchen. But the sounds started almost immediately. The rattle of loose porch boards, a shiver in the glass panes, a low groan in the walls. She froze.

After washing her hands in the bathroom, she stepped back into the hall and stopped cold. A shadow drifted past the porch light outside, stretching long across the wall as if someone were walking by. Her pulse quickened.

She hurried to the front door, heart pounding, and reached for the knob. It turned under her hand, but the door would not move, as though something pressed firmly from the other side.

"Hello?" Her voice cracked. "Who's there?"

Silence answered.

Swallowing hard, she leaned toward the narrow window beside the door. At first, all she saw was her own reflection, pale and frightened. Then her eyes adjusted. Behind her likeness, another shape resolved. Two red points, hovering at the level of a face.

Eyes.

Her breath caught. She panicked, then tried to tell herself they were not eyes. Maybe a reflection, maybe the porch light warped in the glass. She pressed closer, squinting, trying to force sense into the shape.

But the longer she stared, the more certain she became. They were eyes. Watching her.

Her throat went dry. With trembling fingers, she pulled out her phone and typed quickly.

Janice: Something's wrong.

The red points blinked. Then, slowly, they shifted, tilting from side to side as though assessing her, like a predator testing the bars of a cage.

A strangled cry tore from her throat. She stumbled backward, her heel catching the bottom step of the staircase. She hit hard, scrambling up the riser as though it could carry her away.

Her chest heaved. The window loomed ahead, the glass empty now, no eyes, no glow, nothing at all. But the image of that blink, that tilt, burned into her mind, hammering against her ribs until her vision blurred.

Matty: On my way.

The minutes crawled. Every board in the house creaked, every shadow seemed to swell. Janice gripped the 2x4 she used to brace the back door, holding it like a bat, her knuckles white.

Then footsteps pounded up the front porch. Janice raised the board, ready to swing.

"Janice!"

The voice broke through the night. Blonde hair

caught the porch light as Matty froze at the sight of the weapon.

"Shoot!" she yelped, hands flying up.

Janice dropped the board with a clatter, her knees giving out in relief. "Oh my God, I almost hit you." She pulled Matty close, both of them trembling.

"Are you okay?" Matty asked, her breath unsteady.

"Yes," Janice whispered, though her voice shook. She turned back toward the empty window.

Inside, Janice flicked every switch she could find until the house glowed. The brightness was overwhelming, but it felt safer than the dark.

Matty busied herself in the kitchen, pulling tea from her bag as though she had known she would need it. Her voice was quiet but steady. "You made it worse, you know."

Janice frowned. "What do you mean?"

"Turning the light off," Matty said. "My grandma always told me you never give the dark all the power. You think it hides you, but it doesn't. It invites them in."

The words landed heavy.

Matty placed a steaming mug in Janice's hands and looked her square in the eye. "She made me promise three things, and now you need to promise them too. Never let the house go completely dark. Never answer if you hear your name after sundown. And never whistle at night."

Janice swallowed hard. "Why not whistle?"

Matty's gaze slid to the orchard. Her voice was barely more than a whisper. "Because you don't know what you're calling."

Janice's stomach tightened. She clutched the mug as if it were the only warmth left in the world.

"I can't stay here alone tonight," she admitted softly.

"You're not," Matty said quickly. She pulled a chair into the living room, curled up with a blanket, and settled in. "You've got me. I'll stay until you feel better."

Relief rushed through Janice. She lay on the couch, watching Matty drift into a doze, her blonde hair falling loose across her shoulders.

Every lamp in the house blazed, and still, Janice felt vulnerable. The farmhouse glowed like a beacon in the night, exposed from every window. She rolled onto her side, watching Matty breathe softly, grateful she was not alone.

Even so, unease coiled in her stomach. Even with the house lit like day, she could not shake the sense that the night outside was bidding it, patient, just beyond the glass.

Sleep came slowly, and when it did, it was shallow, haunted by the memory of red eyes blinking in the dark.

CHAPTER TWENTY-THREE
◦◦ BE READY

1861, Georgia
Summer

Natalie had begun to find a place for herself in the household. She spent her afternoons in the study with Uncle William, her pencil moving quickly across the pages of his ledgers. Her years of keeping her father's shop accounts had made her nimble with figures, and William praised her skills with open delight. Natalie only smiled politely and let him think she was gifted. Better he believe she had a talent than know how many long nights she had spent over her father's books back home.

That afternoon, she was bent over the ledger on the couch, the scent of old paper and ink in the air, when a sharp knock broke their quiet. She began to rise, but William lifted a hand.

"Stay," he said with a reassuring smile. "It's a friend stopping by. It won't take but a moment."

The door opened, and a tall figure strode in, still in his riding boots, jacket dusty from the road. Natalie's heart lurched. Walt.

Her stomach knotted so tightly it felt as though she had swallowed a stone. Heat rushed up her neck. She couldn't tell if it was fear, anticipation, or guilt. Would he betray her and speak of the letters? Did he mean to expose her in front of Uncle William? She forced herself to keep her eyes on the book, though her hand trembled on the page.

Walt's gaze found hers. For the briefest moment, he nodded as if greeting an acquaintance. Then he turned smoothly to William, taking his hand with practiced ease.

"Should I...?" Walt asked, his eyes flicking back toward Natalie.

"No need," William said, his tone genial. "That's my niece."

Walt's eyes lingered longer this time. Natalie held her spine straight and lowered her gaze to the figures before her, as though the pages demanded her attention. Inside, her heart pounded so loudly she was certain both men could hear it.

William poured a drink and gestured to the chairs, but Walt shook his head. "Not here for pleasure, I'm afraid. The Senate isn't budging. Pressure's mounting from all sides. They're speaking openly now of putting an end to our way of life."

William's face hardened. "What are you saying?"

"I'm saying war is coming," Walt replied. His voice was even, but there was an edge of steel beneath it. "And if the South means to win, it will not be won with words."

A sharp gasp escaped Natalie before she could stop herself. Both men turned. Her cheeks burned. She rose quickly, bowing her head.

"My apologies. If I may be excused…"

"No." Walt's interruption was soft, yet commanding. "What needed saying has been said. I'll see myself out."

He crossed the room, boots striking the floorboards in deliberate steps. As he passed her chair, his back turned toward Uncle William, his hand reached for hers. To anyone watching, it was no more than a courteous farewell. But when his fingers closed around hers, she felt the firm press of something folded into her palm. His hand lingered just long enough for her to see the flicker of a wink, the faintest spark in his eyes that said everything. Keep it hidden.

"Pleasure meetin' you, miss."

Her stomach twisted tighter. She nodded almost imperceptibly, slipping the folded scrap into her pocket. Her pulse hammered. She knew without reading it that it would change everything.

The door shut behind him, leaving a silence as heavy as stone. She turned and found William watching her. His expression was tired, older somehow, the weight of unspoken thoughts hanging between them.

"Please, Natalie," he said quietly. "Say nothing of this. Let me speak to the family first."

She forced a small nod, murmured something about resting, and gathered her things.

In her room, she closed the door and perched on the edge of the bed. Her fingers shook as she drew the note from her pocket. She unfolded it carefully.

Your letters were mailed. Be ready. You are needed by the recipients. Find a place to hide people on the grounds. Destroy this now.

Her breath caught. For a moment, she simply stared, the words blurring as if the ink itself burned. Then, with trembling hands, she tore the letter into shreds no bigger than seeds and stuffed them into her boot.

Be ready. The words repeated in her head. Be ready. For what? For whom?

She wrapped her arms around herself. She had betrayed the trust of the family who had welcomed her, especially William, who called her "niece" with such pride. She should have been ashamed, and part of her was. But beneath the guilt was something stronger.

Conviction.

Yet conviction wasn't enough. She needed help. Someone who wouldn't betray her. For a brief moment, her thoughts turned to Alice. Alice had been nothing but warm, embracing her like a daughter. Maybe she would understand. Maybe she could be trusted. But then Natalie remembered the way Alice's hands shook when Billy grew violent, the way she folded into silence instead of standing against him. Alice loved deeply, but fear had bound her. Trusting her might endanger them both.

Natalie thought of Miss Patty, whose sharp eyes missed nothing, whose presence in the house was steady as the earth itself. But Miss Patty had her own quiet burdens to bear, and if exposed, the cost to her would be too great.

That left Lucy. Silent, bruised, but unbroken. A girl who had already learned how to endure without surrendering her spirit. Natalie's chest tightened. Lucy was the one. She was young, but she carried the kind of strength born of survival. If Natalie were to choose someone, it had to be her.

Natalie sat in the stillness of her room, her heart pounding with the enormity of what she had agreed to. She pressed her palms together and whispered to herself, as though saying the words aloud would steady her. "Be ready."

JOURNAL ENTRY-

There is a weight running through this house since Walt came. Uncle William is quieter. Alice sets fewer dishes on the table. Even the pantry looks sparse, as if the whole household knows to brace for what's coming. They whisper of war. Some pray for it. Others dread it. But either way, it's on the wind.

I walk past the cotton fields, and at first, they look like beauty, white and endless against the red clay. But if you look closer, you see the cost. The bent backs. The blistered hands. The silence of those who cannot speak. That silence is what keeps this house standing. That silence fills the table. It breaks me each time I sit down to eat.

Uncle William is kind in his way. Alice holds me close like family. Little Abby throws her arms around my neck with love so pure it makes me ache. But what would they do if I spoke the truth? That I do not believe this life is right. That I cannot accept a system that owns other people's lives as if they were coins to be spent.

And then there is Billy. His presence pulls all warmth from the room. Even Alice stiffens when he enters. Henry stays pressed to her skirts. Miss Patty mutters prayers under her breath. It feels as though the land itself changes when he walks through it.

And the land. I cannot shake it. At night, it whispers. The trees shift with no wind. The orchard feels alive. Lamps are left burning all night, though no one admits to it. Miss Patty pours little mounds of salt on the window ledges and says it is for protection. Protection from what? No one will answer.

But I have my answer, pressed into my palm by Walt. Be ready. The words are carved into me now.

I cannot stop a war. I cannot end centuries of wrong. But I can do something. I can be someone. And I will.

Be ready.

Natalie

CHAPTER TWENTY-FOUR

⚲ NO GOOD AFTER DARK

Janice had spent the early part of the morning trying to decipher the delicate journal she found beneath the staircase behind the false wall. The pages were so fragile that she feared they might disintegrate if she turned them too quickly. The leather binding creaked when she opened it, and the paper inside crumbled like pressed petals. She caught glimpses of names, scraps of phrases, and what looked like dates. But without context, it felt like trying to read someone else's memory in a language that had no direct translation.

Next to the journal, she had found a folded piece of paper, a letter, brittle and sealed with a bit of wax. It had no address, only an elegant looping initial on the back: N. She had no idea what it said. The ink had faded into the parchment like veins, and the script was too fine, too chaotic to read in the dim light of the hallway. She placed both gently on the kitchen counter and stepped away, knowing she needed a break.

Outside, Guy and his crew were still hammering

away out front, and the AC repairman had just left to fetch a part. The orchard behind the house beckoned to her like an open door, the kind of place that tugged at your curiosity until you gave in. She grabbed the folded map she had found with the journal and stepped into the heat.

She moved slowly, letting her eyes adjust to the shifting light, the air thick and motionless like it hadn't been stirred in a century. Mosquitoes buzzed in maddening loops around her head. The cicadas shrieked their song somewhere above, a sound more like insect rebellion than birdsong. She pressed on, her boots parting the grass until pine straw took over, softening each step beneath the canopy of trees.

The deeper she went, the quieter it became. She was almost certain she had seen movement in this direction the night before, just a flicker of something. Now she wasn't so sure.

Up ahead, through a break in the trees, a clearing appeared. Wrought iron fencing stood sentry, rust-flecked and half-eaten by time. Within the boundary lay headstones in various states of surrender, some crooked, some toppled, all aged to the point of being nearly illegible. She approached with care, walking between concave patches in the grass, careful not to step on anyone's final resting place.

Names carved into stone whispered of lineage: Cheneys, Huxleys, and a handful of others she'd seen in the family Bible. Some markers were tall and stately, Civil War-era granite sentinels. Others were crude and short, no more than a name and date carved by an uncertain hand. The wealth of the dead seemed to fade the closer she came to the fence's entrance.

She paused by one on the right side, a square slab with no base, just a single letter visible beneath the grime: W.

Janice crouched, wiping at the lichen and moss with the sleeve of her hoodie. The stone was thinner than the rest and oddly tilted, as if someone had shoved it into the earth in haste. Her fingers traced the letters.

"WC," she whispered. A jolt ran through her chest.

Could that be William Cheney?

She pressed her palm over her heart, startled. Her grandmother's great-great-grandfather had always been somewhat of a myth in their family lore. He was "the one who owned the plantation," "the one no one talked about." If this was him... why no full name? No dates? No sentiment?

She stood, dizzy with questions. Her eyes scanned the tree line. Why bury someone like this? Alone. Almost hidden.

The hairs on the back of her neck rose.

That's when she saw it, off to the left, half-concealed by brush and bramble, a brown historical marker. Janice walked toward it. Raised lettering spelled it out: **Trail of Tears.**

Her stomach dropped. She looked down at her boots, at the soil beneath her feet. This path, the one she had been casually strolling, was once walked by people forced from their homes, marched hundreds of miles in grief, hunger, and pain.

She sank to an overturned log, her mind spinning.

How could she be thinking about rental prices and kitchen tiles when she was standing on ground soaked in sorrow? This wasn't just a renovation project anymore. It was something else. Something layered and unsettled.

Her thoughts spiraled as she mapped it out in her head. This land had absorbed some of the lowest points in American history: the Trail of Tears, where children were buried along the roadside; slavery, where entire generations were worked, sold, and silenced; and later, the brittle newspaper clippings she had unfolded; *Local Girl Missing After Church Picnic, Sheriff Urges Caution: Curfew in Place After Fourth Incident.*

They hadn't called it a serial killer then, but that's what it read like now, horror layered upon horror, packed into the soil like strata of grief.

She realized this wasn't history most people wanted to admit, let alone talk about. But she was going to learn what happened here. She had to. Driven by something she couldn't yet name, Janice felt as though the land itself demanded it of her.

She looked again at the graveyard, at the names no one cleaned anymore. She'd promised herself she'd sell the house, start fresh. But now? Now she felt like she owed them something.

As she turned to go, the cicadas suddenly went silent, as if someone had pressed pause. She looked back once more at the grave marked WC.

"I'll come back," she murmured aloud. "I'll clean you up. All of you."

The forest seemed to relax.

Then the silence broke. The cicadas resumed their song as she crossed the invisible line between shadow and sunlight.

Her phone buzzed. It was Jeff.

Jeff: How's it going down there? House driving you crazy yet?

Janice smiled faintly, thumbs moving.

Janice: Crazy doesn't even begin to cover it. I'll tell you soon. You'll think I'm losing it.

Jeff: Nah. You've got this. Call me later; we'll talk it out. Love ya.

Janice: Love you too.

She pocketed the phone, but her thoughts drifted to her mother. Ruth's health weighed on her heavier than anything she'd found in the house. Early retirement, the treatments, the way her voice sometimes shook when she swore she was fine. This place was supposed to be a safety net for her. Fix the house, rent it out, keep the family afloat. But every day it became clearer: the house held more than old wood and peeling paint. It held a reckoning.

Before heading back, she shot a quick text to Matty:

Janice: Hey, thanks for coming over the other night. I'll stop by the café soon to fill you in on what I've learned.

She slipped her phone away, then paused to look once more at the woods.

Her grandmother used to say nothing good ever came from being outside after dark. Ruth had repeated it to her more than once, warning with that same firm tone: *Nothing good after dark, Janice. Remember that.*

For the first time, Janice understood exactly what they meant.

CHAPTER TWENTY-FIVE
⚨ WHERE THE LAND SPLITS

A knock on the screen door broke Janice's concentration.

She flinched, nearly closing the browser tab on the digital archives she'd been poring over. For hours, she'd been staring at lists of names tied to the Trail of Tears, thousands of them, and the grief behind those names seeped into her like ink through paper. She rubbed her eyes, realizing how heavy her chest felt.

She rose and opened the door. Guy stood on the porch, hat in hand, his face flushed from the sun.

"Sorry to interrupt," he said, shifting from one boot to the other, "but I think you're gonna want to see this."

Janice followed him across the yard toward the far edge of the property. The crew had finished mowing and pulling brush, exposing something long hidden beneath stubborn vines and tall grass. As they drew closer, she saw the outline of a square foundation—bricks still mortared together in places, blackened in others.

"This here," Guy said, pointing with a callused hand, "I'm pretty sure it's an old summer kitchen."

Janice crouched, brushing loose dirt from one of the blackened hearth walls. "Detached from the main house?"

"Exactly," Guy said. "That way, cooking didn't heat up the house or risk burning it down. I've only ever seen ruins like this down in the low country. But this one's in damn good shape, all things considered."

She traced her hand along the soot-stained brick. Something caught the light, faint but deliberate—etched into the corner of one stone. A symbol.

It wasn't a letter or a number. It looked almost like a playing card, a heart split down the middle with a sharp vertical slash.

Guy leaned over her shoulder. "You see it too?"

She nodded slowly. "That's not decorative, is it?"

He shook his head. "Markers, maybe. For folks who knew how to read them. Escaped slaves, I'd bet. I've read about signs like this."

Janice's breath hitched. The hidden journal. The map. The grief-stricken tree. The women's cries she'd thought she heard in the orchard.

This land had been more than a home. It had been a passage. A haven. A graveyard.

She sat back on her heels, staring at the structure as though it might tell her more if she just looked hard enough. "Guy... how long do you think it's been here?"

He stepped back, scanning the foundation, the woods beyond, the sweep of land that rolled toward the orchard. He gestured with a wide circle of his hand. "I'd say it belonged to the Bigger Chaney house originally. There were probably slave cottages out here too, scattered around. And before these pecans in the field?" He tilted his head toward the orchard. "Most likely cotton. Could've even been tobacco, depending on the soil."

Janice's throat tightened. "You mean this could be from the Civil War?"

He gave a slow nod, wonder settling in his expression as his gaze lingered on the orchard and fields.

Janice stood slowly, brushing her palms on her jeans. Her mind spun. She felt both dwarfed by the weight of what she was learning and electrified by the discovery.

"How would I even go about learning more about something like this?" she asked. "Do you think there's a way?"

Guy tipped his cap back, squinting in the sun. "Call the local college. History department, maybe archaeology. They'd eat this up. Folks out there will know how to date the bricks, tell you who built it, maybe even find more under the soil. You've got something worth documenting."

Janice pulled her phone from her pocket and snapped photos, crouching for close-ups of the etched heart, the soot stains, the bricks still clinging to each other after more than a century. She felt almost feverish with energy.

Invigorated.

That was the only word for it. She had to start recording everything, every brick, every headstone, every mark on this land, before she forgot, before it all slipped away. It wasn't just research anymore; it felt like an obligation.

Her eyes drifted past the old kitchen to the orchard.

The map. The one she'd found tucked into the cedar box beneath the stairs. She remembered its scribbled note: *where the land splits.*

The words echoed in her mind now like a riddle.

She took one last photo of the kitchen hearth and slipped her phone back into her pocket. The sweat on her neck cooled in the breeze, leaving goosebumps on her skin.

This wasn't just renovation anymore. This was an excavation of the land, of history, of secrets someone had once tried to bury but couldn't.

And she wasn't sure if she was uncovering it, or if it was uncovering her.

CHAPTER TWENTY-SIX
◦◦ LETTERS IN THE DIRT

1862, Georgia
Summer

The day's heat clung to the house even as the sun sagged low, pressing close as a fever. Curtains were drawn, windows propped open, but the air would not move. Aunt Alice sat on the porch with a cloth pressed to her throat, her face pale in the amber light.

Natalie slipped out with a murmur about stretching her legs. Alice only waved, grateful for the quiet.

Bitsy hurried behind as always, light on her feet, her braid bouncing against her back. "Where we goin'?" she whispered, eyes shining as if they carried a secret.

"Just a walk." Natalie touched the girl's hair briefly. "But if you come along, you must keep your eyes peeled. That's your task."

"I will," Bitsy said proudly. "I won't let nobody sneak on us."

The barn's wide doors yawned at the orchard's edge.

The last sunbeams stretched long across the yard, catching motes of dust that spun like flecks of gold. Inside, it was cooler, the air carrying the scents of hay and leather.

Natalie reached for a brush that hung on a nail. The chestnut mare flicked her ears when Natalie set the bristles to her coat. The rhythm was steady, soothing, each stroke releasing the day's heat from her shoulders as much as the horse's hide.

Isaac was near the lantern, straightening tack. He looked up when he heard the brush strokes. For a moment, the only sound was the mare's breath and the soft rasp of bristles.

Natalie smoothed the mare's neck, then asked, "Tell me something, Isaac. If you knew how to read… what would you read first?"

His gaze lifted, startled. "The Bible, I reckon. My mama always said it held answers we never got to hear."

"Only the Bible?"

A faint smile tugged at his mouth. "Maybe a newspaper. To know what's comin' before it's here. Not just scraps of talk."

Natalie set the brush aside and crouched on the dirt floor. She picked up a stick and pressed its tip into the earth. "Do you know any letters already?"

Isaac hesitated, then knelt across from her, his broad frame folding into the dim glow. "Some. I've seen 'em, heard 'em said. A few."

Natalie scratched a line and bar. "This one?"

His brow furrowed. "A."

She smiled. "Good. And this?" She curved the stick.

"B."

"That's right."

Bitsy leaned against the doorframe, proud as if she had answered herself. "See? He knows!"

Natalie pressed on. "C."

He echoed, his voice steadier.

She drew another shape: H. "Try this one."

"H," he said, rough at the edges.

"Good. Now this." O.

"O."

She added P.

"P," he repeated.

Finally E.

"E," he said.

Natalie pointed to the string she had written. "Now, one by one. Slowly."

"H... O... P... E." His voice was halting, but true.

"Now together."

He drew in a breath. "Hope."

Natalie's throat tightened. "Hope," she echoed softly.

The barn seemed to still, as though the word itself commanded silence.

She added more, her stick scratching. F-R-E-E.

"F... r... e... e," he tried, stumbling once but finding it whole. His eyes met hers. "Free."

"Yes." Her pulse quickened. "Free."

For a moment, she only listened to the crickets tuning outside, the lantern's hiss, and the mare stamping gently at a fly. Then the question pressed from her lips. "Isaac... why has no one stopped him?"

His eyes narrowed. "Who?"

"You know who. Billy. Everyone whispers. The bruises. The girls gone missing. Why does no one act?"

Isaac's jaw tightened. His fists curled on his knees. At last, he spoke, voice rough. "Because he is William Cheney's son. Because his name shields him, and his skin. The law won't touch him. And those who could act..." He shook his head. "We'd be the ones buried."

Natalie's voice shook. "So we do nothing?"

"We endure," he said. "Or we die for nothing."

Her anger flared, hot and helpless. She opened her mouth, but her voice broke instead.

Isaac reached across the dirt. His hand settled on her arm, warm, steady, protective.

Natalie froze. The touch was no claim, only anchor. Warmth spread through her sleeve, into her skin, steadying her racing heart. Her face flushed; she did not move. The dusk hid the color, but not the heat. Something dangerous and sweet bloomed between them.

"I won't stand idle," she whispered. "If the world won't act, then we must find another way. Words. Knowledge. Hope."

His hand lingered, then slipped away, leaving its warmth behind like a promise.

Natalie forced her breath to steady. She swept the letters smooth with her palm. "Enough for tonight."

Isaac's gaze flicked toward the orchard, now heavy with shadow. His voice was low. "Best keep yourself from lingerin' under those trees after dark. My mama said the orchard carries what ain't at rest. Some nights it cries out. Don't ever go there alone."

Natalie shivered, though no wind stirred. She tried to laugh it off, but the sound failed in her throat.

At the doorway, Bitsy whispered, "I've seen it once. Somethin' movin' in there. Like shadows walkin'."

Suddenly, she stiffened, clutching the frame. "Miss Natalie, look! Out there!"

Natalie rose quickly, skirts brushing straw. "What did you see?"

"A shape. Between the trees." Bitsy's voice cracked.

Natalie drew the girl close, feeling her small frame tremble. "It's only dusk settling," she soothed, though her own pulse raced. "You've done well, keeping watch."

Isaac's voice carried, grave. "Best listen to her fear. That orchard holds its own company."

Natalie guided Bitsy away, her arm firm around her. The cicadas swelled, the orchard looming black beside them. At the quarters, Bitsy broke into a run, burying herself against her mother's apron, words tumbling about shadows. Natalie smoothed her braid, gave comfort, then turned back alone.

The orchard loomed, branches stretching against the darkening sky. Natalie walked faster, heart pounding. Her arm still tingled where Isaac's hand had rested.

Journal Entry-

This evening, I dared to ask if Isaac knew his letters. He did, some. Enough to begin. We spelled HOPE, then FREE. The words were halting on his tongue, yet they shone like lantern-light in that barn. I thought I might weep to hear them. Bitsy kept watch at the door, proud as any soldier. She swore she saw a shadow in the orchard as we finished. Perhaps she did. The trees have long memory, though no one speaks of it plain.

I asked Isaac why Billy roams unchecked. His answer was the truth I already knew, but could not say aloud; his name and his skin shield him, while others would die for nothing. My fury rose hot, and in that storm, his hand found my arm. Warm, protective, steady. I flushed like a child, yet it gave me strength. I cannot name what I felt, only that it bound me closer to him.

He warned me never to linger in the orchard after dark. Said it carries what is not at rest. I believe him. Tonight, the trees loomed close, the air heavy with their watching. Perhaps one day I will write more. For now, I carry the words we shaped in the dirt: HOPE. FREE. They will not be erased.

CHAPTER TWENTY-SEVEN

✿ THE HISTORIAN

J anice had a pleasant conversation with her parents that morning while at the grocery store. Her mother was doing well and had thrown herself into researching the family tree, brimming with a kind of new energy Janice hadn't heard in her voice in months. When Janice asked about what she had learned about the land, Ruth explained that while the surrounding two hundred acres had once belonged to the Cheneys, much of it had been sold or gifted away after the war.

She still couldn't find a date of death for Will Cheney, which bothered her, but she had spent most of her time tracing the smaller house, the one her grandmother was raised in, where her mother grew up, and where Janice now stood. The records showed Thomas Cheney with his name on both houses. But here was the odd part: the larger house passed to Thomas's son, while the smaller house went to Benjamin.

Ruth's voice softened, puzzled. "Family lore always tied that smaller house to Natalie. But if that were true, it would have had her husband's name on the deed. Women couldn't own property back then. It just doesn't add up."

Janice gave a small nod, tucking the detail away. Interesting, but not something she was ready to puzzle out now.

Janice could hear the joy in her mother's voice, which brought a lump to her throat. Her father chimed in to say her mother was following the doctor's orders and letting him take care of her. Janice smiled softly, sensing how much he relished the role.

"What about your job, Mom? How did they take it, you retiring early?"

Her mother laughed. "They didn't take it well at all. They told me to take as much time as I needed and even offered to hold my job part-time when I'm ready to come back. Can you believe that?"

"Oh, Mom, that sounds perfect. If you're happy, I'm happy," Janice replied, imagining her mother's smile through the phone.

"Enough about me. How are you doing in Georgia?" Her mother's voice softened on the word Georgia.

"Honestly, I'm amazed. It's beautiful here, and everyone's been so kind."

"It's a different way of life. When the lightning bugs come out, make sure you sit on that porch and take it all in. They're only there for a few weeks."

"I will. I sure miss you and Dad," Janice murmured, blinking back tears in the cereal aisle.

"Take your time, dear. We're set here, and I'm on the mend. Just call me every once in a while, okay?"

"Yes, ma'am," Janice said in her best Georgia peach accent.

Her mother laughed. "That does suit you. Be careful now. You may never come back."

Janice froze for a beat. She hadn't considered not going home.

As she reached for a box of Frosted Flakes and headed toward the dairy section, her mother's voice returned. "Janice?"

"Sorry, Mom. Just this morning, I realized I need to find someone who can help me with the outside kitchen."

"The what?"

"There's a pile of bricks out back. Guy thinks it might've been an old kitchen the household used."

"Well, I'll be. Let me know what you find out."

"I will. Love you, Mom. Tell Dad I love him too. Gotta go."

She balanced the phone under her chin as she reached for the almond milk.

"Love you too, sweetheart," her mother replied.

Janice ended the call, slid her phone into her pocket, and checked out. Her basket was an odd mix: frozen pizza, cereal, and milk, but she didn't care. No one knew her here, and she wouldn't be around long. At least, that had been the plan.

She stopped by the house next door, the so-called big house, on a whim. Maybe someone there could confirm the kitchen theory. The building had once been a showstopper, but its grandeur felt hollow now. Walking up the grand staircase, she pushed the door open, wincing as it stuck from the pressurized seal of the

AC. She shivered, uncertain if the chill came from the air conditioning or something older, something watching.

The house manager greeted her politely but admitted that the family hadn't lived there in decades. Still, he handed her a business card for a professor at Kennesaw State, a chairman in the history department who might be able to help.

She made the appointment on the spot, scheduled during the professor's lunch hour. But she had walked to the store and had to jog back to the house for her car. By the time she arrived at the university, she was sweaty, flustered, and ten minutes late. The campus was crawling with students, and parking was nonexistent. The chaos reminded her of college.

She rushed toward the cafeteria, scanning the room. A hand shot up across the tables. She stepped sideways to see who it belonged to: a man around her age with dark hair, glasses, and a casual jacket over a polo shirt. Definitely not a student.

"Hi, I'm Janice. Are you Professor Menendez?"

"Please, Gabriel," he said, gesturing for her to sit. "And don't worry about being late. I was just taking a moment to eat."

"Thank you. I appreciate it," she said, trying not to sound winded.

"So, what can I do for you, Mrs…?"

"Ms., yes. Sorry," she replied, smiling more than she meant to. She pulled out a tablet and a pen from her bag. "Gabriel, do you know the Cheney home?"

He set down his fork. "Of course. I moved here

because of the South's history. That home has quite the reputation. But that can't be your only question."

"It isn't," Janice said. "My family owns the smaller house next door. I'm related to the Cheneys and came down to fix up the property."

His eyebrows lifted. "Now that is interesting."

Janice explained what Guy had found: bricks out back under the pile of overgrown grass and ivy, possibly from an old kitchen, and how she didn't want to touch anything without knowing its significance. Then, hesitating for a moment, she pulled from her purse a folded photo of the sealed letter she had discovered and mentioned the journal she had barely begun to read.

Gabriel's curiosity visibly sharpened. "A sealed letter and a journal? That could be a treasure trove of personal history. Do you mind if I take a look when I come by?"

"I'd love that," Janice said. "There's a lot I'm trying to piece together. I think these may hold some real answers."

He nodded, rubbing his hand over his goatee. "The kitchen, the journal, the sealed letter, it's all part of the same tapestry. Would Saturday morning work? Before the heat sets in? Say…around eight?"

"Perfect. Do you drink coffee?"

"Of course. I'm human, aren't I?" he teased.

She laughed, feeling herself relax. "Great. I'll see you Saturday with gloves."

As she stood and thanked him, she sensed his eyes following her out of the cafeteria. She didn't look back. Instead, she pulled out her phone and dialed Jeff. It made her look occupied, just in case Gabriel was still watching. But it also gave her a moment to collect herself.

There was something about Gabriel, his presence, his attention, the way he listened as if she mattered. She wasn't sure what it meant yet, but she felt the stirrings of something new, something she hadn't allowed herself to feel in a long time. He was cute, and she couldn't deny the way her heart skipped.

She would wait to tell Jeff about the journal and the sealed letter. Something in this place was shifting. Maybe Gabriel could help her unravel it all.

Janice didn't go straight back to the house. Instead, she found herself turning toward the café, needing somewhere to process the day. Her feet moved on instinct, the way they used to after finals in college, when she needed comfort, caffeine, and company that didn't ask too much of her. She didn't expect the café to feel like that already, but somehow it did.

The familiar chime over the door rang as she stepped inside. A few late-afternoon stragglers lingered over pie or laptops. Matty looked up from behind the counter, her blonde curls tied in a messy bun and a damp towel slung over one shoulder.

"Hey, stranger," she said with a grin. "Come to give a Yelp review in person?"

Janice laughed. "Actually, I was thinking of leaving a five-star Google review for the coffee and the company."

Matty wiped her hands on her apron and gestured to the counter. "Well, in that case, pull up a stool and make my day."

Janice did just that, taking the mug Matty filled without needing to ask. "So," she said, warming her hands around the cup, "I had a very interesting meeting today."

"Do tell," Matty said, sliding into a seat across the bar. "You look like you've got something to spill."

Janice took a sip, then smiled. "I met with a history professor, Gabriel Martinez. The guy and the museum director both recommended him. I asked if he could help me figure out what's behind that pile of bricks in the backyard."

Matty leaned in. "An outside kitchen?"

Janice nodded. "He's coming to the house on Saturday to take a closer look."

Matty raised her eyebrows. "Okay, wait, Gabriel Martinez? College professor with dark hair and smart-guy glasses?"

"That's the one," Janice said, chuckling.

Matty gave her a teasing look. "Well, now I definitely want a review. On the man, not just the meeting."

Janice blushed slightly. "He's... smart. Helpful. Cute. The kind of guy who doesn't interrupt you when you're rambling about old brick piles and family journals."

"Mm-hmm," Matty said, stirring cream into her coffee. "Sounds dangerously decent."

Janice rolled her eyes affectionately, then turned a little more serious. "While I was out there the other day, I found something else: A marker, partially hidden in the vines. It said, 'Trail of Tears.'"

Matty's teasing tone faded. "You found it."

"I didn't even know it passed through here. But now I can't stop thinking about something you said... about the orchard crying and women burying what couldn't be spoken."

Matty nodded slowly, her voice quieter. "That's exactly

what my grandma meant. She used to say the land out there was soaked in sorrow and that the trees never stopped weeping." She hesitated, then added, "She wouldn't even drive past your property, you know. Not once. She'd take the long way around every time, like even glancing at it would stir something up."

Janice blinked. "Seriously?"

Matty nodded. "She believed in signs. Said that land was claimed with silence, like something sacred had been buried and no one dared speak of it."

Janice's fingers tightened around the mug. "I don't know what I'm supposed to do with that."

"My grandma believed one day, someone would come along who could feel it. Who wouldn't turn away."

Janice looked down at her cup. "I don't know if I want to be that person."

"You don't always get to choose," Matty said gently. "But you can decide what you do with what the land gives you."

They sat in silence for a beat, the hum of the cafe soft around them. Outside, a single crow landed on the sidewalk and cocked its head toward the window.

Janice finally smiled again. "That better be in your Google review."

Matty grinned. "You solve buried mysteries, and I'll handle the ratings."

CHAPTER TWENTY-EIGHT

◦◦ THE CHOICE

1862, Georgia
Summer's End

Natalie had a choice: return home to the comfort of familiarity and safety, or remain in Georgia, where war stirred like thunder on the horizon and injustice festered in the open air. Yet every time she thought of leaving, she remembered Lucy's face, the trembling voice that cried out for her mother, and the shadows in Isaac's eyes, the weary resolve in Ms. Patty's hands.

Natalie had already chosen, even if she hadn't said the words aloud.

Over the past few weeks, she, Ms. Patty, and Isaac had created a subtle but effective code. It had started over evening chores and soft-spoken stories, whispers in the kitchen between slicing onions and folding linens. Ms. Patty, once a seamstress for a freewoman in Savannah, had long ago learned the power of quiet signals: A crooked hem, A misplaced stitch, A spoon turned upside down.

Natalie had added her own touches, small disruptions to her routines, invented ailments to keep the family from wandering the grounds when a hiding was in motion. Isaac, who drove the carriage by day and moved messages by night, coordinated with the workers on Walt's estate. Together, the trio operated like threads in a tightly sewn quilt, each tug pulling another into motion.

This night, the spoon on her tray had been turned handle-down. It meant someone was coming.

Later, as she walked the edge of the fields, she spotted Isaac working on a buggy wheel near his quarters. She approached slowly, pretending to read beneath the tree. "Where do you hide them?" she asked in a hush.

"It's better you don't know, Miss Natalie," Isaac replied without looking up.

"You should trust me by now," she said, her voice low but firm.

He paused, the wheel creaking under his weight. "It's not you I don't trust."

Then, the crack of a whip split the air.

Natalie's head snapped up. Billy rode his chestnut horse like a tyrant surveying a kingdom, grinning as the whip snapped down near bent backs and startled faces. Another foreman laughed beside him. They rode like boys playing war.

But then Billy dismounted, slithering down like a shadow unfurling. Natalie's stomach turned cold. He was heading toward someone. She followed his gaze. Lucy.

Billy grabbed her arm and flung her into the dirt. "What did you say to me?" he snarled.

Lucy said nothing.

"Oh, you're going to get it now."

Natalie stood, heart racing, and looked to Isaac. In a flash, he dropped his tools and rushed forward. "Mister Billy, sir. I apologize for whatever Lucy did."

Billy ignored him until Isaac dared to touch his arm.

Lucy whimpered, "Please!" Her cry cracked the stillness of the fields. Again, she screamed. No one moved. Not one soul dared.

Natalie covered her mouth. She couldn't breathe. Couldn't think. Until she did.

She ran.

"Billy, no!" she shouted.

By the time she reached the quarters, it was already too late. Billy had dragged Lucy inside. Blood streaked down the girl's face, her lip swelling grotesquely. He had her pinned over a wooden table, one hand fumbling with his pants, the other yanking her wrists high above her head.

Natalie gasped. "Billy, stop!"

He looked possessed, sweat glistening, eyes wild. "Every time you speak, I'll hit her," he growled, and he did, again and again.

Lucy's voice was barely audible. "Please, Miss Natalie. Go." She was resigned to her fate.

Then Patty's hand was on her shoulder. Isaac's too. Pulling her away. Shielding her. Natalie stumbled back, unable to comprehend what she had seen, what was still going to happen.

She broke free. Ran.

By the time she burst through the doors of the main house, she was breathless and shaking.

"Whoa there, where's the fire?" Uncle William appeared, concern creasing his brow.

"He's, he's..." She gasped, pointing. "Billy. He's hurting her. He's going to rape her."

He flinched, only slightly. "Who?"

"Lucy!"

"Damn it." His voice was flat. He turned to the window. "Stay here," he muttered.

Natalie watched in horror as he called for Henry, instructed him to stay with her, and then walked, *walked,* toward the quarters.

"Please hurry," she begged.

Henry sat beside her. "Why is he like this?" she asked him, pleading for answers.

"Momma says he was swapped out with the Devil's child," Henry said. "Wasn't supposed to be born alive."

Natalie stared at him, the words not even fully registering. Her body ached with helplessness. Her soul screamed with rage.

THAT NIGHT, Alice came to her room. She closed the door softly, her face pale in the lamplight. For a long moment, she said nothing, only clasped the shawl tight at her throat.

Finally, she spoke. "You must understand. Billy has never been like other children. When he was born, he did not cry. Not a sound. He only stared. And the moment he came into the world, a shadow passed across the chimney. The root doctor who delivered him was so spooked she swore she'd never return to this house."

Natalie's stomach turned. "Then why does no one stop him?"

Alice's mouth pressed thin. "Because he is my son. And because William will not hear of it. He dismisses his temper as nothing more than the ways of men. But I see it. I know there is something darker in him."

Her eyes lifted to Natalie's, sharp with both warning and sorrow. "The land marked him that day. And once it marks a man, there is no undoing it."

Alice fell silent, as though she had said too much. Then she rose and left without another word.

Natalie sat frozen, unable to steady her hands.

JOURNAL ENTRY —

I can still hear her screams.

The look in her eyes. The blood. The way he hit her like she was nothing.

And my uncle, his reaction wasn't horror. It was an inconvenience.

He knew. And I suspect it wasn't the first time. He looked out the window, not in shock but with calculation.

I do not belong in that house. I will not belong to silence. What happened to Lucy is unforgivable, and I will not let it go unanswered.

Every woman here, enslaved or free, young or old, deserves protection. And if no one else will offer it, I will.

I'm writing to Mother and Father tonight. They'll beg me to come home. But I won't. I've made my decision.

What happens to one of them happens to them all. And I will not look away.

Not anymore.

—N.

CHAPTER TWENTY-NINE
⚘ ASH AND EVIDENCE

While arranging bricks into a rough border along the crumbled foundation wall, Janice knelt down to adjust a crooked edge when she suddenly lost her balance. Normally, she would have expected the usual thud on her backside; she'd had her fair share of clumsy landings. But this time, the fall felt different. The ground beneath her had given slightly, as if something under the surface had shifted.

She frowned, brushed the dust from her hands, and glanced around the clearing. The sun was dipping low, stretching shadows across the yard. She wanted to get this spot in better shape before Guy and his crew returned the next day. Despite its disrepair, she liked the feel of this space. She could almost see it as a barbecue area, with a fire pit and rustic furniture. She made a mental note to ask Jeff if that would add to the home's value.

Still sitting in the dirt, she bounced lightly on her heels again. There it was, the same strange give. She stood, scanning the ground. This part of the yard had clearly once been enclosed. In the box under the stairs, tucked between brittle letters and warped old photographs, the hand-drawn map had shown a faint rectangle, an outbuilding or addition that no longer existed. Now she wondered if she was standing right on top of it.

"Another secret door, huh?" she muttered to herself, remembering the false wall under the stairs where she had found the box. A smile tugged at her lips. "Always wanted to be Indiana Jones... or Lara Croft."

She hurried to the porch and grabbed her work gloves and flashlight. Back at the spot, she brushed away layers of leaves and brittle grass until her gloved hand struck something solid. Wood.

Not charred or splintered, but old and intact. A floorboard, maybe. She ran her fingers along the edge, searching for seams. The wood was springy under her touch. Could it be an underground room? The idea bloomed in her chest. A forgotten cellar? A storage space? Something else?

She shifted the flashlight to her other hand and leaned closer, her heartbeat picking up.

By now, the sun had vanished behind the trees, and darkness crept into the yard. The flashlight beam quivered slightly as she moved it across the ground. The air had grown unnaturally still.

She stood slowly and turned toward the house. The porch light glowed warmly in the gathering dark, but she lingered, glancing back once more. Everything looked the same. Yet the itch at the back of her thoughts told her something was different.

The orchard flickered in her mind, unbidden. Those

red eyes she had seen, glowing like marbles in the dark. A shiver ran through her. She glanced up toward the trees, half-expecting to see them again, shadows shifting at the edge of the light.

Her pulse quickened. She whispered, "It was just that one night," and forced herself to look away.

Inside, she shut the door firmly. Locked it. Then locked it again. She moved from room to room, closing blinds and clicking on lights. Only when the house was fully lit did her nerves begin to settle.

On the kitchen counter, the folded map caught her attention again, its pencil lines leading her gaze back to the very spot she had uncovered. She pressed her fingers to the paper and whispered, "Always another secret."

After splashing her face with water in the bathroom, she picked up her phone and typed out a message.

Janice: Hiya! It's Janice. I hope this isn't weird, but I found something outside I'd like your take on.

The reply came quickly.

Gabriel: Sure thing. What did you find?

Janice: Not sure... but would it be weird to find a wooden floor beneath a kitchen that caught fire?

Gabriel: Lol no. So what's weird about it?

Janice: It's... bouncy.

Gabriel: Ok, too many questions. I know we said the afternoon, but is the morning okay?

Janice: Morning works. I'll be here with coffee ready. Oh and ty.

Gabriel: My pleasure :)

Janice stared at the smiley face a little longer than she meant to, then smiled back at the screen.

Janice: :)

She set the phone down, her heart fluttering slightly. Ridiculous, she thought. She felt like a teenager again.

Before bed, she made one last round of the house, checking locks and lights. In the kitchen, she paused at the window, gazing across the yard to where the ground had shifted. The spot looked ordinary in the dark, yet something about it tugged at her.

Sleep came slowly.

And then *it* came.

The summer kitchen stood whole again, glowing with firelight as if nothing had ever collapsed. Pots hissed. A dog barked in the distance. And when Janice turned, she froze.

A girl no older than sixteen stood inside the doorway. Her head was tilted at a grotesque angle, her neck broken, yet she remained upright. Her dark eyes stared directly at Janice, steady, unblinking. This was not the girl from the newspaper clippings. This one was younger, enslaved, her apron torn, and her face streaked with dirt. She swayed, but she did not fall.

Janice couldn't move. The girl's lips parted as if she wanted to speak, but no sound came. Just the silent, impossible weight of her stare.

Janice jolted awake, gasping. The room was dark. The hallway light glowed faintly.

She pressed both palms to her eyes, willing her heart to slow. "It was just a dream," she whispered again, though her voice trembled.

She lay back down, forcing her eyes shut. Willing herself to believe it.

It was just a dream.

CHAPTER THIRTY

⚘ THE REVEAL

T he next afternoon, Gabriel pulled into the gravel driveway in his gray Nissan Rogue. Janice had just finished her last call and was ticking through a mental checklist when she spotted him from the window. She closed her notebook, smoothed her hair, and stepped outside to meet him.

He was rummaging in the backseat, half-buried in a bag of gear.

"Hello," she called.

"And hello to you too," he said, straightening with a grin. He held up a long rod with a flat, circular plate at the end.

Janice squinted against the sun. "What is that?"

"Metal detector," Gabriel said, giving it a little swing. "These old places always have stories buried under the dirt —buttons, nails, tools. Sometimes it's the little things that tell you the most."

Janice smiled, shading her eyes. "So you're hoping for treasure?"

"Always," he said lightly. "Didn't you say you tripped over something odd out here?"

She led him across the yard toward the ruins of the outdoor kitchen. The sun beat down hard, shimmering off the brick outlines.

"I was working right over here," she said, pointing. "I lost my balance, but the ground didn't feel right. Almost like it moved under me."

Gabriel crouched and pressed his heel against the earth. A dull creak answered. He brushed away grass and soil with his hands, and slowly, the edge of a weathered plank appeared.

"This isn't random debris," he murmured. "This was set here on purpose."

He found a raised seam and tugged. The plank resisted, groaning with age, then lifted on stiff hinges to reveal a dark opening.

Janice's breath hitched. A narrow staircase dropped into the earth.

"Holy smokes," she whispered.

Gabriel shone his phone's flashlight into the space. The beam cut through dust and cobwebs, tracing stone steps that led down into shadow.

"This isn't a root cellar," he said. "It's too deep. Too hidden."

A rush of cool air spilled upward, damp and heavy, as though it had been sealed for a century.

Gabriel started down, his steps slow and careful. Janice followed, one hand sliding along the wall for balance. The temperature fell immediately, wrapping her in clammy silence.

At the bottom, the room opened, a low stone chamber. Crates lay splintered along one wall, a wool blanket moth-eaten and curled in the corner.

Gabriel's light froze. He crouched, steadying the beam. "There's... someone here."

Janice stepped closer, her stomach lurching. In the far corner lay bones curled in on themselves, clothed in scraps of Civil War–era fabric. Knees drawn close, arms tight, as though death had come while waiting.

Her throat closed. This was no storage cellar. It was a hiding place.

Gabriel brushed debris carefully aside. Beneath the skeletal arm, half-wrapped in the tattered blanket, rested a rusted tin container. He pried it open. Inside, folded parchment crackled with age.

"It's a letter," he murmured. The fading ink revealed words like fragments of a prayer: *freedom... safe... blessings... Quaker.*

"This was a stop," he said reverently. "A station on the Underground Railroad."

Janice's skin prickled. She stared at the staircase, at the hidden chamber itself. All of it had been waiting, buried under their feet.

Her gaze drifted to the shelves still clinging to one side of the wall. A honey jar, its lid corroded but intact, sat beside a pair of scuffed leather shoes. A boy's shirt, yellowed with age, was folded with surprising care. A strip of dried meat, wrapped in waxed cloth, lay crumbling to dust.

Janice reached out, brushing her hand along the glass of the jar, and for a moment her vision blurred—

.   .   .

◇◇

Lucy knelt in this very corner, candlelight trembling across her face. She set the honey jar down with careful hands, whispering a prayer as she did.

"For strength," she murmured. "And sweetness, to remind them the world still got good in it."

Beside it she placed dried venison, tied with a strip of cloth, and then the pair of mended shoes Isaac had repaired. Not new, but strong enough for another hundred miles. At last, she folded a boy's cotton shirt, tucking a sprig of mint inside for luck.

From outside came the call of a whippoorwill, the signal. Travelers were near.

Lucy's heart raced. She had seen too many arrive barefoot, children clinging to weary mothers, their bellies hollow from days without food. Here, at least, she could give them something: a meal, a covering, a chance to keep moving.

She pressed her palm to the stone, whispering again, "Be safe. Keep walking."

Above her, Natalie's lantern cast a soft glow near the hidden door. Their eyes met, unspoken but sure. Together, they were holding the line.

⚓

Janice blinked, her hand still resting on the honey jar. For a moment, she could have sworn warmth lingered there, like another hand laid on top of hers. She stepped back quickly, chest tight.

But then her eyes fell back to the skeleton. The skull was fractured at the temple, a jagged break that wasn't natural. The curled fingers still clutched a rusted horseshoe.

Gabriel leaned close. "That's blunt force trauma."

A wave of grief rolled over Janice, followed by something darker. Not just sorrow—rage. This body didn't belong in the refuge around it. The air itself seemed to reject him.

"He doesn't belong here," she whispered.

Gabriel looked up. "What do you mean?"

"The room feels... sacred. Like sorrow and hope and memory all live here. But this body, this feels wrong. Violent."

She hugged her arms tight across her chest. The figure seemed coiled, clenched, as if rage had seeped into the bones themselves.

Gabriel nodded slowly but stayed quiet.

Janice drew a breath, then turned to him. "There's something I haven't told you."

His brow furrowed. "What is it?"

She hesitated. Then, softly, "There was more I the box than what I told you."

She swallowed. "Inside was a map. Hand-drawn. Pencil lines faded, but it showed this place, this cellar. A rectangle marked with an X."

Gabriel's gaze shifted back to the bones.

Janice continued. "A button. A piece of embroidered cloth. And a letter... to someone named Meredith. It began: Should I not return…" Her voice caught. "It read like a goodbye."

She glanced again at the skeleton. "I think this place was meant to be found. But not him. Not this one."

The chamber pressed in around them. Dust, stone, silence, all heavy with meaning.

Gabriel finally exhaled. "Then maybe you were meant to find it."

Janice didn't reply. Her eyes stayed fixed on the curled bones, the clenched horseshoe. She could feel it in her gut: the room had been a sanctuary once. But his death had spoiled it.

And now the land itself refused to forget.

CHAPTER THIRTY-ONE
∘∘ UNDERCOVER OF THE STORM

1863, Georgia
February

Uncle William and Aunt Alice were pleased when Natalie announced she would stay longer. What they didn't know was that her decision had little to do with Southern hospitality and everything to do with Lucy, Isaac, Bitsy, and the others who had carved their way into her conscience.

She found Lucy behind the outdoor kitchen, where workers were busy framing a small shelter for the cook. Sawdust floated in the humid air. Isaac stood nearby with a board balanced on his shoulder, sweat darkening his shirt. Lucy looked smaller than usual, her hair tucked into a faded kerchief, her eyes watchful.

Natalie went straight to her and wrapped her arms around her tightly.

"Oh, Lucy, I am so, so sorry. Are you all right?"

Lucy held her just as firmly. Natalie felt the damp heat of tears seep into her collar. She pulled back, cupping Lucy's face in both hands.

"I never meant to cause you pain," Natalie whispered. "I just didn't want him to hurt you anymore."

Lucy lifted her chin, her voice steady but low. "Miss Natalie, the Devil will get his own. It may not be by my doin', but it will happen."

Natalie's chest tightened. She nodded, unable to speak. To shift the weight between them, she glanced at Isaac. "How's it going over here?"

"Laying out the boundary for the new kitchen house," he said, setting the board down and brushing his brow.

Natalie smiled faintly. "Is there anything you can't do, Isaac?"

He grinned. "Haven't found it yet, Miss Natalie."

His laugh was brief but genuine, and even in the heat, it brought a flicker of hope.

Natalie turned back to Lucy, lowering her voice. "Lucy... next time there's a group leaving, you could go with them. You should go. Be safe."

Lucy clutched the bundle Natalie had pressed into her hands, shoes and bandages, and shook her head. "Abby still needs me," she said softly. "And what kind of person would I be to do that to a little girl?"

Natalie's throat tightened. She wanted to insist, to beg her to choose freedom, but she saw it in Lucy's eyes; she would never abandon Abby. Not while she drew breath.

Later, Natalie lingered near the stables, a carrot pulled from her apron as an excuse. The bay gelding nuzzled her palm before crunching down, each bite sharp in the humid stillness. The smells of hay, leather, and summer pressed close, thick as cloth.

Inside, Isaac worked with a pitchfork, his movements sure and steady. A low rumble rolled across the fields, the air heavy with the promise of rain. When he caught sight of her, he leaned against the stall door, breathing hard, his shirt clinging to his back.

"The horses seem fond of you," Natalie said, stroking the gelding's mane.

"They like anyone with a pocket full of carrots," Isaac answered with a quick grin. His eyes slid toward the house; his voice dropped a notch. He seemed to weigh his next words, the shovel handle tapping once against the boards, quiet as a metronome.

Natalie's breath hitched. He wasn't talking about horses anymore.

Finally, he said, rough and quiet, "The train is on its tracks. North."

The carrot snapped in the gelding's teeth. Natalie stilled, heart thudding. Pride flared hot in her chest, proof she had done something, that her letters and courage had not been wasted. The line was moving; people were running for freedom. But pride's edge was sharp. Every mile forward meant lives balanced on a blade.

She hesitated before she whispered, "What about Billy?"

The gelding's ears flicked back. A sharp whinny tore from its throat, high and fearful, and it struck the stall wall with a sudden kick that rattled the boards. Dust sifted from the rafters. Natalie jumped back, hand flying to her throat.

Isaac's jaw tightened. He set the fork aside, eyes gone dark. "Even the animals know him." His voice came low, almost reverent, as if he'd seen this before. "No one can stop him. He's a demon walking this earth. Best thing you can do is stay out of his way. God'll sort him out when his time comes."

Natalie pressed her cheek to the gelding's neck, feeling the tremor beneath its hide. Billy's name seemed to sour the very air, to ripple through the rafters. His absence weighed heavier than presence, like a shadow that clung no matter the light.

Isaac straightened, his tone louder now, ordinary. "Storm's coming. Best get inside."

She nodded, forcing calm, though her knees still shook. She turned toward the house with Isaac's warning and the horse's terror lodged in her chest. Pride, fear, purpose, danger: she carried them all at once.

Later that night, Natalie found Lucy again near the back door, where the smell of supper still lingered. The kerchief had slipped from Lucy's hair, a strand curling damp against her cheek.

"Thank God you're here. I don't think I could face it all without you." Lucy said softly, her hand brushing against the front of her apron as though by habit, her voice carrying the weight of someone who had learned not to waste words.

Natalie's throat caught. She smiled instead, lifting her skirts as she turned toward the stairwell. "Y'all are stuck with me now."

For the first time in weeks, she felt a flicker of something steady. A place. A purpose.

The next day, the fields steamed under a sweltering sun. Cotton bloomed in white tufts against the red earth, and workers bent low, hands moving in a rhythm older than the house. Lucy moved among them, humming a tune. Natalie caught it at once, not just a song but a message. A warning. A signal.

Her uncle stood at the rise, arms folded, but he didn't notice. None of them did. Natalie's pulse steadied, just a little.

Billy hadn't been seen for days. William had sent him to town to work off Lucy's doctor bills. Whether it was penance or pride, Natalie couldn't tell. His absence felt like thunder that never quite arrived. Even without him, the storm lingered in every flinch at a slammed door, every drop of silence when his name was spoken.

That Sunday, the storm arrived, but not Billy. The skies split with rain, and the clay roads dissolved into mud. Church wagons stayed empty. The household gathered in the parlor, sluggish and damp, the air thick with humidity.

The parlor was dim, heavy curtains pulled against the downpour. The windows rattled with each gust, rain lashing so hard it sounded like stones striking glass. The children squirmed at first but eventually settled; Natalie played a simple hymn on the piano, Henry humming along, both trying to lighten the mood. Alice sat with her embroidery hoop balanced on her lap, though her needle slipped more than once in the bad light.

At the hearth, Abby crouched near the fire, a primer spread across her knees. Lucy sat beside her, shoulders nearly touching, her lips shaping the words softly as Abby worked her way through the line.

"Do… to… oth…ers… as… you… would…" Abby faltered, then pressed on, her voice small but steady. "… have them do… to you."

Lucy's mouth curved. "That's right. Again, slower this time."

Abby gave a proud little nod, her finger moving under each word as though they might slip away if she didn't hold them in place.

"That's a good one to keep in your heart," Lucy said quietly, watching her. The irony wasn't lost on her.

Natalie's chest lifted at the sight, a white child and an enslaved girl near Natalie's own age, bent over letters in the same glow. For a moment, she let herself believe the world could tilt that way, quietly, toward right.

William's voice cut through. "That's enough of that."

Abby looked up, startled, the primer slipping in her lap. Lucy's hands stilled, her eyes lowering in the practiced way of someone who knew where danger lived.

"Reading in plain view," William muttered, jaw tight. "What's next?"

Alice did not lift her eyes from her embroidery, but steel threaded her voice. "Plain view of whom, William? We are all family here."

The fire popped. Silence pressed in, heavier than the rain. William's gaze lingered on Lucy. His mouth thinned, as if to argue, but something in Alice's tone held him. He turned away with a grunt.

Abby clutched the primer closer, and Lucy's hand brushed over hers in quiet reassurance. Abby whispered,

"We'll finish later." Her face flushed with small, fierce pride. Lucy gave the faintest nod.

William rose, restless. "Cards," he announced. "Best way to pass a storm."

"It is still the Sabbath," Alice said.

He waved her off, already fetching the deck. "Sun is down. Sunday's done."

Chairs scraped as they gathered. The lamplight cast small golden halos, shadows pooling in the corners. The air carried damp earth and wet wool.

Natalie fanned her hand of cards, trying to appear calm. Her fingers trembled on the pasteboard. She could hear her own pulse.

Then, outside the parlor window, a light flickered.

William paused mid-shuffle. "Now, who could that be?"

Natalie's stomach clenched. The plan. She'd assumed it was canceled for the rain. Her eyes darted toward the tree line where a faint lantern bobbed. Too quick. Too purposeful.

"I'm sure it's someone checking the horses," she said, forcing calm. "The storm may have spooked them."

"They're going the wrong way," William said, narrowing his eyes.

"Maybe they already checked on them," Natalie replied too quickly.

William pushed back his chair. "I should see."

Panic coiled in her chest. She pictured the fugitives in the rain, wet faces, shaking hands, gripping one another as they hurried through the mud. If William stepped out now, he'd see them. He'd know.

"Henry," Natalie blurted, "could you check for your father? Let him know if anything looks unusual."

Alice's voice slipped in smoothly before Henry could move. "Yes, let Henry go. Besides, William, it's your turn."

The words landed with precision, a stitch placed exactly where the seam might give way.

Natalie's eyes flicked to her aunt. Chance, or intention?

William hesitated, gaze fixed on the distant light. A slow rumble rolled over the house. By the time he looked back, the glow was gone.

"Perhaps you're right," he muttered. "Still felt… off."

"This whole day has felt off," Alice replied evenly. "Now sit. I mean to win this hand."

The game resumed, though Natalie barely registered the cards. Every nerve ran taut. She kept her gaze on the window, praying the light would not reappear. Outside was nothing but a gray blur.

When Alice finally laid down her cards with a small triumphant smile, William groaned, and Henry laughed. It looked ordinary, like family at leisure on a stormy night.

But Natalie knew it was not.

As Alice rose, she touched Natalie's shoulder lightly, the pressure deliberate. "Come on, children. Time for bed."

Natalie stayed in her chair long after the others left, trembling. Alice had known. She had to have known.

· · ·

JOURNAL ENTRY-

Tonight, we won.

It was quiet. No fanfare, no waving lanterns. Just rain on the roof, cards on the table, and a single hand resting on my shoulder that told me everything.

I don't know how many passed. I may never know. But I saw the light vanish, not because it was stopped, but because it had gone far enough to be safe.

Aunt Alice surprised me. I don't know how long she has known, but I felt it in her touch: solidarity, warning, or both. Resistance doesn't always roar. Sometimes it knits quietly in a corner, or distracts a husband at a card table, while lives slip into the night.

This afternoon by the stables, Isaac told me, in the way we tell things now, that the train is on its tracks. Pride and fear came together in me like two sides of the same coin. Pride, because the work is real. Fear, because every mile means a life held out to the dark and asked to cross.

Billy's absence is no comfort. We breathe easier only until he circles back. Even the horses shied at his name.

Still, tonight I will sleep lighter. Lucy smiled. Isaac laughed. Abby sounded out her letters by the fire with Lucy's hand steadying hers, and Alice called us family with her chin up. And a path was walked under cover of storm.

Maybe next Sunday, someone else will make it through.

Maybe this is how the world changes,

one game of cards at a time.

—N.

PART THREE
LIGHT AND LEGACY:

The truth rises, the past breathes, and the living must decide what to carry forward.

"The light shines in the darkness, and the darkness has not overcome it."
— John 1:5

CHAPTER THIRTY-TWO

◦◦ DIAMONDS IN THE CELLAR

1863, Georgia
April

I t had been six months since that night. Six months since Lucy's cries split the quarters, since Natalie had sworn in her journal never to look away again. Six months of moving carefully through shadows, whispering messages between kitchen work, and turning grief into resistance.

Billy had returned to the estate. His presence was never steady; some days he sulked in town, while others he prowled the fields, but he was always there, like thunder in the distance. Lucy carried the proof of his cruelty in her body now, her belly just beginning to swell. She moved slower in the fields, humming the coded hymns that stitched their secret world together. The sight of her resilience hardened Natalie's resolve.

The new outdoor kitchen stood proudly behind the house, but only a few knew the truth. Beneath its fresh boards and stone hearth lay something far older: a forgotten root cellar. Isaac had stumbled across it during construction, noticing how the soil dipped oddly, how the bricks didn't match. Together, he and Natalie had rebuilt it in silence—new beams for support, seams reset to vanish, an entrance disguised so well even William himself would not notice.

To most, it was storage.

To them, it was sanctuary.

Natalie and Lucy had scratched maps into its stone walls. Starbursts for the Mason-Dixon line. Diamonds for movement. Spades for caution. A rough river etched like a scar to mark the Chattahoochee. They wove signals into daily life: a hymn hummed slightly off-key, a jar of pickled okra turned inward, a hem stitched the wrong way. Even Aunt Alice helped, sometimes distracting William with a card game or a question just long enough for a shadow to slip across the yard.

Natalie thought of Walt often. Six weeks earlier, during one of Uncle William's endless games of whist, he had taught her to read the cards differently. The Queen of Hearts followed by the Eight of Spades: "Questions heard. Eight safe." A knuckle tapped twice on the wood: "Check the cellar." No one else at the table suspected. To them, it was a harmless game. To Natalie, it had become scripture.

Later, he had tucked a note into her hymn book: "*Southwest route compromised. Use the mill run. Leave Sunday after service. Two.*"

She burned it that same night.

Now she stood in the cellar with Lucy and Isaac. Rain lashed the kitchen roof above, rattling shingles and flooding the yard. A young couple waited in the shadows, a man clutching a toddler, his wife swollen with pregnancy. Isaac guided them down the narrow steps, his movements steady despite the storm.

Natalie passed down a bundle: shoes, bread, and a quilt. "He said two," she whispered.

Lucy nodded, hand on her belly. "Then they best be ready after the sermon."

Natalie scratched a small diamond into the stone wall. Two souls marked for north.

The next morning, the storm had broken into thin sunlight. The family dressed for church, carriages slick with mud. Natalie climbed into the wagon beside Abby and Alice. Isaac helped her up, his fingers brushing hers for a fraction longer than necessary. Their glance held, a quiet signal of its own.

Abby fidgeted with excitement. "I can't wait to see my friends again! I miss Sunday school."

Natalie teased her. "You have friends at home. Am I not enough? Is Henry not enough?"

Abby giggled. "You're old. And Henry's a boy."

William laughed. "Apparently anyone older than Abby is ancient, my dear niece."

When they arrived, something was wrong. People clustered in knots outside the whitewashed church, voices low, faces pinched. The bell rang, calling them in.

Pastor Dale stood at the pulpit, hands gripping the Bible. "I know some of you are shaken by the passing of young Rachel Doling," he began. A ripple of gasps swept the pews.

Natalie's stomach lurched. A child?

"She was found yesterday by the Chattahoochee," the pastor continued. "Her death was unnatural. Let us not seek vengeance, but leave it to the Almighty to bring justice."

A man shouted from the back, "Best find the son of a bitch that did it!"

Whispers filled the air. Natalie leaned forward, catching scraps:

"They said her head was near off."

"Bet it was a runaway."

Natalie slipped from the pew and found Isaac near the drivers. "Rachel was killed by the river," she whispered.

He nodded grimly. "They're blaming runaways."

Her chest tightened. "What if it was someone we helped?"

His eyes darkened. "No. The folks we help want to live, not kill. But listen, two Black girls were found dead earlier this year. Same age. Nobody spoke of it. Not a word."

Natalie's breath caught. "What?"

He held her gaze. "Silence swallows some lives whole. But Rachel's family has money. Now people talk."

Her heart pounded as she returned to the pew. The storm inside her felt greater than the one that had soaked the fields the night before.

JOURNAL ENTRY-

I don't know who killed Rachel Doling, but it was not one of the souls we've helped. Walt told me once: A runaway doesn't stop to spill blood. They run toward life, not away from it.

Still, fear gnaws at me.

The code is working. Two diamonds etched in stone mark the couple hiding beneath the kitchen now. Walt's cards. Lucy's songs. Isaac's signals. Even Alice's steady hand at the card table. Together we weave a net fine enough to catch hope, if only for a moment.

And yet, I lie awake wondering if it will ever be enough.

This morning, Isaac brushed my hand as he helped me into the carriage. It meant nothing to anyone else. To me, it was everything. He is the best man I've ever known.

I can never say it aloud. Not in this world.

So I write it here. If these pages outlive me, let them carry this truth:

I loved him.

~ N.

THAT NIGHT, as the house settled into silence, Natalie passed the hallway window and froze. Billy stood out by the orchard, lantern in hand, his face lit in cruel orange. He wasn't looking for cattle. He wasn't even moving.

He was staring at the kitchen.

At the ground beneath it.

At her.

Natalie pulled the curtains tight, but her hands shook long after.

CHAPTER THIRTY-THREE
∘∘ BORN IN THE SHADOWS

1863, Georgia
June

They came and got Natalie in the middle of the night. Isaac's voice was urgent but hushed as he knocked on the side door of the house.

"It's time," he said.

Natalie barely had time to throw on her cloak before following him into the cold. The air was heavy with moisture and the scent of hay, the moon a pale eye in the sky.

She found Lucy in the stable, writhing in pain, biting down on a piece of leather. Patty crouched at her feet and Bitsy sat behind her, small but mighty, letting Lucy lean back into her lap for support. Bitsy kept pressing a cool rag to Lucy's temple, whispering steady words. Isaac's family was already there, every pair of hands ready.

The lanterns swayed faintly from their hooks,

throwing thin shadows across the stalls. Horses shifted restlessly in their bays, snorting, hooves scraping straw as if they, too, sensed the urgency. The air was hot with the mingled scent of animals, sweat, and something metallic.

Lucy wasn't ready to be a mother. But ready or not, it was time.

The men tried to usher Isaac out, but he wouldn't leave. Every time he turned toward the door, he doubled back, face drawn tight with dread. He caught Natalie's eye, the weight of his guilt plain. She tried to reassure him with a small shake of her head—there was nothing he could have done to change what Billy had forced. Still, he couldn't let go of the burden.

The rocking pain came in waves, then constant, as if Lucy were being squeezed past breaking. She cried out, begged Natalie to make it stop. Natalie could only hold her shoulders, murmur comfort, and pray.

Patty worked quickly, her voice calm and commanding. "Push now, girl. Push."

Bitsy leaned in, letting Lucy grip her legs like rails. Natalie steadied her from behind, whispering encouragement. Patty looped leather reins under Lucy's arms and tied them to a beam so she could squat and bear down.

Lucy groaned, body trembling, slick with sweat. The sound of her struggle filled the stable, rising and falling like thunder.

"You're almost there," Natalie whispered in her ear. "You're not alone."

Isaac rushed back to her side, gripping the reins where

Bitsy had been. He pressed his forehead to Lucy's for one fleeting moment, whispering something only she could hear. Then he braced his body and spoke low and steady. "Breathe. I'm right here. You can do this."

His voice grounded her. Natalie felt it too.

With one last desperate push, Lucy gave everything she had. A slick sound, a cry that split the night—and the baby was born. Patty caught him in her waiting hands. She tied off the cord with practiced speed and bundled the child.

Lucy collapsed backward, eyes wide with disbelief. Natalie leaned in, voice trembling.

"It's a boy," she whispered.

Lucy blinked slowly. "A boy?"

Patty nodded. "Strong one, too."

Lucy stared at the ceiling, tears slipping into her hair. "I hope he never becomes like *him*."

Bitsy smoothed damp curls from her brow. "He won't. He's yours now. And he's safe."

Isaac lowered himself onto the hay beside them, a hand pressed over his mouth. His shoulders trembled with quiet relief.

Natalie glanced toward the house, fear catching in her throat. What would Billy say if he returned? She prayed he never would.

Lucy's voice was soft but sharp. "Is he all right?"

"He's perfect," Patty said firmly. "Ten fingers, ten toes."

Lucy exhaled and closed her eyes. "Thank the Lord."

Natalie tucked a folded blanket beneath Lucy's arms,

easing the child into them. The baby's tiny fists stretched and curled. His first cries echoed in the rafters, hushed by the sound of steady hands.

"You're safe. He's safe," Natalie said.

The horses nickered, quiet and respectful. In the small stable, time seemed to pause. A new life had come into the world. For a fleeting moment—even in Georgia, even in the shadow of cruelty—there was peace.

Lucy looked down at the swaddled baby, awe breaking across her exhausted face. "His name is Benjamin," she whispered. "Ben for short."

Natalie blinked back sudden tears. "That's a good name."

Lucy managed the faintest smile. "It was the name of the man you told me about. The one from the North who writes about freedom. You said he fights for us. If this boy grows up, I want him to be like that."

Natalie's throat tightened. She nodded slowly. "Then it's perfect."

JOURNAL ENTRY -

Tonight, I watched a child be born into a world not yet kind. Lucy, too young to carry so much pain, brought forth a boy with more strength than he knows. I saw Isaac tremble, saw Bitsy and Patty hold the line like seasoned warriors. I felt the pulse of something ancient in that stable—grief, yes, but also hope.

For a moment, the war and Billy both felt far away. But I know they will come crashing back too soon.

There are horrors I cannot undo, but tonight I held something whole. I pray this little one never learns the true reason for his beginning. Let him grow in love, not legacy. Let the sins of men die with them.

His name is Benjamin.

—N.

CHAPTER THIRTY-FOUR

⚥ NOT IN MY HOUSE

The bell over the café door chimed as Janice stepped into the cool, coffee-rich air. It was Saturday late morning, and the place was alive in that gentle way between the breakfast rush and the lunch crowd…

Forks tapped on plates. Someone laughed near the pastry case. Ice slid in a glass and cracked with a soft pop.

"Hey, you," Matty called from behind the counter, towel looped through her apron tie. "Your booth is open. I saved it with a decoy mug and everything."

Janice grinned and slid into the red vinyl. The decoy mug steamed. A strand of sunlit dust drifted lazily in the beam that cut across the table. The room smelled like butter and cinnamon and a little bit of grill smoke. It smelled like a place people stayed.

Carlos moved past with a gray bus tub against his hip. He was nineteen at most, quick and careful, curly hair tucked under a cap. "Morning, Ms. Janice," he said with that shy smile he had when he was not sure if he should look you in the eye.

"Morning, Carlos. Are you saving any biscuits back there, or are you letting Matty sell them all out from under us?"

He laughed. "I will try."

Matty set a plate on the table without asking. "Cornbread with honey. Because you look like you need it." She topped off the coffee and drifted away to the register, where a couple was deciding between peach pie and pecan.

Janice took a bite of cornbread and felt that easy warmth travel up from her stomach. The café's air conditioner hummed against the Georgia heat. A toddler squealed two booths over, then dissolved into giggles as his grandmother bounced him on her knee. Somewhere behind the line, a cook sang a line of a hymn out of tune, happy and unselfconscious.

The door chimed again.

A man in a camo cap and mirrored sunglasses walked in with another guy a step behind him. He pulled the hat off and stuffed it in his back pocket, already scowling at nothing in particular. They took the table near the front window, the one that basked in light nobody wanted in August.

Matty brought menus. "Morning, gentlemen. Y'all doing alright?"

"Coffee," the first man said, flat. "And a plate of bacon. Real bacon, not that turkey mess. Don't try to sell me that."

Matty's mouth stayed kind, but her eyes cooled a

degree. "We only serve one kind here. Is that all right with you?"

He gave a tight nod without saying thank you. Carlos arrived with water glasses and set them down. The man watched his hands. He watched the way he moved. Something ugly woke up in his face, small at first, then bigger.

"Hey," he said loud enough for the nearby tables to hear. He snapped his fingers. "Boy. Wipe this. It is sticky." He added a word after "boy" that turned the room brittle. A slur that made the air tilt.

Carlos flinched. The water trembled in the glass. Janice felt that tremor travel through her own hands even though she was nowhere near them.

For a breath, the café went quiet. Forks hovered. Someone's phone lock screen lit and then went dark again. The toddler stopped giggling.

Janice's chair scraped as she stood. She did not think about it. Her body was moving before her brain caught up. She crossed the room and put herself between the man and Carlos with nothing but a cloth napkin in her hand. She did not raise her voice. She did not need to.

"Do not talk to him like that," she said.

The man leaned back, surprised, a smirk forming, the out of place kind you learned in bars when you thought you knew exactly how far you could push.

"Who are you," he said. "His lawyer?"

"I am a customer," Janice replied. "And a person with ears. You do not get to come in here and insult the people who keep your coffee hot."

He smiled wider, like he had found a new toy. "Oh.

We got ourselves a hero." He turned his head and pitched his voice to the room. "Relax, lady. It was a joke."

Carlos stared at the floor. The muscles in his jaw fluttered. Janice felt a pressure rise in her chest, that same pressure that had chased her along the edge of the orchard. She kept her tone even.

"It was not a joke," she said. "It was an insult. And you will not use that word in this room again."

Chairs shifted. Someone at the counter murmured, "Amen."

Matty was already moving. She did not hurry. She did not need to. She reached the table and set down the coffees she had poured, then stood straight with her towel in her hand like a flag she could drop at any moment.

"House rules," Matty said. "No slurs. No threats. No bullying my staff. You can eat with respect, or you can stand outside and get sunburned. Your choice."

The man scoffed. "You serious?"

"Very," Matty said. "And before you ask, yes, I do own the place. You are in my living room. We keep it clean."

His buddy tried to cut the tension with a laugh that fell flat. "Come on, Dale. Coffee is coffee. Sit down."

Dale took the mug anyway and drank. "You got signs for your rules?" he asked.

Matty gestured toward a small framed card by the register. **We reserve the right to refuse service.** Another card beside it read: **Be kind or be quiet.**

Dale snorted. "Looks like California to me."

"Looks like decency to me," Matty said.

He looked past Matty to Carlos again, and something

sly crept into his voice. "You wanna earn that tip, kid, or do you need the lady to fight for you every time?"

Janice felt heat rise under her skin. She opened her mouth. Matty laid two fingers lightly on Janice's forearm, a signal to hold.

"This is how it works," Matty said, still calm. "You can apologize to my employee and order like a grown man. Or you can leave your coffee and go. If you stay and mouth off again, I will call the sheriff. He plays cards here on Thursdays. He knows where my spare key is."

A chuckle rolled from the counter. It was not mean, only true.

Dale's face did a slow turn from red to pale and back to red. He tugged at the brim of the cap in his pocket, set it on the table, and stared at it for a long moment like it might tell him what kind of man to be. His buddy cleared his throat and pushed a napkin toward him. The moment stretched. Someone's fork clinked on china. Then Dale looked up at Carlos.

"Sorry," he said. It came out stiff. "That was out of line."

Carlos swallowed. "Thank you," he said softly.

Matty nodded once. "Good. What will you have with that bacon?"

"Eggs," he muttered. "Toast."

"Wheat or white."

"White."

"Hash browns or grits."

"Hash browns."

"Fine," Matty said. "It will be out when it is out." She

turned, caught Carlos's eyes, and tipped her head toward the kitchen. "Take five and get some water."

Carlos vanished behind the swinging door. His shoulders slackened as soon as he crossed the threshold.

Matty faced the room. "Y'all good?" Heads nodded around the café. Conversations stirred back to life, tentative at first, then warmer.

Janice let out a breath she did not know she had been holding. Her hands shook as the adrenaline leaked away. Matty saw it and made a come-here motion with her towel. They stepped into the narrow space behind the pastry case where the smell of sugar was strongest.

"You all right?" Matty asked.

"Yeah," Janice said. "I just… I could not sit there and let it stand."

"I know," Matty said, and there was something like pride in her voice. "Thank you for stepping up. That is what it looks like. In the real world. Not just a share online."

"I did not make it worse, did I?"

"You drew a line," Matty said. "He crossed it. That is on him."

Carlos pushed through the door with a glass of water. His eyes were bright in a way that made Janice want to put a hand between his shoulder blades and steady him. Matty took the glass and handed it back to him.

"You did fine," she said. "Go wipe down the patio, then come back in. "You can help me ring for a while."

He nodded. "Thanks, Ms. Matty."

The cook slid two plates through the pass. Matty carried them out. Janice walked with her. Dale kept his eyes on the window. His buddy murmured thanks and a quiet, real apology to Matty that she accepted with a nod.

At the booth again, Janice stared at her coffee and realized it had grown cold. She did not care. Her chest ached in that strange way it did when a thing was both heavy and right. She watched Carlos on the patio through the glass. He moved slower now, less rushed, every motion careful. A girl at a table outside caught his eye and gave him a small thumbs-up. He smiled, quick and real.

Matty returned with fresh coffee and a side plate of sliced peaches. "On the house," she said. "For nerves."

Janice laughed, a little shaky. "Does this happen a lot?"

"Less than you would think," Matty said. "More than it should."

"What do you usually do?"

"Same as today," Matty said. "Be plain. Be firm. Let folks know what kind of room they are in. You would be surprised how many people have never heard the word 'no' said like it means something."

Janice glanced at the sign by the register again. **Be kind or be quiet.** It was simple. It was everything.

"Can I ask you something?" she said.

"Shoot."

"Have I made it harder for Carlos by getting involved? I do not want to be that person who wades in and then leaves him to deal with the fallout."

Matty studied her. "You are not here for one day. You are part of this place now. There is a difference. We stand up, then we stand with. You already know how to do both."

Janice felt her throat tighten. She nodded and forked a peach slice to give her hands a task. It tasted like sunshine.

The door chimed again. A retired couple Janice recognized from other mornings came in. They took a table by the wall and waved at her. The café regained its rhythm. The sizzle from the flat top rose and fell. The toddler resumed his giggles. The heat outside thickened, but inside it felt clean again.

Dale and his buddy finished in silence. He left cash tucked under the rim of the plate, more than the bill but not enough to look like atonement. Before he reached the door, he paused. He looked back at Matty. He looked at Carlos through the glass. He looked at Janice and did not hold her gaze. Then he left. The bell chimed once.

"All right then," Matty said softly.

The room seemed to breathe.

Carlos came back inside, pink-cheeked from the sun. Matty slid him behind the register. "You ring. I will run."

He glanced at Janice, then at the floor, then back up. "Thank you," he said. It was quiet and big at the same time.

"You do not owe me thanks," Janice said. "You are part of this place. So am I."

He nodded and focused on the next guest with a steadier voice. "How was everything today, ma'am?"

Janice leaned back in her booth and let the weight ease out of her shoulders. She thought of the orchard and the red eyes she had seen and the nights she had stood with a board in her hand while the shadows pressed up against the porch light. She thought of the cellar and the bones and the letters tucked into the past. There were battles in the dark, and there were battles at noon in a room that served pancakes, and both mattered. Maybe this was how the world was changed, a little at a time. You held your ground when a thing tried to step over it.

Her phone vibrated on the table. Jeff.

Jeff: How is Sunday in the land of peaches?

Janice: Eventful. I will call later. Remind me to tell you how I got myself banned from being quiet.

Jeff: Proud already. Do you need bail money?

Janice: Not today.

Jeff: Love you.

Janice: Love you back.

She set the phone down and watched Matty pass a plate to a man at the counter and clap a regular on the shoulder as she moved. It struck Janice that the café was not just a business. It was a boundary. It said, "This is who we are, and this is who we are not." She felt grateful to sit inside its circle.

When she stood to leave, Matty met her at the door with a paper bag. "Biscuits for later. And for Wednesday, if you want them before the professor arrives. I can have the porch light fixed by then too. My guy can run by."

"Curtains first," Janice said. "Then the light."

"Curtains always first," Matty agreed. Her smile softened. "You did good today."

"So did you."

Matty tipped her head. "It is my house."

Janice stepped into the heat and the bright white glare of the sidewalk. The bell chimed behind her, then stilled. She stood for a second and let the sun press its warm hand across her shoulders. Somewhere a crow called from the line of pecans behind her property. The sound skittered down her spine, then faded.

She tucked the paper bag under her arm and headed toward the gravel drive. The day felt larger than it had a few hours earlier. She did not know why that felt like courage, only that it did.

CHAPTER THIRTY-FIVE

⚓ COFFEE AND CLUES

A week later, on Sunday morning, the diner had settled into a rhythm Janice had come to rely on. Matty, always playing the role of hostess, greeted Professor Gabriel with a knowing smile and guided him to Janice's favorite booth...

Two cups of coffee arrived shortly after, filled to the brim with cream and sugar, just how he liked it. Even now that summer was in full swing, he couldn't bring himself to drink it iced. Somehow, it didn't seem like coffee could do its proper work unless it was hot.

This morning, Gabe entered just as the mugs were set down, sliding into the red vinyl booth across from Janice.

"Perfect timing," she said, noting the tired look in his eyes.

"Aww, I need this," he muttered, reaching for the coffee like it was a miracle cure.

"Tough night?" she asked.

He nodded, lifting the mug. "Yeah. The neighbors had some kind of party. The bass was shaking my dishes."

"Yikes. Why didn't you say something?"

"I don't know," he said, shrugging. "I guess I wanted to be the cool neighbor."

Janice raised an eyebrow. "Well, next time get an invite. And if not, definitely tell them to turn it down."

Matty refilled their coffee and took their orders without the need for menus. There was a comfort in the familiarity of it all.

Gabe took another sip. "Do you mind if I come by and take a look at the family grave you mentioned?"

She leaned back. "Sure, but... why?"

"No real reason. I just want to get names and places clearer. My work-study students made copies of the journal and worked on enhancing the faded writing. That probably explains why I was up so late last night."

Janice's expression lit up just as the waitress returned with two large plates of food. "That makes sense now," she said.

She moved her over-hard eggs onto her pancake, buttered the stack generously, and searched for syrup.

Gabe grimaced. "How can you eat that... mixture?"

Janice grinned and made a point of saying "Yummmm" as she took a bite.

Gabe shook his head and started in on his carefully separated scrambled eggs and hash browns. He was one of those people who preferred his food to never touch. Janice found it endearing.

"So," she said between bites, "did you find anything out?"

"Yes," he said. "Turns out, the journal was a gift from a girl named Meredith to someone named Natalie. Natalie was sent away for the summer and used the journal to document her time in the South."

Janice dropped her fork. "Wait, *Natalie*? Are you sure?"

"Positive. The name was faint, but after they enhanced the ink, it was clear."

Janice sat back, stunned. "If it's the same Natalie… she's my fourth great-grandmother."

Gabe looked up, chewing thoughtfully. "That's incredible. You'll get to know a lot more about her once they finish scanning and transcribing everything."

Janice's excitement was hard to contain.

"So… does this have anything to do with the graveyard visit?" she asked.

"Maybe," Gabe replied. "You mentioned a headstone marked 'W.C.' I'm thinking there may be more to it, maybe something faint you didn't see. Would you mind if I took a rubbing and a few photos?"

"Of course not," she said. "Especially if it helps connect the dots."

She sipped her coffee.

"Oh, and the porch is almost done," she added. "Next week it gets painted."

"Sounds like you've got a dozen balls in the air," he said, smiling.

"I started back to work too." She sipped her coffee. "When do you want to come by?"

He considered it. "When's good for you?"

She hesitated, then offered, "Why don't you come for dinner? Wednesday, maybe? It should be cooler by evening, and we could walk to the grave afterward."

His eyes met hers, lingering. "I'd like that very much. What can I bring?"

Janice's stomach fluttered. Her throat tightened. This was their fourth Sunday meeting, but something about this felt… different.

"Just yourself. Do you like pasta?" she asked, trying to sound casual.

"Pasta is perfect," he said, his gaze not leaving hers.

"How about six? That way, there's still daylight left for the walk."

She focused on her food, needing a distraction. "Sounds great. Six it is."

Matty returned. "How's everything?" Once she got behind Gabe, she gave Janice two thumbs up.

"Perfect, as usual," Janice said, welcoming the change in topic and trying to stifle a giggle.

Matty moved on, and Janice let out a breath she hadn't realized she was holding.

"So how many history majors do you have working on the journal?" she asked, shifting the conversation again.

Gabe explained the difference between work-study students and full history majors, but Janice's mind drifted. All she could think about was Wednesday. Dinner. The journal. Her fourth great-grandmother and what new light might be shed.

Did she just accidentally make a date? she wondered. Was it really an accident?

She stopped eating, lost in thought.

"Janice?" Gabe's voice pulled her back. "You okay?"

"Sorry," she said quickly. "Got caught up thinking about the journal."

"I'll get you a copy as soon as I can," he promised with a smile.

They finished the rest of their meal, paid their separate checks, and walked out into the warm Sunday morning, each wondering just how much more history was about to be uncovered.

As Janice reached her car, she pulled out her phone, hesitated, then texted Jeff:

Janice: Met with the professor again this morning. He confirmed the journal belonged to Natalie, my 4x great-grandmother.

JANICE: Also... I may have just invited him to dinner. For research. (Maybe.)

JEFF: "RESEARCH," huh? ;)

Janice laughed under her breath, slipping her phone back into her bag. Research or not, Wednesday was going to change something.

CHAPTER THIRTY-SIX

◇◇THE SHADOW STILL WALKS

Henry found her crouched beside Lucy and the baby. There was no question about the child's paternity.

"Natalie, they're coming," he said, breathless.

"How did you know I was here?" she asked, alarm blooming in her chest. If Henry had found her, who else might?

"I knew you were sympathetic," he said quickly. "That's why I didn't say anything. But you have to go. They're almost here."

She froze. "They?"

"The Army," he said, glancing toward the distant glow on the horizon, "and probably the family too."

Natalie's stomach dropped. The Confederate Army was marching north, stripping every household of its sons, husbands, and fathers. She had watched neighbors vanish overnight, young men dragged from fields, old men pressed into ranks despite their trembling hands. Even the halls of the great houses grew hollow, their portraits staring down at rooms emptied of the living. What the South proclaimed as duty felt to Natalie like theft—of lives, of futures, of hope. And caught between two worlds, she felt the loss as both.

"Oh God," she whispered. "What are they going to do?"

Before Henry could answer, Billy stormed into the barn. He stopped cold at the sight of Natalie, Lucy, and the newborn.

"I knew you weren't just getting plump from the cooking," he spat. "You whore."

Isaac stepped forward instinctively, placing his body between Billy and Lucy.

"Isaac, no," Natalie begged.

"What are you going to do about it, boy?" Billy sneered.

"Nothing, if you do nothing as well," Isaac said, his voice even and calm. He straightened to his full height. His threadbare pants barely met his shins, but his frame was solid from a lifetime in the fields.

Billy wasn't used to defiance. He bristled, enraged.

Henry approached from behind. "Come on, brother. They're calling every able man to service. Lee's army is marching north, and we have to prepare."

The orange light flickering on the horizon pulsed like a second sun, rising too early and in the wrong direction. Natalie turned to Henry. "What is happening?"

"The Yankees are pushing closer," Billy answered instead, his voice sharp and full of venom. "They'll strip the land bare, cattle, corn, everything we have. And for the likes of him." He jerked his head toward Isaac.

Natalie stepped forward. "Isaac had nothing to do with this."

Billy's jaw clenched. "Maybe not. But he'll hang for it."

A sharp gasp came from Bitsy behind her. Natalie had forgotten she was there. Billy turned and strode toward the shed. Natalie's heart pounded. She didn't need to follow to know what he was retrieving.

Bitsy helped Lucy to her feet, but the young woman was barely conscious. Her strength had drained with the delivery. She could not save herself or the child.

Billy returned with a rope. He twisted it into a noose with steady, terrifying precision.

"Henry, get Isaac," he commanded.

Henry didn't move.

Billy's eyes blazed. "If you don't, I will kill that thing in Natalie's arms."

Silence swallowed the barn. Even the animals seemed to stop breathing.

Natalie stepped forward, her voice shaking. "Billy Cheney, have you lost your mind?"

"You have no right to speak to me," he growled. "That thing is Satan's child. It doesn't deserve another breath."

She glanced down at the baby. There was no time to reason. Billy's mind was beyond reach.

He lunged toward her. Murder lived in his eyes.

Before he could make contact, Isaac rammed into him with the full weight of his body, sending Billy sprawling to the floor. Dirt and straw lifted into the air like smoke.

Henry covered his mouth with both hands.

Bitsy stood in front of Lucy, shielding her with a courage that defied her size.

Natalie's mind raced. She knew she couldn't win a fight against Billy. Lucy couldn't run. They had no place to hide. Her hands trembled, but something stronger surged through her, a hot, ancestral fire that burned in her chest.

If Billy wanted blood, she would give him reason to fear it.

Isaac and Billy fought like animals, rolling in the dust, fists flying. Natalie placed the baby in Bitsy's arms.

"Go," she said. "Run. Hide."

Bitsy didn't hesitate. She swaddled the baby in her skirt and vanished into the dark.

"Billy, no!" Henry cried.

Natalie turned back. Billy had Isaac pinned and was punching him with a horseshoe gripped tight in his fist. Blood flew with each impact. Isaac's limbs went still.

A crack. A splatter. Isaac's face was no longer recognizable.

Natalie couldn't see. Everything was red.

Red for the blood spilled.

Red for the rage and helplessness she'd carried like a second skin.

Red for Lucy. For the baby. For herself.

She moved without awareness, without breath. Her hand closed around the handle of the horseshoe hammer near the stall.

It felt cold. Heavy.

Billy was strangling Isaac now, both hands locked around his throat.

The barn fell silent.

She stepped forward. She heard a voice, her voice, but detached, as if it belonged to someone else.

"Billy. Stop."

He didn't.

She raised the hammer. Every memory of cruelty, every flash of injustice, every bruised back and broken spirit she had witnessed, lit up her veins.

And then she swung.

The blow connected. His skull gave way beneath the force. Blood sprayed.

Billy's hands dropped from Isaac's neck. His head lolled to the side.

He blinked, dazed, confused.

For one brief second, their eyes met. The monster was gone. Only the boy remained; the boy he might have been.

"Why?" he whispered.

Natalie didn't know if he was asking why she had done it, why she was even here, or why he had turned into something so hollow.

She raised the hammer again, driven by the momentum of survival.

Henry caught her wrist. He shook his head.

Billy collapsed, convulsing. Foam formed at the edges of his mouth. His limbs jerked once, then fell still. His eyes rolled back. His body settled.

She had killed him.

She dropped the hammer, then dropped to her knees.

"I just wanted him to stop," she whispered. Her voice cracked. Blood coated her hands.

She crawled to Isaac. His face was swollen and unrecognizable, but then he coughed.

"Oh, Isaac," she said, brushing hair and blood from his forehead. "I'm here. I'm here."

"Where…" he wheezed, then spat blood. "Where is Lucy?"

Even after all of it, his first thought was of her.

"She's safe," Natalie told him. "Bitsy took the baby. They're hiding."

Natalie dabbed at Isaac's swollen face with a rag torn from her own skirt, blotting blood where it ran down his cheek. His breath rattled, shallow but steady. His gaze drifted past her, fixing on Lucy where she lay in the straw, fingers weak but still clinging to the embroidered linen.

"That cloth—" His voice rasped, broken but urgent. "Where did she get it?"

Natalie followed his eyes. "She's had it since she came. Says it was her mother's."

A sound escaped him, half sob and half laugh. "I knew it. I knew the moment I saw it. That was my mother's. Lucy… she's my sister. They sold me off when she was just little. She wouldn't remember me."

Natalie's throat closed. She looked from Isaac's battered face to Lucy, still clinging to the linen as though it tethered her to life. The truth pressed against Natalie's ribs like a weight. Lucy had family, flesh and blood — and she didn't even know it.

"Don't tell her yet," Isaac rasped. His eyes shone with fierce, desperate love. "She's been through too much already. Just… keep her safe."

Natalie nodded, tears burning hot. She pressed the rag

back against his brow, then glanced at Lucy, her hand curled protectively around the cloth. The thread of family bound them still, even if Lucy never knew.

The barn was no longer empty. Women had come in and were helping Lucy to her cabin. Men stood in a circle, watching. Some furious. Some silent. Some relieved.

Henry stepped forward. He looked at Billy's crumpled body, then at the blood on Natalie's hands.

He turned to the men. "Bury him. Somewhere no one will find him. Don't tell me where."

Natalie looked up, eyes wide. "Henry, why?"

"He was my brother," he said, "but he was also a terrible man. What he stood for was cruel and backwards. No one is born less than another. We were raised in darkness, but I choose to walk in light."

Natalie's breath caught. He looked at her with something like admiration.

"You never stopped believing in something better," he said. "And now, it begins."

Two men lifted Billy's body. Henry turned back one last time. He shifted from foot to foot, his eyes darting everywhere but her face. He sucked in a breath and blurted the words before he lost his nerve.

"So many went north, fighting for the old ways," he said. "But you, you broke it too. Maybe from that... maybe something good could... I dunno... grow." His voice cracked, and he bit his lip, holding himself still.

Journal Entry —
I killed Billy Cheney tonight.

I need to write it plainly, before my mind starts trying to make it prettier.

I didn't grow up with him. I didn't love him like a brother. But for the last few years, I lived under his roof. I smiled when I had to. I looked away when it was safer. But I always knew something was wrong.

I think I knew before the first girl went missing. There was a shadow that followed him. A cruelty that slithered just beneath the surface, even when he wore his Sunday clothes. When the bodies started turning up, or vanishing altogether, I told myself it could have been raiders. Deserters. Strangers. But deep down, I knew.

And I knew that if I left, others would suffer.

That's why I stayed. Not because I believed I could change him. Because I feared I might be the only one who saw what he was capable of.

Tonight, I saw the full truth.

He meant to kill Isaac. There was no reasoning with him. His eyes were wild with hate, his hands wrapped around Isaac's neck like it was a righteous act. And the baby —dear God, he would have hurt the baby too. I saw it in him. He would have burned the whole barn down with Lucy inside, just to prove a point.

So I swung.

The hammer was heavy, but it moved like it had been waiting in my hand all along. I didn't feel heroic. I didn't feel brave. I felt done.

The rage didn't roar. It simmered. Years of small silences, of hands wringing in the dark, of women's names no one said out loud. It all rose to the surface at once.

He looked surprised when I hit him. Like I'd betrayed him. But I never once told him I was on his side.

He said, "Why?" I think it was the first honest word he'd spoken to me.

I didn't answer. What would I have said? Because you were killing them. Because no one stopped you. Because someone had to.

I thought I'd hit him again. But Henry stopped me. And just like that, Billy was gone. The ground shook when he fell. Or maybe that was just me, shaking.

I don't feel proud. I feel hollow. I feel like something in me broke, and something else hardened in its place. Maybe this is what it means to live in a world that punishes those who scream too loudly and praises those who hurt quietly.

The women carried Lucy back. The baby is safe. Isaac is alive, barely. And Henry? He'll cover it up. He said this is the beginning of something new. I want to believe that.

But I know better than most: new beginnings don't come without a cost. And tonight, I paid the debt. And Billy paid for his sins.

—Natalie

CHAPTER THIRTY-SEVEN

◦◦THE HOME THEY BUILT

1863, Georgia
April

The morning after, the house held its breath. Pots were stacked but not washed, a chair lay toppled near the back door, and a lantern sat half-filled on the kitchen table as if someone meant to return. The night had been a siege of its own kind. No soldiers on the road, no bugles or drums, only the cries within these walls and the orchard answering in its low, grieving hum.

Lucy slept at last. Miss Patty had washed her, wrapped the baby close, and set both to rest in Lucy's small room. Alice had gone to the attic that morning and returned with the carved cradle her own children had once slept in, its rails polished smooth by years of rocking. She set it near Lucy's bed herself, spreading the embroidered cloth across its spindles. "This will be Benjamin's now," she said, her voice low. "It kept mine safe, and it will keep him too."

Isaac lay on a narrow cot in the sewing room, his chest rising shallow, his breath dragging like a saw. The basin on the floor was clouded brown with water used to cool his fevered skin.

Natalie rose unsteadily, her bones aching, her mind blurred from the blood and shouting. She drifted to the kitchen and found Alice already there. The ledger lay open in front of her, pencil stilled, her shoulders stiff as boards. Alice lifted her head, and Natalie saw the red rim of her eyes, though her voice came out iron.

"It has to be now," Alice said. "I will not have Lucy and that child hidden in the quarters, whispered about, pitied, or shamed. They will have a home of their own. Walls that are theirs. And we will raise it before word spreads."

Natalie's throat tightened. "So soon? You haven't even…"

Alice cut her off with a glance sharp as a blade. "If we wait, questions will come. If we build now, we choose the story. I will not have her raising that baby in shadows."

By noon, the yard was alive with sound. Henry and Walt bent to ropes looped across their shoulders, dragging sleighs fashioned from scrap boards. The makeshift runners screeched against the clay, leaving furrows in the dirt. Each load carried planks and beams salvaged from the collapsed smokehouse. The Impressment Act had been passed only weeks before, giving Confederate officers the authority to seize horses, mules, and wagons wherever they found them. Squads swept through the county, taking teams for supply trains and cavalry patrols, leaving families to manage as best they could. Alice had tried to hide the last mare in the orchard, but even she was claimed in the end, her bridle looped with army rope and her hooves striking out in protest as she was led away. With the horses gone, every burden shifted to human shoulders, and now it was Henry and Walt who strained against the ropes, dragging beams inch by inch across the yard.

This was the only way.

Uncle William had been gone two weeks, last seen riding Natalie's chestnut mare into town. He had said he meant to join the regiment. Some believed him. Others whispered he had slipped off west to save his skin. Either way, he had not come back.

In his absence, the house had looked to Billy. Alice's mouth tightened at the thought. She would not speak his name. She kept her gaze on Henry instead. He was the one carrying the weight now, hammer in hand, each strike steady, every blow a claim that order could still be held.

Sweat stung Natalie's eyes as she steadied planks, her palms raw with splinters. The ropes cut red into Henry's shoulders, but he never faltered, jaw clenched, step sure. Walt scavenged nails with care, prying them from warped boards, straightening them one by one against a stone. Nails had grown dearer than coin; salt was scarcer still, coffee long gone. Confederate money bought less each month, paper nearly worthless. Families in town spoke of burying silver in orchards, of hiding jewelry in root cellars.

Alice had already pressed a small box of coins, a locket, and a folded letter tied with twine beneath a loose board in the barn, tamping dirt over it with her heel.

"Deserters walk the roads," she had muttered. "Hungry men with guns. Soldiers take what they please. We will not tempt either."

What livestock remained was hidden in the far barn, two milk cows, three hogs, guarded each night by men who dozed in chairs with rifles across their knees. "Coins won't keep us alive," Alice had said. "But these beasts will."

Miss Patty boiled lye soap to scour pitch from skin, then walked the perimeter of the rising frame with a bowl of water and a pinch of salt, her lips moving in a low chant. She pressed her hand to each corner stone as though anchoring the very earth.

Lucy watched from her bed, the baby nestled close. Her eyes tracked every motion outside, Henry hammering, Walt bracing beams, Natalie hauling shingles until her palms bled. Lucy smiled faintly when Natalie looked her way, gratitude shining so fiercely that Natalie nearly dropped her load.

On the third day, the roof went on. Without horses or a hoist, they raised beams inch by inch, shoulders straining, teeth clenched. The wood groaned, then settled into place. Alice exhaled, the first sound of release since she had given her command to build.

When Lucy was carried into the whitewashed room, tears slipped from her eyes. She touched the wall as though she might leave her handprint there. "It feels... different," she whispered. "As if it believes we will last."

Alice followed with the cradle, placing it in the corner and smoothing the embroidered cloth across its spindles. Her voice trembled but held firm. "This is not charity.

This is claiming. This cradle has held my children. Now it will hold yours. You belong here, and so does he."

Benjamin stirred then, fussing at first, then letting out a sharp wail that echoed in the small room. Miss Patty chuckled softly. "That's a good sound. Means he's hungry or wet. A child that cries is a child that wants the world to tend to him."

Alice's face softened. "As it should be."

Natalie glanced at the cradle, remembering what she had been told of Billy's birth, how he had come into the world without a sound, only staring, eyes wide and knowing. Alice herself had said it chilled her, as if something older and darker had come through with him that day and never left. Benjamin was different. His voice rose sharp and sure, the sound of a babe claiming the world's attention. It filled the new walls like a blessing.

That evening, Miss Patty came into Lucy's room with a small bowl of salt. She sprinkled it along the window ledges, pressing each grain into the wood.

"Why salt?" Natalie asked from the doorway.

"To keep out what don't belong," Miss Patty said. Her gaze flicked to Benjamin. "Firstborns draw things near; they always have. This one lies quiet, different from the rest. Seems the curse clung to Billy and not to him. Still, I'll not take chances. The land remembers what it claims."

She pressed the last pinch onto the sill, then paused, her voice dropping to a whisper. "Especially now... since he ain't here no more."

Natalie froze. Her breath hitched, her face hot though her blood ran cold. Miss Patty's eyes met hers, calm but knowing.

Natalie swallowed. Her voice trembled. "What does Auntie Alice think happened to Isaac?"

"The truth," Miss Patty answered, tying her apron strings tighter. "'Twas Billy. He carried the ruin in him, and he brought it down on Isaac. Alice feels it, though she don't speak it. The orchard does."

Natalie blanched. Heat surged through her face, memory crashing, the hammer in her hand, the rage that blinded her, the blood she could not wash clean. Miss Patty reached out and touched her arm lightly.

"Don't fear me, child," she said softly. "I know what I know, and I'll hold it quiet. Some truths are for the earth to keep."

That night, the family gathered on the porch. Henry sat with boots off, Walt stretched his sore arms, Miss Patty shelled peas into a wooden bowl. Alice rocked the cradle with her heel, Lucy dozed in a chair. Natalie swept the new floor with a broom of twigs, the boards creaking under her steps.

The house was more than shelter. It was proof. Every salvaged nail, every blistered palm, every board dragged by rope had spelled a word in the dirt and hammered it into wood: **HOPE.**

For the first time in weeks, Natalie let her shoulders ease. The house stood now at the orchard's edge, square and proud against the dusk.

No one spoke Billy's name. The orchard would answer in its own time.

Lucy's voice wavered as she hummed, rocking Ben in the fading light. Isaac bent closer, his low voice joining hers until the two sounds braided together, old and familiar. For a moment, it was as if the past sat with them on the porch.

Lucy faltered, her voice catching. She looked at him, startled. "How...?"

Isaac's gaze softened. He reached to rub Ben's small back, his hand steady and gentle. "My mother also sang this song when she did her chores," he said quietly. His eyes dropped to the linen folded across Ben's blanket. "And she would place this cloth on the table when she wanted to feel fancy."

Lucy's breath caught. Her hand smoothed the fabric, her fingers trembling over the worn stitches. It was then she understood what he was saying. A single tear slipped down her face. "Why didn't you say something?"

He held her gaze, his thumb still moving in slow circles over the baby's back. "Because I didn't want to cause you any more pain if something happened to me. But I always did what I could to keep you safe."

She reached for his hand then, lifted it, and pressed it against her cheek, holding it there as her tears ran freely. "Isaac..." Her voice broke into a whisper. "You've always kept me safe."

His eyes shone, brimming. "Lucy, you're my sister. Then and always." He glanced down at Ben nestled between them. "And you two are not alone."

From the doorway, Natalie stood silent, her own tears welling. She was happy for the two of them, happy they had found one another, even in a world determined to tear families apart. She knew she would write it down later, so this fragile piece of joy would never be lost.

· · ·

Journal Entry -

We built with bare hands, dragging sleighs of wood across clay where horses once pulled. Alice's husband is gone—a fortnight now—and no word. Some say he rides with the regiment. Others say he saved only himself. He left Billy in his place, and we saw what came of that. Now Henry hammers the nails, steady and young, and the weight rests on him.

Miss Patty salted the windows, whispering that firstborns draw danger. She said Benjamin lies differently, that the curse seemed to cling to Billy instead. Tonight, I believe her. For when Benjamin fussed, it was for milk. When he cried, it was for wet linen. His voice rose sharp and clean, the sound of a babe needing the world to tend to him. Billy never cried that way. He came into this life silent, staring, as if he already knew. Something came through with him that day and stayed with him ever after. The orchard has never forgotten it, nor have I.

Tonight, I also saw a gentler truth: Lucy and Isaac finding one another again, brother and sister made whole by a song, a cloth, and the child between them. It was a moment I will not let the world erase.

It frightens me to be seen, but it steadies me too. Miss Patty spoke the truth of Billy, and I know she will keep it as the earth does. We will guard this child. HOPE, Isaac shaped that word with me in the dirt, and now it stands at the orchard's edge in wood and stone. The house and the cradle are its proof. Whatever comes, it will not be erased.

CHAPTER THIRTY-EIGHT

⚓ BETTER AND BEST

J anice woke to sunlight warming the fresh paint on her bedroom walls. The pale gold light slipped through the curtains and caught the edge of a picture frame she had hung the week before, making it glow as though it belonged in a gallery. She lay still for a moment, her body sunk deep into the mattress, listening to the hum of cicadas outside. Her muscles ached from the week's labor, every joint stiff, but the ache felt earned, like the soreness after planting something new and watching it take root. For the first time in a long while, her spirit felt light.

The air carried a faint sweetness, lavender rising from the sachet tucked beneath her pillow. She breathed it in, closing her eyes, letting the scent remind her that the house was changing along with her. What had once been filled with dust and silence now offered something like comfort.

Her gaze wandered upward to the ceiling beams. The wood was darkened with age, pitted and scarred by smoke and time. She imagined the lives they had looked down upon, the voices they had heard, the secrets pressed into the grain. Dust motes shimmered in the beam of light above her, drifting like tiny constellations. She had spent hours painting these walls, pushing new color over old grime. Yet even beneath the fresh coat, the house breathed with memory. She could feel it like a faint hum inside her chest, steady and insistent.

The night before, she had called Jeff and her mother on a Facetime group. It had begun as a simple check-in but turned into an hour of laughter, the kind that left her ribs aching and her eyes wet. Jeff teased her mercilessly about becoming a country woman.

"If you stay down there much longer," he had said, his voice full of mock warning, "you'll be raising chickens, wearing gingham, and entering the pie contest at the county fair."

She had laughed so hard she nearly dropped the phone. "If I bake a pie, you'll be the first to eat it," she shot back.

"Not unless you ship it express," Jeff had replied. "I've seen you cook, sis."

Her mother had been quieter but amused, listening in the background, humming once or twice as if the sound of her children bickering was its own comfort. When Janice mentioned Gabe, her mother's eyebrows had lifted in that familiar way that mixed curiosity and suspicion. Janice had insisted it was not a date, but her mother's smile had lingered, patient and knowing.

She rolled out of bed slowly, stretching until her joints gave a series of small cracks. The floor was cool beneath her bare feet, the boards groaning a little as she crossed to the window. She padded into the kitchen, still in her cotton nightshirt, hair pulled into a messy knot. Coffee was already on her mind.

She measured the grounds carefully, the earthy scent rising as she scooped. The percolator sputtered to life, filling the quiet with its gentle rhythm. The sound soothed her, grounding her in the morning. While she waited, she moved through the house, straightening stacks of books and folding the blanket draped across the couch.

She paused by the dining room window, pressing her hand to the new plaster. The surface was smooth under her palm, cool to the touch, yet there was a warmth beneath it she could not explain. Sometimes she felt as though the house leaned toward her, pressing itself against her hand, acknowledging her. She shook the thought away but could not escape the sense that this place was no longer just walls and boards. It breathed with her now, and she with it.

The coffee finished with a soft hiss. She poured a mug and carried it to the porch. The air outside was warm already, heavy with the promise of summer. The orchard rustled in the slight breeze, pecan branches swaying like old women whispering secrets. She sipped slowly, savoring the bitterness, the heat sliding down her throat. The cicadas' hum wove through the stillness, steady and ancient.

For a few precious minutes, she allowed herself to simply exist, watching sunlight move across the grass. The orchard shimmered faintly in the heat, the moss dripping from its limbs like gray-green lace. She thought she saw movement deep between the trunks, a shimmer, a shadow, but when she blinked, it was gone.

Her phone buzzed on the porch rail. She set the mug down and picked it up.

Gabe: Hi.

A smile crept across her face before she could stop it.

Janice: Good morning. You are not canceling on me, are you?

Dots appeared, disappeared, reappeared.

Gabe: What? No. Actually, the opposite. I have an update.

Her pulse quickened.

Janice: About?

Another pause.

Gabe: Can I come over?

Her eyebrows shot up.

Janice: Now?

The reply was immediate.

Gabe: NM. It has waited 160 years… what are a few more hours?

Her grin widened despite the nervous flutter in her stomach.

Janice: No way. Get over here. I am brewing coffee now.

She had just set the phone back on the rail when she heard tires crunching on gravel. She startled, laughing at how quickly he had appeared, as though he had been waiting just down the road. She stepped down onto the porch, shielding her eyes from the sunlight. His car rolled to a stop, the metal catching a flare of gold from the rising sun.

Gabe stepped out, tall and easy in his movements. His shirt sleeves were rolled to the elbow, forearms tanned. He looked up, and his smile was unguarded, wide and unashamed, as if seeing her was the highlight of his day. The sight made her heart stutter. For a moment, she imagined him always walking up this path, imagined the sound of his voice carrying across the porch, imagined years weathering them both but softening rather than breaking.

He climbed the steps, leaned in, and kissed her cheek before she had time to react. The touch was brief but warm. She stood frozen as he passed her into the house, her hand rising instinctively to her cheek where his lips had brushed.

"I have good news," he said, his voice bright as he set his satchel down.

She blinked, struggling to gather herself. "Well?"

"Actually, I have better news and best news." He grinned at her, playful. "Which one do you want first?"

Her laughter came out thin and nervous. "Coffee," she muttered, escaping toward the kitchen.

She poured two mugs, her hands trembling. She fixed his the way she had seen him take it at the diner, black with the faintest splash of cream. She inhaled deeply before returning to the living room and setting his mug before him.

"Thank you," he said. "So? Better or best?"

She tucked her legs beneath her on the couch, curling into herself. "Better. Ease me in."

He pulled his laptop from the satchel and flipped it

open. The screen lit his face, casting shadows that sharpened his features.

"They came through," he said.

Her brows drew together. "Who did?"

"The students," he replied, fingers moving quickly.

Her heartbeat picked up. "Already?"

He nodded. "Remember the letter to Meredith? The handwriting was hard to read; some of it had faded. They scanned it, cleaned it, and reconstructed the missing sections."

He turned the screen toward her.

Janice set her coffee aside. Her palms were clammy. She leaned in, the words pulling into focus on the glowing screen. It felt as though a hand reached from the past and held her still.

"Did you read it?" she whispered.

"No," he said softly. "I waited. This is yours to read first."

He stood and walked away, giving her space.

Her throat was tight. Her fingers trembled on the trackpad as she scrolled.

Dearest Meredith,

How I long to speak these things to you face to face, yet Providence forbids it. I cannot leave, and so I put my heart to paper, trusting it may one day reach your hands.

Janice swallowed hard, her fingers trembling on the

trackpad. The words felt alive, pulsing against her eyes, as if Natalie herself were whispering them.

THERE WAS A MAN HERE, a wicked man, who threatened all I held dear. Though I did not intend it so, I struck the blow that ended his life. I shall carry that burden through every waking day and restless night. The man was my cousin, William, called Billy. He was a violator of women, and I believe he took the lives of many young girls in this county.

THE BLOOD DRAINED from Janice's face. She dragged her hands through her hair, tugging at the roots until her scalp stung. The room pressed in on her, heavy with the scent of old wood and paint. She could almost hear the orchard groan.

WE HAVE TOLD the world another story, but you must know the truth. We are raising his child as our own. To all, I am the mother, yet in truth, it is Lucy. The boy's complexion is light enough that the lie has endured, and when the war was done, the world asked no questions. Thus, we have kept the secret, to protect him. To protect her. Lucy, Benjamin, Isaac, and I, we are bound together as family, though few would understand the shape of our bond. I love them with all that is in me. Isaac and I have joined in the old way, yet I dare not give him children of my own, lest it cost him his life.

. . .

JANICE'S BREATH CAME RAGGED. She pressed the heel of her palm against her forehead, dizzy with the weight of it.

THIS LAND BEARS a curse of sorrow. Their suffering still lives in the orchard, and Lucy says only their people may bless the ground again. Until then, the spirits will not rest. Keep the lamps burning. And never bear your first child upon this soil.

THE WORDS SHIMMERED on the screen, and Janice could almost smell iron, blood, or ink, and feel the air shift with the hush of spirits.

BILLY'S BODY lies not where the map marks his grave. I placed something there instead, something meant for the family. He cannot use it, but perhaps you can.

HER THROAT TIGHTENED.

FORGIVE ME, Meredith. I pray you will find peace and understanding in these words, though they be heavy. I send my love and the wish for your happiness, always.
   Natalie

THE SIGNATURE BLURRED. Janice blinked hard, her eyes

burning. She pushed the laptop back gently, her fingers trembling as though the keys had scorched her skin.

"Wait," she whispered. Then louder, "Wait… so that means…"

She stood, pacing, her hand pressed to her forehead. Her breath came in ragged bursts.

"Gabe," she called, half laughing, half sobbing, "read this."

He stepped forward, reading quickly, his eyes scanning each line. She stared at the ceiling, the plaster above her swimming as though the house itself leaned closer.

Her great-grandmother was not Natalie. It was… is… Lucy.

Her knees weakened. She sank onto the couch, her palms pressed into the fabric, grounding her against the tilt of the floor. Her voice broke.

"Lucy is my fourth great-grandmother. Not Natalie."

The words rattled inside her chest, heavy and light all at once. Her great-grandmother had been born enslaved, had endured, had raised her son, and that was the start of her line.

Her throat closed. Tears burned hot. She ran her hands through her hair, fingers tugging at the roots as if to anchor herself. And then, almost without breath, the word slipped out of her:

"Wow."

It was not shock. It was pride, fierce, aching pride that Lucy had survived, that her name had endured, that Janice carried her blood.

Gabe sat very still, his palms pressed together,

fingertips brushing his mouth. His eyes softened, filling with understanding. He didn't need to speak.

"All this time we carried Natalie's name," Janice said hoarsely. "Benjamin carried it first, so he could move safely through the world. And every generation after, we repeated the story because it was easier than the truth. We thought Natalie was our root. She is family, Billy's cousin, my aunt across the branches, but it was Lucy all along."

The names in her family tree suddenly felt like masks, one draped over another until Lucy's face vanished beneath them. But now Lucy stepped forward, unmasked, demanding to be remembered.

Janice laughed through her tears, the sound bitter and joyous at once. "That was the better news. What on earth is the best?"

Gabe hesitated, then closed the laptop carefully. He set it aside, his expression tender. "They digitized the journal too."

Her breath caught. "The journal?"

He nodded, sheepish. "The one you said was too faded to finish. The students transcribed it. I did read it. I am sorry. I could not help myself."

Her heart raced. "What did it say?"

He lowered his voice. "Natalie and Lucy ran a stop on the Underground Railroad. Right here. On this land."

Janice let out a choked laugh that collapsed into a sob. She pressed her face into her hands. The weight of it was overwhelming. Lucy, enslaved, yet sheltering others. Natalie risking everything to stand beside her. Isaac, Henry, Alice, together they had carved freedom into this soil.

She felt the house shift around her, the old timbers creaking as though the walls themselves leaned closer to witness her tears. She could almost hear hurried footsteps on the stairs, whispers in the dark, the scrape of a latch closing over a hidden door. For an instant, lamplight flickered across the far wall, though no flame burned in the room.

Janice dragged her hands through her hair, leaving it wild around her face. Her voice cracked, the single word spilling out in wonder:

"Wow."

Gabe's fingers came together again, brushing his lips as though holding back his own emotion. He gave a single nod, quiet and sure, a gesture of respect for the women who had lived, and endured, before them.

He crossed the floor and lowered himself beside her. His arms wrapped around her shoulders, strong and steady. She buried her face against his chest and let the sobs come. Not grief, but joy, fierce and raw. Joy that she finally knew who she was. Joy that Lucy had endured and that her line had not been lost.

When the storm of tears slowed, Janice pulled back, chest still heaving. She reached for the notebook on the table and scrawled quickly, her hand shaking so the ink bled unevenly on the page.

Lucy is my ancestor. Not Natalie.

The words sat stark and crooked before her. She stared at them until her breathing steadied.

Her thoughts turned, inevitably, to her mother. How could she tell her? Her mother had spoken of Natalie with reverence, carrying her as a matriarch of strength. Would this truth sound like betrayal? Would her mother feel as though Janice had stripped Natalie of her honor?

She pictured her mother's reaction. Silence first, brows drawn tight, lips pressed thin. Then perhaps a measured response, slow and cautious. But she also imagined her mother's softness, the way she often hummed hymns under her breath while folding laundry, the way she spoke of resilience as though it were stitched into their very blood. Perhaps she would understand. Perhaps she would see Lucy's survival not as shame but as strength.

"I will have to tell my mother," Janice said aloud, her voice unsteady but sure. "She deserves to know who we really come from. Even if it hurts at first."

Gabe tilted his head. "Do you think she doesn't already?"

The question caught her. "What do you mean?"

"Sometimes families carry truth without words," he said gently. "Sometimes silence itself is the knowing."

She thought of her mother's eyes the day she had first mentioned Georgia. Suspicion, yes, but also something else. Perhaps her mother had always suspected the story was not as simple as they had been told.

"I don't know," Janice admitted. She pressed her palms flat to her knees, grounding herself. "But I am going to tell her. I cannot let Lucy stay a secret another generation longer. She deserves her name back."

The words solidified inside her like stone. For the first time, she understood that uncovering the past was not about tearing down lies but about giving truth a place to stand. And she would stand with it.

She rose slowly, the house groaning in the quiet as

though acknowledging her vow. At the upstairs window, the orchard stirred in the dusk, its moss-draped limbs swaying like a congregation of witnesses.

Her lips parted, and with quiet certainty, she spoke the word that had followed her since the night of discovery:

"Wow," she said again.

The sound lingered in the stillness, a whisper of awe carried into the pecan trees. Janice ran both hands back through her hair, exhaling hard, as though trying to release the weight of generations from her body.

Gabe stepped up behind her, his hands folding, fingertips grazing his mouth. His breath shuddered softly, and when she glanced at him, his expression said everything: he understood.

CHAPTER THIRTY-NINE

⚓ THE CALL

Janice sat at the kitchen table long after Gabe had gone. The candle from dinner had burned to a crooked stub, wax hardened along the rim of the glass jar. Her notebook lay open before her. Lucy's name filled the page in uneven strokes, written again and again as though the repetition could fix her into history.

The silence pressed heavy. She could not carry the truth alone, not even for one night. She picked up her phone, scrolled to **Mom**, and pressed call.

It rang twice before her mother's voice came through, warm but wary. "Janice? You sound awake. What's wrong?"

Her throat tightened. "Nothing's wrong. Not like that. Can you put me on speaker? I want Dad to hear too."

There was a pause, the muffled sound of a button pressed, then her father's voice joined. "You've got both of us. What's going on?"

Janice hesitated. She wasn't ready to drop the weight

of what she had learned all at once. "First, how are you feeling, Mom? How are your appointments going? Are the treatments helping?"

Ruth exhaled softly. "Some days are better than others. The new medication makes me tired, but the doctors say the numbers are looking stronger. We just keep moving forward."

Ed added quietly, "She has been braver than she lets on."

Janice pressed the heel of her hand to her chest. "I wish I were there with you for all of it."

"You are with us," Ruth said gently. "Even if you are far away. Now tell us what's on your heart?"

Janice gripped the phone. "I found something. About the family. It changes what we thought we knew."

The line went quiet. She could picture them sitting side by side in the den, her mother leaning forward, her father adjusting his glasses.

She forced herself to go on. "You know how the story has always been that Natalie was Benjamin's mother? That she was widowed young and raised him herself?"

"Yes," Ruth answered quickly. "That is the story. That's what my grandmother told me, and I told you."

Janice pressed her hand against the table, steadying herself. "It isn't true. I read a letter Natalie wrote. She admitted that Benjamin wasn't hers. He was Lucy's."

A long silence followed.

Her father's voice came, cautious. "Lucy?"

Janice closed her eyes. "Lucy was an enslaved woman in the Cheney household. She was young when she came there. She lived close to Alice and helped in the house.

Natalie wrote that Benjamin was Lucy's son, not hers. His father was Billy."

Ruth gasped. "Billy?"

"Yes," Janice said, her voice catching. "Natalie's cousin. That makes Natalie family still, but not the way we thought. She wasn't Benjamin's mother. She was his cover. She claimed him as her own to protect him and to protect Lucy. To the outside world, she was a widow with a child. Inside that house, Lucy was his mother."

Another silence stretched long and thin.

Her father finally asked, "And you know this from the letter?"

"Yes," Janice whispered. "Natalie wrote it to her friend Meredith. Not family, but the friend she trusted most back home. She confessed things to her she could not have told anyone here. In that letter, she said, 'To all, I am the mother, yet in truth it is Lucy.'"

Her mother's voice trembled. "And how do you have that letter?"

"I found it in a box under the stairs. The students scanned it and restored the faded ink. I read it with my own eyes," Janice said. "And there's more. Natalie began keeping a journal too. At first, she thought she would go back north someday and give it to Meredith. It was meant as a record of her life here, something her friend could hold if she never made it back in person. But she never left Georgia. The journal stayed here. It is unfinished, but it has pieces of the truth. That's how I know."

On the other end, Janice heard her mother shift, a chair creaking. "All this time..." Ruth murmured. "We carried Natalie's name. We thought she was the root. And Lucy's name was never spoken."

Janice pressed her hand to her mouth, tears spilling over. "That's why I had to call. We cannot let her stay hidden. Not another generation. Lucy is our line."

The line was quiet except for the faint static. Then Ruth spoke, her voice steadier. "If Lucy is the root, then we will carry her name now. She survived. She raised her son. She gave us life. We will not lose her again."

Ed cleared his throat. "And Natalie still matters. She stood in the gap. She chose the lie that saved them. Both women are part of you, one by blood, one by sacrifice. That doesn't make Natalie any less important. It makes her choice all the braver."

Janice nodded, though they could not see her. Relief and grief washed together. "Yes. Both of them. Together."

Her mother's voice softened. "You were brave to tell us, Janice. I know it was not easy. But I am glad you did."

"I was terrified," Janice admitted with a shaky laugh.

"You never have to be afraid to tell me who we are," Ruth said firmly. "Even if it changes the story. Especially then."

Ed spoke again, his tone quiet but steady. "So, what happens next?"

Janice looked toward the dark window, the orchard beyond, the land heavy with secrets. "There is more. Natalie left clues in her journal. There may be something hidden on the property. I have to keep looking. And I will tell you everything as I find it. No more silence."

Her mother exhaled, the sound like a prayer. "Then

keep digging. And keep telling us. We will stand with you."

Ed added, "You are not alone in this. You never were."

Janice pressed the phone to her chest, overwhelmed. When she lifted it again, her voice was steadier. "Thank you. Lucy matters. Natalie matters. And so do we."

"We do," Ruth said quietly.

They stayed on the line a while longer, speaking of smaller things. The garden. Jeff's visit. The weather back home. Everyday words that reminded Janice she was still tethered to them.

When the call ended, the house felt lighter. She turned back to her notebook. Lucy is my ancestor. Not Natalie.

She added a line beneath.

And I will speak her name.

She closed the book and sat in the quiet, feeling generations shift around her. The silence was no longer empty; it was waiting to be filled.

CHAPTER FORTY

∘∘AFTER THE GUNS WERE SILENT

1863, Marietta, Georgia (in the shadow of Chickamauga)
October

When the shooting finally stopped, the quiet felt heavier than thunder. Fences leaned, smokehouses yawned open to the weather, and the orchard stood thin and sallow where shells had torn the branches. The road into town showed more ruts than wagons. Paper money crumpled to dust in a person's hand.

Wagons rattled past the road into town, heavy not with cotton but with men broken from the fields of Chickamauga. Some they carried; some limped beside, blood soaking through their bandages. They asked for water, for bread, for a place to lay their heads. Alice sent Abby inside, but Natalie and Lucy carried buckets to the gate and pressed cool cloths to fevered brows until the wagons moved on.

Alice's husband never came back. Some said he fell with a gray regiment. Some said he rode west. He had taken Natalie's chestnut mare the day he left, promising to send word. No word ever came. No stone ever carried his name.

Henry took the weight instead, quietly, without announcement. Isaac was there beside him, steady and unshaken, his hands blistered on the same rope, his breath lifting in the same cold air. Together they cut timber from the far wood, dragged it home on sleigh runners, and raised walls until their arms shook. Walt came to help too, bent by grief but grateful for work. They said cholera had taken his wife during the war, and though sorrow shadowed his face, he lent his strength as if it might ease his own burden.

Even while they cut timber, the sound of hooves came at odd hours, gray uniforms slumped in the saddle, boys no older than Abbigail. Some stopped to beg for water. Others only stared, hollow-eyed, before the road pulled them along.

By day, the orchard seemed distant, a line of trees across the field. Sunlight spilled through the branches and softened their edges until they looked almost harmless. Birds nested and sang. Sometimes a squirrel ran along a limb and made the children laugh. When the shadows began to stretch, the orchard changed. The safe distance folded away. A listening started at the edge of things.

The house at the orchard's edge, born in a hurry and fear, did not stay small. Each season added something, a porch brace here, a wider hearth there, a stair that rose to a loft, and then a proper second floor. The roofline lifted. The windows looked out farther. It was never grand, but it stood honest and square, saying what needed saying. We endured.

Miss Patty walked the new corners with a pinch of salt and a murmur. She pressed grains along sills and into seams where wall met floor and floor met door. "It is not that the devil is gone," she said. "It only moved." She did not have to name where.

They learned the orchard's new language. It no longer lay still the way it had when Billy was alive, that terrible hush that pressed on the house like a weight. Now it was restless, breaking its own silence. At dusk, it began with the cracking of branches, though no wind moved them. Then came the rustle of leaves like voices whispering in a crowd. As night deepened, the sound rose to a thin keening that swept across the yard. Fruit fell before ripening and struck the ground with hollow thuds. Once a pear landed on the porch roof and rolled into the yard, though the air was still. Another night, a limb clawed at the glass, though no breeze carried it.

Benjamin was walking by then, legs wide and sure, curls stiff from heat and sun. In town, when they went for lamp oil or flour, he held Natalie's hand and called her Momma. That was decided. Alice had said it plain. "The world is not ready for our truth. It will be kinder if Natalie is the mother the town sees." Lucy had nodded, jaw tight, eyes bright. At home, when the door was closed and the orchard's edge was all their world, he climbed into Lucy's lap, pressed his cheek to her shoulder, and called her Momma too. He did not see the difference as a burden. He saw two arms and a single place to lay his head.

When Isaac came in from the fields, Benjamin ran to him, wrapping little arms around a leg or reaching up to be lifted high. Isaac would hoist him to his shoulders and let him tug at the curls at his temple. 'Pal," Isaac called him every time, and Benjamin laughed and answered it back. "Pal." No one outside their house knew what it meant, but the sound of it settled something in the boy, as if he had claimed a word no one could take from him.

Bitsy had found her place as the seasons turned. She lived with Alice and Henry in the big house, in Lucy's old room, made hers. She kept a basket of needles and thread by the upstairs window where the light ran true. Her fingers were small, quick, and sure. Bitsy shaped dresses that fit like a second skin and hems that never wavered. People came from miles with bolts of cloth wrapped in paper, asking for her hands and her eye. Every stitch she pulled seemed to answer the orchard back, saying beauty could rise even where grief had taken root.

She sewed Benjamin a new shirt from a scrap no one wanted, collar sharp and cuffs neat. He strutted the yard as if he wore a judge's coat. Lucy clapped. Natalie laughed. Alice's tired eyes softened. Bitsy lowered her head, shy of praise, but pride glowed all the same. At night, she folded her work and set her thimble on the sill of Lucy's old window. She looked across the field. In the morning, the trees were only trees again. At dusk, they gathered themselves and troubled the glass.

Abbigail's gift ran in words. Alice's daughter wrote at the kitchen table when the others slept, her lamp a small circle against the dark. The local paper printed the columns under a man's name, never suspecting. Henry carried the folded pages into town with eggs and nails and came back with coin. Neighbors read aloud in the store and said the writer knew their very hearts. Henry only nodded. Abbigail kept her secret and scrubbed the ink from her fingers as best she could.

At night, when the house went still, Isaac came the way only he knew. He had built it in a long winter, a narrow run between walls with a tight ladder. The boards closed behind him. A door opened in the back of Natalie's wardrobe. No one heard him come or go. No one saw. It was a husband's right made into a secret, and he had carved it with his own hands.

Sometimes she waited with the quilt turned down. Sometimes she slept, a candle guttering on the table. He brushed fine dust from his sleeves, set his palm on her cheek, and stood quiet with her. Their vows did not need repeating, yet they spoke them, soft words in the dark that steadied them against the orchard's noise.

Benjamin learned the sound too. The faint creak of the hidden door woke him sometimes, and he stirred as if to say he knew Isaac had come home. Once, when Natalie carried him past the wardrobe, he patted the door and whispered, "Pal." She hushed him quickly, heart racing, but Isaac only smiled and gathered the boy into his arms.

They kept on as people must. Henry turned up earth that had not been turned in years, the first furrows shallow where roots had crept under. Isaac yoked himself to the plow when the mule faltered, his back bowed and unbroken. Walt brought seed saved in cloth bags and traded for what he could not spare. Miss Patty rendered fat and boiled soap. Alice counted everything: the nails, the eggs, and the hours Henry and Isaac spent mending the fence where hogs had pushed through. Sometimes she touched the carved cradle without looking, her fingers moving along the rail as if reading a line she knew by heart.

By day, Benjamin spun in the yard, and the orchard looked ordinary. Birds flashed in and out. A small wind ran through the leaves. When the sun leaned west, the edges stretched. Branches turned to black lines. The safe distance of daylight gave way to something else. That was the hour when the cries began again, high and thin, riding dusk like a warning no one wished to hear.

Alice heard it and set her jaw. The orchard had been silent when the thing wore her son's face. She knew Billy was gone because the silence had gone with him. The noise was proof. She did not speak his name. She did not need to. Some nights she stood at the back door and listened. "It is only wind," a person might say, but she knew the difference between wind and a voice that has lost its body.

Billy's name did not pass anyone's lips. The orchard had made its statement days after he vanished. Where once it had been suffocatingly quiet, now it rattled and spoke, loud and unshy. Buds burst early on branches no one tended. Fruit hung heavy and sweet like an insult. The haunting had slipped its skin.

Natalie kept her eyes low when Miss Patty spoke on the porch. "He was the face it wore," Miss Patty said softly. "What haunted this land put itself in him. When he died, it went back here. Do not think that means it is gone. It is louder now, but it is not wearing a man."

Natalie did not ask for absolution. She did not believe in it. When Isaac's fingers laced with hers later, she let herself breathe. Some nights, with the orchard whispering and the red eyes flashing, she leaned against his chest and thought the land would have to wait its turn.

ONE AFTERNOON IN LATE WINTER, when mud clung to boots and the sheep had not yet lambed, Alice took Benjamin out to the small house by the orchard, the first room they had raised, and showed him the corner where the embroidered cloth still lay under the cradle. "This cloth was mine," she said, "and then it was your Momma's, and now it is yours." He ran his fingertips along the stitchwork and looked up at both women to make sure he had heard right. He grinned as if they had given him a secret and a crown and went on tracing the thread.

Bitsy watched him twirl in the shirt she had made and smiled to herself. Her work had begun to pull wagons to their yard. Dresses, coats, riding skirts, all passed through her fingers. She measured and pinned with care and sent each piece out into the world neat and true. She kept her coin under Alice's eye and learned to bargain for thread and buttons. At night in Lucy's old room, she folded the next day's work and laid it in a clean stack. She looked across the field and told herself a person could live with a loud orchard if there was good stitching to hold the day together.

Abbigail's words found their way back as well. After Henry returned from market, he set the paper on the table, and Lucy read a column aloud, her voice trembling at the truth tucked inside it. Natalie looked at Abbigail across the lamplight and saw the spark of pride she tried to hide. Bitsy listened with her hands quiet in her lap. They all knew whose voice it was, though the town never would. Sometimes Abbigail folded a page into Henry's satchel for the next day and pressed his arm with a grateful smile. He never said the name printed there. He did not need to.

They did not stop the small protections. Salt at the sills. Sage in a twist above the back door. A broom turned bristles up at night. If a fox took a hen, Henry set a trap and moved the roosts. If the red eyes blinked and held, Miss Patty tapped the window twice and said, "Not tonight." Most nights that worked. On the nights it did not, someone sat up with a lamp and waited the dark out while the orchard cried against the glass.

Once Benjamin woke crying hard, the kind of cry that says more than "wet" or "hungry." Lucy carried him to the porch and let the cool air wash over his neck. Natalie brought a cloth and laid it damply on his forehead. Isaac wrapped a blanket around them, his hand steady on the child's back. "Easy, Pal," he whispered, the word as gentle as a lullaby. Benjamin hiccupped, grabbed at their fingers, and kept one hand in each until his breath steadied. When he slept again, Lucy left her palm on his spine and said what she had said a hundred times in the dark. "We are here."

The seasons made their slow turns. Wheat came up thin the first year and generous the next. Pigs farrowed, and sometimes they did not. A pane in the upstairs hall cracked on a hard freeze, and Alice left it that way until Henry could trade for glass. The crack spread in a clean white line and became part of the house like a scar becomes part of a face. No one apologized for it.

Miss Patty aged into a different steadiness. Her steps were slower. Her hands did not lose their knowing. On Sundays, she set a dish of milk at the back step for luck and said if luck was not real, milk still was, and something living would drink it. She was right both ways.

By day, the orchard kept quiet enough to pass for ordinary. The children could play in the yard then, and Bitsy liked to stitch with the window open while Abbigail read a paragraph aloud to test the rhythm of a sentence. By evening, the world tilted. The branches lengthened into claws. The voices woke and crossed the field. Alice would close her eyes and listen. She told herself that to listen was a kind of prayer, not for mercy but for strength.

When the first harvest after the war came in clean and decent, they held a small supper on the porch. The table was set with cracked plates and a mismatched line of tin cups. Walt said a prayer that came out crooked and true. Benjamin banged his spoon. Lucy laughed. Bitsy set out bread she had bought with her own earned coins. Abbigail tucked one of her folded pages into Henry's satchel for the morning. Isaac squeezed Natalie's hand under the table, and she did not pull away. For a single moment, hidden in plain sight, she felt the world shift in their favor.

Isaac was stitched into everything they built. His hands were in the walls they raised, in the furrows turned, in the arms that lifted Benjamin high. Benjamin laughed hardest when Isaac called him "Pal" and answered it back as if the word belonged to no one else.

At night, when silence settled, Isaac came through the narrow way he had built behind the closet wall. The door in Natalie's wardrobe creaked open. For a few hours, their vows lived whole. The family that could not be spoken of in daylight rested in one room, bound by love stronger than the world's law, while the orchard wailed beyond the walls.

Alice lay awake more often as the year turned. She listened to Bitsy moving in Lucy's old room and felt a quiet ease at that sound. Bitsy was safe. She heard Abbigail's tread in the kitchen at first light and the scratch of a pen. Words and cloth, Alice thought. That is what we have. Timber and nails and words and cloth. She rose early and counted the breakfast eggs, and measured the coffee thin. She watched Henry walk out with Isaac and felt the steadiness those two carried between them like a beam. She watched Natalie and Lucy move together in the kitchen with the grace that makes a home where a lesser kindness would fail.

By the time Benjamin could run the length of the yard and not fall, the house had settled into itself. The second floor held heat in winter and let it go in summer. The stairs creaked in the same places each night. If you stood at the top and looked down, you could see the door and the line of the orchard beyond like a horizon you could walk to if you went straight enough. The red eyes blinked some nights and not others. The leaves kept their counsel. The land remembered. People did, too.

On a late spring evening when the air smelled of rain and new leaves, Benjamin lay between both women on a quilt near the porch and named what he could see. "Roof," he said. "Chimney. Tree. Momma." He pointed first at Natalie, then rolled and pressed his face into Lucy's shoulder. "Momma," he said again, not choosing and not required to. He fell asleep there with one hand holding Natalie's sleeve and the other curled in Lucy's skirt. Isaac came quietly from the yard, crouched beside them, and laid his palm on Benjamin's back. "Pal," the boy murmured in his sleep. Isaac bent low, and his cheek brushed his nephew's hair.

Henry's shadow crossed the yard with the slow confidence of a young man who had measured a life and found it sound. He checked the shed and set the latch. He looked once into the orchard and then looked away. It looked back as it always did. He did not bow to it, and he did not taunt it. He went inside and washed his hands while the trees whispered their grief behind him.

The house breathed like a living thing. Boards dragged on sleigh runners. Nails hammered straight against stone. Window glass bartered from a man who had lost all but a crate of panes. Everything carried its story and held together anyway. There are fortunes built on less.

When night fell, Natalie wrote one more page in the journal and slid it behind the board.

· · ·

JOURNAL ENTRY -

The war has not ended but it feels f it has already collected its toll from us. We pay not only in fields left fallow, but in the fences broken and the bones in our backs. Chickamauga bled straight down the road to our door. We gave water where we could, cloth torn for bandages, bread broken into smaller pieces so it might stretch farther. Still the wagons rolled on, groaning like coffins with wheels.

Alice's husband never came home. People will say what they say. There is no grave. Billy's name is not spoken. Miss Patty calls him what he was, the face that the haunting wore. When he died, the thing that had poured itself into him slipped back to the orchard. It is louder now, never resting.

THE HOUSE *we raised was a small form of repayment to the woman who had endured more than any soul should be asked to bear. It is not fine, but it is ours. Henry cut the timber, Isaac set the braces, Walt lent his strength, Alice counted nails, Miss Patty salted the corners. Lucy and I made curtains from scraps and painted the upstairs hall. The pane that cracked last winter holds. We live with what holds and mend what doesn't.*

Benjamin calls us both Momma. In town, he takes my hand. At home, he sleeps on Lucy's shoulder and reaches for me without opening his eyes. He fusses when he's hungry and cries when he's wet, the way a child should. Alice says, Billy never cried like that. He came into this life silent, as if he already knew too much. Something rode in with him and stayed until the day it left him and went back to the trees. I write this down because I need the truth where I can see it.

I keep the first letter Isaac ever wrote to me hidden behind the board in the little room. Paper is dear, but this is dearer. The words are simple, but they are his, and I read them when I need to remember that our love has a voice that even the orchard cannot silence.

CHAPTER FORTY-ONE

⚲ THE DIG

Janice had not stepped into the root cellar since the day the county morgue came to take the skeleton away. Even now, weeks later, she could not pass the kitchen door without glancing at the ground, half expecting the shadow of the trapdoor to stir on its own. The space was empty, swept clean, but the air around it still felt heavy, as if the soil remembered what had been buried there.

At night, the memory came back sharpest. She would wake to the faint scrape of wood against earth, a latch shifting where no latch remained. Sometimes she dreamed of the cellar filled with water, voices bubbling up like breath through silt. Other nights, it was Lucy she saw, a shadow at the bottom of the stairs, eyes lifted, lips pressed tight around a secret she would never speak. Janice would jolt awake, heart hammering, certain she had heard the trapdoor rattle.

She remembered the morning the officials had come. Two men in plain uniforms carried the remains out in a dark bag, careful but brisk, their faces set in professional lines. They did not look at her when they passed, and she was grateful. She did not want to see her own fear mirrored in their eyes. When the door closed behind them, silence fell so thick she thought she might choke on it. Even now, the memory clung to her.

Lucy must have lived with that silence every day of her life, Janice thought. Watching, guarding, keeping the secret. Janice felt the weight of that vigilance as she passed the kitchen door each morning, knowing she was only brushing the surface of what Lucy had endured.

That morning the air hung heavy with heat, cicadas droning like a chorus of warnings. Janice sat on the porch steps, notebook in her lap, when the crunch of gravel drew her eyes up. Gabe's car turned into the drive. He climbed out with a quick wave.

"Morning," he said, searching her face. "You eaten yet?"

Janice shook her head. "No. Too wound up."

"Then let's grab a bite first. We will need the fuel."

Her stomach answered before she could. She gave a small laugh. "Fine.

The bell over the café door jingled as they stepped inside. Morning rush. Coffee steamed, bacon and frying potatoes perfumed the air, and the clatter of plates filled the room.

Matty was everywhere at once, apron tied tight, blonde hair pinned back, her pencil tucked behind her ear. She spotted them and grinned, already motioning to an empty booth.

"Well, well," she said, sliding a pot of coffee onto their

table before they even sat down. "You two look like you are carrying either very good news or a small bomb. Sit. Eggs, toast, or pie?"

"Eggs and toast," Janice said, then after a beat, "and pie."

Matty winked. "Knew it." She scribbled and spun away, delivering plates to a family of four and topping off an old man's mug in one fluid motion.

The café buzzed with forks against china, the hiss of the griddle, and the constant shuffle of feet. Snippets of gossip drifted from the counter. "That Cheney place... bones in the cellar..." Janice stiffened.

Gabe brushed her hand under the table. "Ignore it. Focus on us."

Matty returned, sliding plates down, eggs steaming, toast golden, and pie off to the side like a dare. She leaned her hip against the booth. "All right. Talk fast. No, wait. I want the long version, but table six wants more coffee. Give me the headline first."

Janice's throat tightened. She had not planned how to say it. The words slipped out raw. "It was not Natalie. It was Lucy. Lucy is my fourth great grandmother."

Matty's eyebrows shot up. For a beat, the noise of the café dulled. Then a voice called her name. She jolted, pointed at them, and hurried away. "Do not move."

She darted between tables, sliding checks, laughing with a toddler, grabbing an order from the pass-through. When she came back, she leaned low, pencil poised. "Go on. I heard Lucy. Who is she?"

Janice gripped her coffee mug. "She lived here. She worked in the house. Billy—Natalie's cousin—hurt her.

He forced himself on her. When the baby came, she loved him. Loved him so fiercely she gave him everything. But because his skin was light, they let the world believe he was Natalie's child. They let the lie stand to protect him. No one questioned it. No one dared."

Matty's jaw tightened until her teeth showed. "Girl, those bastards did terrible things to women and men both. Everybody knew it, even if they pretended not to." She slapped her palm on the table, making the silverware jump. "It makes my blood boil. If I could meet them face to face right now..." Her breath hissed. She shook her head hard.

Her voice lowered. "You ever hear about that so-called doctor they used to praise, the one they call the father of modern gynecology? He kept an African American woman captive, cut into her over and over, experimenting without anesthesia. No pain killers. Nothing. Tortured her, then built a career out of it. They still had statues of him for years. That is the kind of men we are talking about."

Janice's eyes burned with the truth that had been denied her family. She was amazed by Lucy's strength and saddened that her story had been hidden for so long. "Lucy raised Benjamin. She protected him. She survived. Through her, I am here."

Matty sat back, breath unsteady. Then she leaned forward and gripped Janice's hand. "Then we honor her. We say her name. We do not let anyone write her out again."

A shout from the kitchen made her jump. She squeezed Janice's hand once more, then hurried off to refill mugs and ring up a bill. She returned minutes later, apron still tied, slid into the booth across from them, and fixed Janice with a steady look. "Say it again."

"Lucy is my ancestor," Janice whispered. "Not Natalie. Lucy."

Matty nodded firmly. "Good. Let it sit in the air." She let the silence work, let the words find their weight.

At last, she blew out a breath. "This is the South. Chances are we are all related somehow. The difference is whose names got spoken out loud."

Janice's throat closed. She pressed her hand against her chest. For the first time, speaking it did not feel like a confession. It felt like the truth.

Gabe opened the laptop then, turning it toward Matty. A rough sketch filled the screen. A fence line, a crooked cedar, an X near the place where the land dipped. A note in the margin read: where the land splits.

Matty tilted her head, squinting. Then she let out a short laugh. "Sounds like a treasure map to me."

By the time Matty's shift ended, the café had thinned to a few latecomers. She hauled a cooler of water bottles from the back and slid it into her trunk. Gabe followed in his car. Janice drove behind him, her palms damp on the steering wheel.

The drive back was quiet, each of them turning over the weight of what had been said at the café. The silence did not feel heavy. It felt charged, as though the land itself was waiting for them to return.

They parked at the edge of the property and cut along the fence line. The orchard loomed, branches heavy with heat. Cicadas shrieked so loudly the air seemed to vibrate.

The ground dipped near the old cedar. In winter, water would collect in that shallow bowl and sit for days.

Janice slowed, her throat tight. "Before we go on, you need to understand something. The curse of the firstborn, the one people whispered about, came from here. From the orchard."

Matty's brows furrowed. "From the orchard, how?"

"When the Cherokee were forced through this land, many babies did not survive the march. Mothers laid them in this ground because there was nowhere else. The grief soaked into the soil. It never left. That is why the land feels heavy. That is why people whispered about curses."

Even the cicadas seemed to pause, leaving the silence raw and open.

Matty tightened her grip on the shovel. "That is heartbreaking. No wonder this place feels wrong."

Gabe's voice was steady and quiet. "That grief does not belong to you, Janice. You are right. It is not yours to carry."

She pressed her notebook to her chest. "I am going to call the Cherokee Nation. Ask someone to come. The land needs to be blessed. Until then, the sorrow will keep whispering. It is theirs to release, not mine."

Matty nodded firmly. "We will make the calls after this. But today, we follow what Natalie left behind."

THE FAMILY CEMETERY lay just beyond the orchard, shaded by old oaks. Stones leaned at odd angles, their letters rubbed nearly smooth by time. Janice's eyes caught the marker that had haunted her since the first day she stumbled upon it: W. C. No birth date. No death date. Only letters, sharp and lonely.

Gabe switched on the metal detector. The device hummed as he swept slow, patient arcs over the ground. Thin beeps rose and fell, faint at first, then sharper near the cedar.

"This is the spot," he said.

Matty set the cooler down and drove her shovel into the earth. "Well, what are we waiting for?"

They fell into rhythm. Gabe marked the signals. Matty dug, her movements steady and precise. Janice crouched near the rim, brushing soil back with careful strokes. Sweat trickled down their backs. The smell of clay rose sharp and metallic, like old iron and wet leaves.

A jay scolded from a branch, then fell silent.

"If a skeleton pops out, I am done," Matty muttered, not looking up.

Gabe shot her a sharp glance. Janice's laugh broke the tension, quick and nervous, but welcome.

The detector gave a more urgent tone. Gabe adjusted his sweep, then tapped the earth. "Right here. Narrow band, maybe eight by ten."

Matty cleared another layer. Her shovel struck something solid with a dull clang.

They froze.

"That is no rock," she whispered.

They traded tools for their hands, scraping the soil back until the edge of a rusted metal box emerged. Its surface was pitted and streaked with corrosion, the hinges swollen but intact.

Janice slid the box free and heaved it onto the grass. Metal shifted inside with a muffled weight. The lock had rotted to a fragile scab. Gabe wedged the flat of the shovel beneath the hasp and pressed. The latch snapped with a muted crack.

Janice lifted the lid.

Inside lay a dark block, rough-edged, no larger than a loaf of bread. At first it looked like hardened dirt. She reached in and touched it. The surface was waxy, not earthen.

Matty crouched low. "What is that?"

Gabe leaned in, eyes narrowing. He scraped his thumbnail against the block. A brittle chip flaked free and fell into his palm. Beneath it, something gleamed faintly.

"This is not dirt," he said, voice hushed. "It is sealed. Wax, maybe pitch. Families used this to protect valuables underground. I have read about it, but I have never seen one."

Janice's breath caught. "So, what is inside?"

He pressed harder, prying at another corner. A larger shard broke loose. Sunlight struck the exposed edge and flashed bright. "Gold."

All three drew a breath at once.

Matty pointed. "That is not just gold. Look there." Another glint, silver-bright under the seal.

Gabe nodded reverently. "Southern gold and silver. Sealed and buried to survive. Most were lost or stolen, but this one... it lasted."

Janice lifted the block with both hands. It was heavy, far heavier than it looked, pressing against her palms with the weight of years. She ran her fingers over the hardened surface and felt the ridges of coins encased within.

Matty let out a low whistle. "Always heard stories of families burying treasure before the soldiers came through. My folks used to tell them like ghost tales. But I never saw proof. Thought it was just a way to keep us kids wide-eyed. And here you are, pulling it out of the ground like the old stories were waiting on you."

Janice hugged the block to her chest. The weight steadied her, solid and undeniable. Tears pricked her eyes. "This is it. This is what Mom needed. She does not have to worry about bills anymore."

Gabe rested a hand on her shoulder. "Then the land finally gave something back."

Janice thought of Ruth, the envelopes piled on the kitchen table, the fear etched into her face with every new notice. Relief swelled sharp and sweet. It was not only money. It was freedom from dread.

Matty leaned on her shovel, then pointed toward the far edge of the family graveyard. A narrow stream cut past the fence, twisting into the orchard's shade. She raised both arms, palms up, like a question.

"Where the land splits," she said. "Like the map said. Right there."

Janice followed her gaze. The words on the old page matched the ground beneath their feet. The cedar. The dip. The creek cutting past the graves. It had been there all along, waiting.

The orchard rustled, leaves shifting as though stirred by a breath older than the wind. Janice thought she heard a sigh, deep and low, as if the land itself had been waiting for this moment.

Matty crouched again, brushing soil from her knees. "You carry their names, Janice. Now you carry their gold and silver too. But what matters most is it came to you. That is not chance. That is family."

Janice closed her eyes. She could feel the truth burn steady in her chest. For the first time, she did not feel like an intruder on this land. She felt claimed.

She lifted the block again, pressing it to her chest. "Ready," she whispered.

They carried the past up the path together.

CHAPTER FORTY-TWO
⚓ THE INVITATIONS

The house was quiet when they returned from the cemetery. The three of them carried the rusted box between them, setting it gently on the kitchen table as if the weight of it might shift the floorboards. Dust clung to their sleeves, the smell of earth still heavy in their hair and clothes.

Janice stood with her palms pressed against the table, staring down at the iron chest as though it might open its mouth and speak. She had half expected to wake from this in the night, to realize she had only dreamed of coins sealed in wax and a necklace that matched. But there it sat, undeniable.

Matty clapped her hands suddenly. "We're filthy. If I'm going to toast buried treasure, I'm at least going to do it without grave dirt under my nails."

Janice startled, then laughed, and the sound eased the air. The three of them took turns at the sink, scrubbing soil from their hands, the water running brown before it cleared. Gabe rolled up his sleeves, red streaks rising where the shovel had rubbed against his skin, while Matty rinsed quickly, flicking water from her fingertips as if she could shake the graveyard off her skin.

When their hands were clean, Janice reached for the pitcher cooling in the fridge and pulled three tall glasses from the cupboard. She poured slowly, amber liquid sloshing against ice, then set the glasses on the table. "Homemade sweet tea," she said with a small smile, her voice catching. "Just like Mom taught me."

She slid a glass toward Matty, who accepted it with a playful salute. "Well then, cheers to your mama. She raised you right."

Janice nodded, her chest tightening, and raised her own glass. Gabe joined them, the three of them clinking in the dim light of the kitchen, as if this were some ancient rite instead of an impromptu toast after digging up a grave. The first sip was sharp and sweet, and Janice felt it steady her.

Her throat tightened again. "I have to tell them. My parents. Jeff. Everyone."

Gabe set his glass down carefully. "Then that's what we'll do. Tonight."

Janice sat at the kitchen table with the phone pressed to her ear, Gabe on one side and Matty on the other. Both leaned close, silent sentinels. The rusted chest still sat between them, a mute reminder of what they had uncovered.

The line clicked. "Hello?" Ruth's voice was thin but clear, carrying the distance of four time zones.

"Mom, it's me."

"Janice! I was hoping you'd call. How's the house? Have you eaten? Is the roof leaking yet?"

Janice let out a shaky laugh that cracked halfway through. "The roof's fine. Mom... remember the map I told you about? The one we found in that box?"

"I remember," Ruth said cautiously. "What about it?"

Janice swallowed, pressing her palm to the table for strength. "We followed it. It led us to something buried on the property. A chest. Inside were coins and silver. And one of the coins—it matched the necklace you gave me."

The silence stretched long enough that Janice thought the line had dropped. Then Ruth let out a trembling laugh, brittle but real. "Lord, Janice. All this time, and you're the one to uncover it."

Her throat burned, and the words tumbled out in a rush. "It's real, Mom. There's enough in it that you and Dad will never have to worry again. Not about the bills. Not about the lights or the pills. You'll never have to worry anymore."

Her voice cracked, tears spilling. Matty wordlessly pressed a tissue into her hand while Gabe laid a steady palm against her knee under the table.

On the line, Ruth's voice broke. "You don't know what that means to me. I've lain awake nights, wondering how much longer I could keep everything afloat. And now—" She coughed lightly, then called out, muffled, "Ed! Come here. You need to hear this."

A rustling followed before her father's steady voice filled the receiver. "Janice? What's going on?"

"Dad, it's true. The map was right. We found the chest. It belonged to the family."

Ed was quiet for a long moment before he spoke, careful and practical. "If that's true, we'll need to get lawyers involved. Paperwork. Proper channels. You can't just sit on something like that."

"I know," Janice said, brushing at her damp cheeks. "But before any of that, I need you both here."

Ruth broke in, fierce now. "Yes. We'll come. Even if Ed has to wheel me onto the plane, we'll come."

"You don't have to—"

"I do." Ruth's tone left no room for argument. "Send us the details. I want to see it with my own eyes."

When the call ended, Janice sat with the phone still in her hand, her pulse racing. The room felt strangely lighter, as though Ruth's determination had spilled into the house itself.

Gabe leaned forward, thoughtful. "Since your mother's going to be here, maybe this is the time to reach out to other family. Now that we know the Benjamin Freeman Cheney line, we could try to find them."

Matty's eyes brightened immediately. "Oh, I like that. Why not make it bigger? A real gathering."

Janice hesitated, then gave a small, almost nervous smile. "Only if you two will help."

Matty slapped the table, grinning. "I love a good party. I've got the foldable tables."

"And I can hang string lights," Gabe added. "Maybe even tiki torches. Dress the place up a little."

"What about the cellar?" Matty asked carefully.

Janice's stomach clenched. "I think everyone should see it, if they want to. It belongs to them too."

Matty chewed her lip. "Yeah, but that's deep stuff."

Gabe's voice was steady. "It could be cathartic. For everyone to know what happened, to face it. If we fail to remember the past, we're doomed to repeat it. That goes for both the cellar and the Trail of Tears."

Silence stretched a beat, heavy but purposeful. Janice reached for her notebook, tapping the edge of it against the table. "Then we'll do it. We'll invite them all."

THE HOUSE HAD GONE dark by the time Janice worked up the nerve to call Jeff. She paced the front porch as the phone rang, cicadas singing in the humid night.

"Janice?" His voice was rough but quickly sharpened. "What's wrong?"

"Nothing's wrong. At least, not exactly. "Jeff... we found something. On the property."

"That doesn't sound like 'nothing's wrong,'" he said dryly.

Janice hesitated, then spilled it in a rush. "The rusted chest. The silver. The coins sealed in wax. The match to Ruth's necklace." By the time she finished, her chest was heaving.

Jeff whistled low. "Well, leave it to you. Most people go off to flip a house and find mold. You go and dig up buried treasure."

Despite herself, Janice laughed. "It doesn't feel like treasure. It feels like... desperation. Like history."

"Then that's exactly why you've got to tell it," Jeff said. "You said you've been scribbling in that notebook all summer. You've already started a book, whether you know it or not."

"I'm not a writer."

"You are now. You've got the story. Nobody else could tell it."

Janice leaned against the porch rail, staring at the dark orchard. "Will you come? To the gathering?"

"Of course," he said without hesitation. "I gotta get my eyes on this hunky professor. Besides, I also want to meet this Matty you keep talking about."

Janice smiled, her heart easing. "She's... one of a kind."

"I'll be the judge of that," Jeff teased.

JUST BEFORE MIDNIGHT, the three of them were at the kitchen table again, this time with stacks of paper spread across the surface. Janice dipped a pen into ink, her hand trembling as she wrote the first words:

"In memory of Lucy. In honor of Natalie. For the family they saved."

Each invitation carried the name of a cousin or descendant she had traced through the family tree, some barely connected by blood but still tethered to the same root. Gabe folded the letters neatly, Matty slid them into envelopes, and together they sealed them by the light of a lantern.

Matty tapped one envelope against the table. "You realize what you're doing, right?" This isn't just letters. This is the start of a book. You literally dug one up."

Janice shook her head, though her cheeks warmed. "Don't start. I swear you and Jeff already know each other. He just said the same thing."

"Well, he ain't wrong," Matty replied, standing and stretching

Jeff's words echoed in her mind: *You're already writing it.*

Gabe leaned back, folding his arms. "She's right, you know. Someone has to put this into words. Otherwise, it all goes quiet again."

Matty brightened suddenly. "And while we're on the subject of keeping things from going quiet, Janice, you need a dog or something fury"

Janice blinked. "A dog?"

"Obviously. You can't rattle around this place alone. A house like this? You need something with four legs and a bark."

Gabe smirked. "Or at least one that likes belly rubs more than ghosts."

Janice laughed, the tension in her shoulders easing. "You're both ridiculous."

"Ridiculously right," Matty said. "Mark my words, you'll thank me when you've got a puppy keeping you company."

Janice shook her head, but she smiled as she sealed another envelope. The idea stuck, warm and persistent.

That night, after the last letter was addressed and the lantern extinguished, and Matty and Gabe called it a night, Janice stepped into the orchard. The air was still, the trees whispering faintly in the dark. She carried her notebook, its pages swollen with scribbles and fragments.

"I don't know who will come," she whispered to the night. "Maybe no one. Maybe everyone."

She touched the necklace at her throat, the coin cool

against her skin. Somewhere in the silence, she imagined Lucy standing guard, Natalie with her pen, the Cherokee mothers laying their children to rest. All of them waiting for someone to remember.

Janice closed her eyes, steadying her breath. She had thought she was only here to flip a house. Instead, she had uncovered a home.

CHAPTER FORTY-THREE
⚲ THE GATHERING

Ruth and Ed arrived the night before, a rented car bumping up the gravel drive under the hush of cicadas. Ed stepped out first, stiff from travel, but his eyes were sharp as he surveyed the house. Ruth followed more slowly, leaning on his arm, a scarf looped loosely around her neck. Her lipstick was a shade brighter than Janice had ever seen her wear, defiant against the pale of her skin.

Janice ran down the porch steps. The hug nearly undid her. Ruth was thinner, yes, but there was a spark in her eyes that hadn't been there when Janice left Seattle.

"You made it," Janice whispered.

"Of course," Ruth said, straightening. "I told you I would. But before I sleep, I need to see it."

Inside, Janice led her to the kitchen table where the box rested, lid pried open, its contents carefully arranged. The map and Natalie's letter were tucked into protective plastic sleeves, their fragile paper guarded against further wear. Ruth lowered herself into a chair and reached for them with trembling hands. She studied the letter first, her fingertips grazing the faded ink as though she could feel Natalie's urgency pressed into every stroke. Then the map, the arrow marked *where the land splits* still clear despite the years.

Her breath caught. "So it's true," she whispered. "Not just stories. Not just shadows."

"It's true," Janice said softly.

Ruth set the pages down with reverence and looked at her daughter, tears shining. "Then I can rest tonight. I had to see it with my own eyes."

Only then did she allow Ed to guide her upstairs, where she collapsed gratefully into bed, the orchard framed beyond the window.

Ed lingered downstairs with Janice and Gabe, shaking hands firmly.

"So, you're the one helping my daughter dig holes," Ed said, studying Gabe with a level gaze.

Gabe glanced at Janice, then back to Ed. "Not just holes. Trying to help her fill some of them too."

Ed's mouth twitched, the closest thing he gave to a smile. "Good answer."

By morning, the house hummed with motion. Matty burst through the door, balancing two casserole dishes and a tin of her famous cornbread, a towel slung over her shoulder like a uniform. "Don't worry, I brought reinforcements," she announced, setting the food on the counter. "And there's more in the car."

Together, they carried folding tables to the backyard,

Gabe stringing lights between pecan branches while Matty taped down tablecloths against the breeze. Janice set out jars for candles and flowers, her hands steady even as her stomach fluttered with nerves. It was supposed to be a handful of cousins, maybe a dozen at most. She hadn't dared to expect more.

But by noon, the gravel drive was full of cars. Families stepped out, carrying coolers and trays as if they'd rehearsed it. Fried chicken, potato salad, pies in dented tins, macaroni and cheese, green beans cooked with ham hocks, dish after dish arrived unannounced, the tables bending under generosity.

Janice stood in the kitchen doorway, stunned. "I didn't ask them to bring food."

"Family doesn't wait for permission," Matty said, already slicing cornbread into neat squares. "They show up with enough to feed an army." She clapped her hands together. "We're officially in reunion territory."

Ruth appeared then, rested from her nap, and wearing a pressed blouse Janice hadn't seen her in for months. She stepped onto the porch and stopped short, her eyes widening at the yard full of strangers-turned-cousins. For a moment, she swayed, hand at her chest.

"I thought... I thought it would just be a few," she whispered.

Janice slipped an arm around her. "So did I."

Matty appeared at their side with a roll of masking tape and a black marker. "If this is a reunion, then we're doing it right. Name tags, everyone. Write your name big enough for the people in the cheap seats." She tore off three strips, pressing one to Ruth's chest with exaggerated care. "There. Official."

Ruth let out a startled laugh, the sound so alive that Janice nearly wept.

By midafternoon, the yard had become a living quilt of stories. Cousins traded memories and pieced together half-remembered names. Children darted between tables, chasing fireflies in broad daylight. Jeff arrived with his usual irreverence, immediately falling into easy banter with Matty. Janice caught them laughing by the drink table, heads bent together like old friends.

At the center of it all sat the remembrance table: Natalie's journal, the letter to Meredith, Lucy's embroidered cloth, the hand-drawn map, and photographs, both sepia-toned and fresh from cell phones. Candles flickered, their small flames steady in the late afternoon breeze. Flowers from home gardens spilled across the cloths, sunflowers, zinnias, roses, and rosemary. A simple sign rested at the front: *In Memory of Lucy. In Honor of Natalie. For the Family They Saved.*

One by one, people came forward to speak. A woman with silver curls said her grandmother had whispered of a woman named Lucy who must never be forgotten, though her name was never spoken outside their home. A tall man in his forties remembered an uncle who insisted they came from strong women but had never explained what that meant. A young woman held her baby against her chest and said she had always felt there was something unsaid in their family line, a silence that lived in the pauses of elders.

When it was Janice's turn, she stood with Natalie's journal in one hand and the fragile letter to Meredith in the other. Her voice trembled as she told them what she had learned, that Benjamin's mother was Lucy, not Natalie, that Billy had fathered him. That Natalie had chosen the lie of widowhood to shield Lucy and the boy. That the orchard carried grief older still, Cherokee mothers who had buried their children under its roots. She read Natalie's words aloud.

When she finished, silence fell heavy. Then a woman with skin as dark as rich earth stepped forward and took Janice's hand. "We wondered," she said softly. "We always wondered. And now we know." Others followed. Some were darker, some lighter, some in between, but all were family, all carried Benjamin's line. The dam of silence broke. Janice sobbed openly in their embrace, clinging to them as if she had always known them.

Later that afternoon, the visitors from the Cherokee Nation arrived. Janice met them first at the edge of the yard, her voice steady though her hands shook. "Please, stay. Be our guests of honor tonight. This is your land too. Your stories belong here."

The elder woman inclined her head, silver hair glinting in the late sun. "Then we will sit with you."

Chairs were pulled forward, plates filled, and hands passed dishes from stranger to stranger until no one could remember where the meal began. Between bites, the elders spoke softly of what their grandparents had told them, of children buried beneath the march, of songs sung to keep grief from shattering the living, of the land itself refusing to forget. Every word settled into the gathering like a stone dropped into still water, sending ripples outward.

As dusk neared, the family and their guests walked to the orchard where the grief was thickest. The elder woman pressed her palm to the soil and began to sing. The younger man scattered cornmeal in a fine thread, a blessing stitched into the ground. They spoke words Janice could not understand but felt in her bones.

Then they asked everyone present, the descendants of Lucy, of Natalie, of Benjamin, of all who had walked these fields, to join hands. Circles formed around the orchard, around the old trees that had carried centuries of sorrow. The elder's voice rose clear.

"Let the smallest be gathered. Let the mothers be comforted. Let the firstborn walk free."

Hands squeezed. Tears fell. And for the first time in generations, the orchard seemed to relax.

When the blessing was done, Janice led them to the summer kitchen. "There is something more," she said. She opened the trap and let the cellar breathe its cool air.

They descended in turns. Some pressed palms to the clay walls and wept without speaking. A few folded their hands and prayed, words muffled into the damp air. Others couldn't bring themselves to go down, standing instead at the doorway with tears streaking their cheeks. Every reaction was its own kind of testimony.

"This is where Lucy stood guard," Janice told them. "This is where Natalie wrote about keeping the lamps burning. People were hidden here. People lived because of this place."

A hush filled the cellar. Not silence, it was too full of

breath and memory for that, but a pause that steadied everyone who stood within it.

When they emerged, the sky was already violet, and the first stars winked into place. The tables glowed under strings of white lights, lanterns swaying in the warm night air. Cousins traded plates and stories, children darted after fireflies, laughter rose and mingled with the ache of what had been revealed. The Cherokee guests remained at the long table, welcomed as kin, their presence stitching together old wounds with new ties.

As the evening closed, Janice stood at the family cemetery. She placed a flat stone beneath the oak and wrote one word on it in chalk: *Lucy.* She told them a proper marker would come, but this would keep her name from silence tonight.

Back on the porch, the lights Gabe had strung still glowed, steady as the stars appearing overhead. Ruth sat in a chair, her hand in Gabe's, Ed standing behind her with quiet strength. Matty leaned her head against Janice's shoulder, Jeff's fingers linked easily with hers.

Janice lifted her glass high, her voice carrying clear. "Keep the light on."

Every voice rose with hers, steady and sure, a chorus that carried across the orchard and into the night.

For the first time in generations, it was not a warning whispered in fear, but a toast, a promise, an anthem, a way forward.

And Janice knew, with certainty at last, that the house, the orchard, and the lives bound to them were no longer just shadows of the past. They were hers. They were theirs. They were home. She felt then, as the orchard hushed and the house seemed to breathe around her, that Lucy, Natalie, her grandmother, and all the women who had suffered on this ground had at last been laid to rest in the clay—and were finally at peace.

The orchard exhaled, and the clay's long-buried tears turned to song.

EPILOGUE

A year later, the house was quiet again. Not heavy, as it had once been, but settled, like soil after rain. Out back, the pecan trees stretched wide, their branches heavy with green. The string lights still hung between them, weathered now, but Janice left them up as a reminder of the night the family came home to each other.

Ruth had passed in the spring. She left the world full of stories, surrounded by Ed and Janice, her questions finally answered, her laughter still echoing in the halls. The orchard had seen her off beneath a sky streaked with violets, the same way it had welcomed her back to Georgia months before.

Gabe had been the one to place the soft bundle in Janice's arms not long after. "You shouldn't be here alone," he'd said. The one-eyed golden retriever blinked up at her, scarred but gentle, already loyal. They named him Captain Jack, though most of the time he was simply Jack.

Now he stretched at her feet on the porch, his head heavy against her boots. Janice scratched behind his ear with one hand and rested the other on the notebook in her lap. A fresh copy of her first book lay beside it, still carrying the faint scent of ink and glue. She had published it in memory of her mother and of Natalie and Lucy, a story of grief and strength, of women who kept the light burning even when the world tried to snuff it out.

The pages of her notebook were already crowded with more names, fragments of stories, and the beginnings of what would come next. She paused, listening. The house no longer pressed with unease, but the orchard still hummed, a low breath of sorrow and memory. Janice had learned not to fear it. Some pain could never be erased, only carried, honored, and passed on with the telling.

The screen door creaked, and Gabe stepped out, two mugs of coffee in hand. He set one beside her, then leaned against the porch rail, his eyes warm as they followed the line of trees swaying in the twilight.

"You've been buried in your writing too long," he said gently. "What do you say we get away for a weekend? Florida's not far. I know a place in St. Augustine that I think you'd love."

Janice looked up at him, startled, then smiled. The name itself carried a shiver, as though it had been waiting for her. Old stone walls. Salt air. Ghosts she had not yet met.

Jack stirred at her feet, lifting his one good eye toward her face as if he, too, were listening.

"St. Augustine," she repeated softly. She shut her

notebook with care and leaned down to press her forehead against Jack's. "Maybe it's time."

The porch light flickered, steadied again, and Janice lifted her coffee in a small toast toward the orchard. The house breathed, the trees stood, and for the first time, she felt not just at home, but ready for what came next.

AUTHOR'S NOTE

This story began as a whisper, an echo from the past that refused to stay buried.

Tracks Beneath the Clay is fiction, but it is stitched with truths. Truths passed down in family stories. Truths hidden in the silences between generations. It is about legacy, the kind we inherit and the kind we choose to build. It is about the weight of history, the pain of injustice, and the power of remembrance.

Natalie, Lucy, Isaac, and Janice are not just characters to me. They are tributes: to the women who held families together through violence and fear; to the enslaved and the free; to those who hid people under floorboards; and to those who survived long enough to speak. They are tributes to descendants who feel the tug of something ancient in the marrow of their bones, even if they cannot yet name it.

This book is also a love letter to women, the way they carry one another, hold each other up, and bear one another's burdens across generations. They are woven together. And when one woman suffers, all do. Silence can cost lives. But solidarity, that is where change begins. That is how we heal what history tried to silence.

You may notice the symbols at the start of each chapter. The paired diamonds (◇◇) mark the past, while the fleur-de-lis (⚜) marks the present. They are small signposts meant to guide you between timelines, the same way Janice learns to walk between memory and discovery.

I wrote this novel not just to tell a story, but to honor one.

If you are holding this book, thank you for reading with your heart. For bearing witness. For walking these haunted paths with me.

May we always ask questions. May we always seek truth. And above all, may we keep the light on.

With gratitude,

Leia Kay

ABOUT THE AUTHOR

Leia Kay is a Southern fiction writer whose work draws from the red clay, dark history, and enduring spirit of the Deep South. A mother of four and proud empty nester, she writes stories steeped in legacy, loss, and the quiet power of women who refuse to be forgotten.

When she's not writing, Leia spends her time reading, knitting, and sharing quiet evenings with her husband and her two fluffy fur babies. Her stories walk the line between the living and the haunted, where past and present are always entwined.